Clay Legionary

Clay Warrior Stories

Book #1

J. Clifton Slater

This is a work of fiction. While some characters are historical figures, the majority are fictional. Any resemblance to persons living or dead are purely coincidental.

Clay Legionary takes place in 271 - 268 B.C. when Rome was a Republic and before the Imperial Roman Empire conquered the world. While I have attempted to stay true to the era, I am not a historian. If you are a true aficionado of the times, I apologize in advance for my errors.

I'd like to thank my editor Hollis Jones for her work in correcting my rambling sentences and overly flowery prose. Also, I am grateful to Denise Scherschel for her help in structuring the book. Her amazing illustrated book *Zippy McZoomerman Gears Up* is a must read for children with disabilities.

Forget your car, your television, your computer and smart phone; journey back to when making clay bricks and steel were the height of technology.

J. Clifton Slater

www.JCliftonSlater.com

E-Mail: GalacticCouncilRealm@gmail.com

Clay Legionary

Act 1

Prodigy

Merriam-Webster Dictionary defines Prodigy as a young person who is unusually gifted with special talent. These advanced talents, no matter how extreme, tends to be beneficial for those associated with the prodigy.

A prodigy can come from many different fields: musical prodigy; mathematical prodigy; engineering prodigy; literary prodigy; or artistic prodigy.

Usually, the talented child poses no threat to strangers who encounter the youth. However, dig a little deeper into the Latin origin of the word and you'll uncover a threatening dark side.

The Etymology of prodigy is prodigium. Prodigium means omen or monster – Thus the gifted can then become the feared. Now, imagine the gifted youth as a Swordsman Prodigy.

Chapter 1 - Cooperative Village

Alerio Sisera broke from the corner of the school house and sprinted away with one thought in mind - escape. The path lay across the yard and threaded between two grain storage buildings. With arms pumping and knees raising and falling, he raced towards the trail leading to his home and safety. The buildings grew closer and his escape seemed assured.

For the last year, three older boys had terrorized him and the younger students in his small class. The bullying began with pushing and verbal harassment. But recently the levels of aggression had sunk to a new low. Physical punishment and petty theft were now part of their itinerary of pain and suffering.

Unfortunately for Alerio, he became a primary target when the older boys discovered his father had been an Optio in the Legion. Each of the three boys' fathers had served short stints in the Republic's army. Their fathers carried resentment for NCOs when they were discharged. They passed on the negative emotions to their boys.

He reached the alley between the grain buildings with a vision of open fields in sight. Relief washed over Alerio and he slowed. Suddenly his attempted escape was abruptly cut off.

"Going somewhere Sisera?" One of the boys asked as the three stepped into his path.

One circled around behind Alerio. The one who had spoken shoved his face in close as if to dare the younger boy to take a swing. The third boy moved close to Alerio's side.

"What, no time to say hello?" he whispered in Alerio's ear. "Got to get home to your stolen land and that pretty mother of yours."

Alerio's hands clinched into fists, his face reddened at the mention of his mother, and he started to punch the boy. But, the boy on his side had placed a foot between his legs and when the boy behind him pushed, Alerio found himself face first on the ground.

A kick to his ribs rolled him over and he lay looking up at three sneering faces.

"What do you have for us today?" One asked as he reached down and plucked the pouch from Alerio's belt. "Your payment for stealing our best land," he explained as he spilled the content of the pouch into his hand.

He distributed the five copper coins to his companions. The iron spinning top he kept for himself. A dried root shaped like a dragon was tossed to the ground beside Alerio. As the young boy watched, a heal pulverized the dragon into shredded mulch.

"Do better tomorrow; I'd like a new knife," another of the boys said as he bent down. He ended the instructions with a hard punch to the center of his victim's chest.

It was then Alerio cried out in frustration. The physical pain was temporary while the mental anguish burned deeply into his mind. Plus, he knew tomorrow would bring more abuse from the older boys.

Chapter 2 - The Sisera's Farm

He left the small village behind and raced down the path towards his home. The trees surrounding the small villa came into view and the dread faded. Faded until he entered the kitchen and met his mother.

In a panic, she asked, "What happened to your face?"

A cloth was dipped in a bowl of water and applied to his cheek. It came away stained with dirt and blood. His mother studied the bruise.

"Was it those boys again?" She asked as she dabbed at his cheek. Then she added. "I'll have your father speak to their fathers."

"No! Ah, no, I fell," he lied.

The thought of his father being involved in the dispute was unbearable. Alerio imagined it would make the assaults worse and he'd rather face the boys alone than have his father interfere.

Over the last year, his father had tried to teach him self-defense. But his tendons were too immature to apply wrestling holds. His arms too thin and under sized for boxing so, after those attempts, his father gave up on teaching him to fight.

The afternoon was filled with chores and Alerio had already put the fight behind him. At dinner, he avoided the eyes of his parents and his two older sisters. They ate and his father talked about planting and the need to rotate fields. Alerio had stopped listening when his sisters interrupted to comment on the scrapes and scabs on his face. His father didn't comment. He simply looked long and hard at the injuries. For the remainder of the meal, Alerio feared that his father would become involved.

After dinner, retired Optio Sisera motioned for Alerio to follow. He guided the boy through the courtyard, around the grain separation racks, and into a storage shed. Three walls of the shed held farming tools. On the fourth hung weapons.

Large heavy infantry shields and smaller shields used by skirmishers occupied the center and lower part of the wall. Shelves above and beside the shields were filled with javelins, bows, and swords. The senior Sisera reached under the shields and moved a barrel filled with arrows. From the recess, he pulled out a wooden sword. He swung it effortlessly a few times before carrying it outside. Alerio followed.

They walked around to the rear of the shed, and Alerio's chest swelled with pride at the farm. What once had been a rocky, barren track was now a field of grain. Stalks swayed in the evening breeze and appeared golden in the light of the setting sun. Between the rock wall at the edge of the field and the shed, a tree trunk had been planted. It stood taller than the boy and was twice his thickness. Stripped of its bark, the post appeared to glow golden in the fading light.

Alerio watched as the retired Optio laid the wooden sword against the shed, struck flint and lit a lantern. He hung the lantern from the roof's overhang before picking up the sword.

"This is a recruit training gladius," his father stated as he walked to the tree trunk gripping the sword in one hand. "You strike the post from the side twice before swinging the sword to the opposite side and striking it backhandedly. Twice and once then repeat."

He demonstrated the two slashes and one backhanded strike before handing the sword to Alerio. The tip of the wooden sword drooped towards the ground.

Alerio had played with his father's gladius when he was younger. It had taken two hands to hold the short sword yet, he had been able to lift it. The wooden sword was almost twice the weight of the metal weapon.

"It's heavy so when you transition to a real gladius, you'll be stronger and better able to handle the drills," his father explained. "Practice until you get tired. Then come in and clean up."

His father disappeared around the shed and Alerio concentrated on lifting the sword tip from the dirt. He managed three repetitions before his right arm gave out.

In frustration, he switched to his left hand and managed only two repetitions. With the sword back in his right hand, he struck twice, but, as he shifted the gladius to the opposite side of the post for the backhand strike, the wooden sword slipped from his hand. It landed in the dirt.

Chapter 3 - The Sisera's Villa

In the weeks that followed, Alerio managed to evade the older boys. When they did catch him, he noticed their punches weren't as devastating. Compared to the burning and soreness from the sword practice, their attempts seemed weak.

One day he returned home to find his father entertaining company. Two big men sat on the patio talking with the former Sergeant. They were laughing and each held a clay mug of vino.

"Alerio come here," his father said calling him over. Dropping an arm over his shoulders, he stated proudly to the men, "This is my boy. Alerio this is Centurion Efrem and Optio Egidius. We served together in the Legion."

Alerio was taken by surprise. His father wasn't expressive with his emotions. He worked hard, treated his family and slaves fairly, but he was stingy with his praise.

"I can see much of you in him," Centurion Efrem observed. "Back when you were a scrawny, raw recruit who didn't know the difference between a shovel and a gladius."

"I know the difference, sir," Alerio boasted.

"Oh, you do, do you?" Centurion Efrem asked. He stood, pulled his sword, and spoke to the other man. "Optio Egidius, give the boy your gladius."

The Optio slid his weapon free and handed it to Alerio hilt first. Compared to the heavy wooden sword, it seemed light.

"Let's see what you know," the Centurion demanded holding out his weapon.

Alerio wasn't sure what to do. He swung twice at the other man's blade before swinging to the other side and backhanding the opposite side. Efrem's sword rocked from the blows.

"Impressive," the man said. "Now, strike harder and I'll provide resistance."

This time Alerio's gladius didn't rock his opponent's blade. It was as if he were striking the unmoving post. On the backhand move, the Centurion's blade struck back.

Alerio's sword stopped cold, jarring him from hand to shoulder. His fingers went numb and the tip of the sword touched the ground. Even in that state, he didn't drop the weapon.

"That wasn't fair to the lad, Centurion," Optio Egidius scolded.

"Better he learned defeat now than think himself an expert and die from ignorance," the infantry officer said. "Had enough boy?"

Retired Sergeant Sisera hadn't said a word during the drill. He did have an odd look on his face.

"No, sir," Alerio replied as he switched the gladius to his left hand. He brought the blade up to guard position and waited.

Centurion Efrem smiled and glanced over at the former Optio. "Sisera. Did you teach him to be ambidextrous?"

"Not me Centurion," Alerio's father replied. "I was never that good a swordsman."

"Alright young Alerio," Efrem said bringing his blade up to touch blades with the boy. "Begin."

This time Alerio was ready for the counterstrike. While it stung, it wasn't disabling and he managed to fend off the Centurion for a flurry before the older man's strength won the drill.

"Optio. If it's alright with you," Centurion Efrem offered. "I'd like to train the boy while we're here. He has promise."

Alerio hadn't thought about being ambidextrous. He'd been switching hands because he could only swing at the post with the training sword for so long with one hand. In order to prolong the training, he had switched from right to left and left to right.

Centurion Efrem and Optio Egidius were on fall furlough from the western Legion. Both men grew up in the Capital and neither wanted to go from the orderly life of a Legionary to the chaos of a city. So, they'd accepted former Optio Sisera's offer of home cooked meals, wine, conversation, and a soft bed in exchange for working the harvest. They'd leave well fed with a few Republic gold coins in their pouches before returning to their duty post.

During the four weeks before harvesting began, Centurion Efrem drilled and taught Alerio. By the time the sickles, shovels, and baskets were distributed, Alerio knew all of the Legionary drills. While not proficient at them all, he knew enough to practice each drill daily.

Chapter 4 - The Harvest

Two years ago, for the harvest, Alerio had been assigned to the separating screens. Along with others, he scooped up handfuls of stalks and thrashed them until all the grain fell from the husks. He hadn't been that helpful but he tried.

Last year, he graduated to shovel duty. As the seeds filled the space under the screens, he and others shoveled the grain from under the trashing racks and into bags. He got more on the ground than in the bags. But he didn't get in anybody's way.

He was standing along with all the able-bodied personnel on the farm, waiting for his father to handout assignments. Alerio eyed the thrashing racks and screens, shovels and bags. If given a choice, he'd rather not be there. Because of the collective nature of thrashing, the people assigned to the racks made small talk and bad jokes from sunup to sundown.

His other option was on the collecting crew. They followed the harvesters picking up armloads of hacked down stalks and placing them in the wagons. When a wagon was full, a handler guided the mule to the thrashing area. The work was hard on the back muscles but the collectors rotated walking the mules and wagons to the racks. They'd get a little rest while the wagon was unloaded. Alerio figured he could do the work, but it was up to his father. So, he waited.

A big hand landed on his shoulder. He turned around to see who owned it.

"You ready, little man?" Sergeant Egidius asked.

"Ready for what, Optio?" Alerio replied.

Egidius placed a sickle in the boy's hand.

"You're with me on harvesting duty," the Legion NCO advised him. "I explained to your father that I needed someone who could keep up with me. He asked me who and I said you. Are you ready?"

The harvesters were the first line attackers. They operated out front cutting stalks as fast as the slowest cutter allowed. Cut too fast and your work went to waste as your stalks lay on the ground absorbing moisture. Cut too slow and you held up the entire operation as the advancing line waited for you to catch up.

"Cut low and keep up," Egidius advised. "But, most of all remember - When hard work has to be done, do it with good humor and a song. Defending a shield wall, breaching a barbarian hoard, digging a ditch or harvesting grain, it's all the same. Hard work."

"Yes, Optio," Alerio replied.

Chapter 5 - The Grain Field

The next morning a line of tall men and one boy stood at the edge of the field. As the sun broke over the horizon, a whistle sounded, sickles swung and tall stalks of grain fell to the ground. The harvest had begun.

Alerio's hand was sweating and his right arm cramped. He switched the sickle to his left hand and kept chopping at the stalks. While not thick, the grain plants were plentiful and each cut dropped a bunch. At one point he staggered from exhaustion but Egidius reached out and steadied him.

"This is hard work, lad," the Sergeant advised him. "What do we do?"

"Thank the Goddess Ceres for the opportunity to sweat in her name," Alerio replied.

"I think she'll take that offering," Egidius said. Then he began to chant:

Up each day to the rising sun,

work all day til the work is done,

sound off, one-two, one-two, three, four.

Sickle in hand and a field ahead,

going to chop all day til I'm dead,

sound off, one-two, one-two, three, four.

I'm a mighty man and can't be beat

mounds of stalks laying around my feet

sound off, one-two, one-two, three, four.

On the second round of the chant, Alerio added his voice. By the fourth rendition, men on the line were chanting along with the Optio. When the sun reached overhead, food was delivered. They walked off the line and collected thick sandwiches.

"Hard work," Optio Egidius stated.

"Time for jokes and singing," Alerio replied.

His face was covered in pollen and dirt. Sweat had long ago dried them in a pattern of streaks. Yet, the most pronounced feature was the smile on his young face.

Former Optio Sisera arrived and began walking the cut. From time to time he stopped and called a cutter over. After pointing out stalks chopped off too high, he moved over to inspect another row. High cuts were a waste as the stalks, after thrashing, were used as animal feed. A stalk cut too high meant less feed per row. Sisera barely looked in Alerio's direction.

"Is something wrong?" the boy asked Egidius. "Father didn't come over."

"Right now, he's not your father," the Sergeant advised him. "He's in command of the harvest. I've seen him like that before. Strolling around in the midst of a savage hoard, calmly directing his Legionaries. The last time I saw him, he was bleeding and fighting off a bunch of barbarians. Between strikes, he issued corrections to reform the battle line."

"So, him ignoring me is a good thing?" Alerio asked.

"Sure. If he'd come over it would be to yell at us about high cuts," Egidius assured him. "When Optio Sisera is working it's best not to draw his attention."

Alerio had seen the medals, the letters of commendation, and the weapon's stash, but he'd never really thought about his father fighting in a battle. He didn't have long to ponder the thought. Egidius lightly tapped him with a fist.

"We're wasting a perfectly good day," the Optio said as he pulled Alerio to his feet. "That grain isn't going to harvest itself."

"Up each day to the rising sun, work all day til the work is done, sound off, one-two, one-two, three, four," Alerio chanted as he marched to the edge of the tall grain stalks.

Egidius cringed and added his voice. He sang louder, as much to mask the lad's rough singing, as to motivate the other cutters.

Chapter 6 - The Great Room

Three weeks later, former Optio Sisera and Centurion Efrem were huddled around a table. While Sisera had run the harvest operation, Efrem had been in charge of accounting with the village's grain commission.

"You mean to tell me we produced more grain and feed stalk than the bigger farms?" Sisera questioned.

"That's correct Optio," the Centurion assured him. "I checked their books. It seems your homestead is tops when it comes to cashing in. I overheard a number of farmers complaining about your choice location."

"Choice location?" Alerio's father spit out the words. "Haven't they noticed the stone walls around my property. Where do they think they came from? The sky? No, my son, my staff and I dug the rocks out one by one."

"Easy there Sisera," the Centurion said attempting to calm the farmer. "They don't have the experience with farming that you do."

"You mean like having fish shipped in. Grinding them up with manure and spreading it over the fields," Sisera replied. "Or, rotating the crops to rest the soil in sections."

"Yes, how did you learn that?" Sergeant Egidius asked from across the room.

Alerio and the Optio had been discussing fighting tactics. They'd barely paid any attention to the conversation until Sisera raised his voice.

It didn't seem as if the retired Optio would answer, so Egidius asked again, "How did you learn about fish and crop rotation? The boy should know."

"During the western campaign there was a big battle," Sisera said. His eyes looked at something beyond the walls of the room and his voice dropped as if the memory was hard to relate. "The battlefield had been a collection of farms. From the stunted crops, I could see the soil was poorer than the farmers working it. We met the barbarians in those fields. We stomped the crops and watered the soil with the blood and bones of Legionaries and savages. Then we retired to our winter quarters."

"How did that teach you about farming?" Alerio asked his father.

"In the spring, we marched by the fields but no farmers remained to plant them," Sisera reported. "But grass grew. Thick and tall, almost as if it had been planted by farmers. The next year, a group of families moved in and planted crops. The crops, where the soil had been so poor the farmers were starving, filled sacks with grain only two years later. Bone, blood and rest were the difference."

"Your father thought and talked about that all winter," Optio Egidius said. "We were ready to bury him in those fields by spring."

"Good thing you didn't," the Centurion remarked. "It was that summer when the steady Optio Sisera saved our lives."

"What, my father saved your lives?" Alerio asked excitedly. "How? Where?"

"When you're older," his father assured him. "Now it's time for you to turn in."

"Alerio. I understand you've had some trouble with three boys in the village," Centurion Efrem said catching the boy before he left. "If you do tomorrow, look on top of the fourth board on the right grain storage building. I left you something."

Chapter 7 - The Cooperative Village

The time off from classes for the harvest hadn't change Alerio's physique. He was still tall and thin with a gangly gait and prone to tripping over his own feet. If anything, the hours of work with the sword and the sickle gave him the appearance of being underweight.

His appearance didn't disturb the three boys waiting for him at the grain storage building. One blocked the alley while the other two spread out so he couldn't escape by going around the structures.

"Your father cheated and it's going to cost the other farmers," one sneered. "What have you brought me?"

Alerio looked from one boy to the other, then at the base of the right storage building. He counted up four boards. As he thought about what the Centurion had placed there, one of the boys closed in on him. The first lesson from the Centurion had been about footwork. It's hard to grab or hit a moving target.

A soft scraping sound behind him identified one of the boys sneaking up. Alerio waited for the shove that would send him tumbling forward or backward to the ground. When the boy in front reached out, Alerio slapped his hands away, danced to the side, and yanked at the boy's arm. Caught by surprise, the boy tumbled forward. The two boys ended up grabbing each other.

"That's sweet," Alerio teased. "Harvest season is the time for love."

While the two boys attempted to untangle their limbs, the third boy ran at him. In the past, Alerio would have panicked and froze in place making an easy target. This time he reached out, grabbed an outstretched arm, and pulled while stepping swiftly to the side. The boy's momentum propelled him into the other two. The three fell to the ground. Alerio ran down the alley to the safety of the school building.

In the afternoon, he didn't see the boys on his way home. He was at the villa before he remembered the present hidden on the storage building.

Chapter 8 - The Bully's Turn

After dinner, while his father and his friends sat talking, Alerio went behind the shed and beat on the post. Between strikes, he danced patterns. For the first time, he understood the purpose of movement in a fight. And, he understood the purpose of keeping level headed and singing. With a steady rhythm, his practice became more intense and more focused.

In the morning, he dressed and jogged to the storage building. Waiting for him were the three boys and a man.

"You there, fish farmer," the man yelled. Then he turned to one of the boys, and inquired. "Is this the one who attacked you?"

The boy nodded shyly and replied, "Yes, Dad. We were just hanging out when he came up and demanded our money."

"What have you got to say for yourself," the man demanded. "You owe my boy five coppers."

Alerio was stunned. For a year, the boys had beaten and robbed him. Now they were accusing him of being a thief? It was all he could do in the face of the absurd accusation, he laughed.

The man took a step forward while asking, "Are you laughing at me? I'll give you something to laugh at."

His hand clamped down on Alerio's shoulder and his fingers dug painfully into the muscles. Alerio bent his knees attempting to retreat down and away from the pressure. The hand followed maintaining the painful clamp for a few seconds.

Suddenly, the pain ended and the farmer lay sprawled on the ground about five feet away. Standing over him was Sergeant Egidius.

"We can do this the hard way or the easy way," Egidius suggested.

"What's the easy way?" asked the farmer.

"I beat you and you bleed," the Optio replied.

"What's the hard way?" the man asked with a hint of terror in his voice.

"I beat you and you bleed," the Optio said with a smile.

"I don't see the difference," the confused man admitted.

"Oh, there's not. But my old Optio said to always give a man a choice in his punishment," Egidius explained. "It helps get him invested in the consequences of his actions."

With the final word, the Sergeant punched the man in the nose. As the farmer reached to cover his bleeding nostrils, Egidius jerked him to his feet.

"Do you like little boys?" Egidius asked as he sank his fingers into the back of the man's thick neck. "How about big boys? We like to play too."

The man shuddered as the fingers closed in and the muscles yielded. He blinked trying to separate the words, from the action causing him pain, and the blood streaming down his face.

Alerio watched fascinated. Optio Egidius hadn't lost his temper. Instead, he talked and destroyed the confused man in just a few moves.

"Listen closely," Egidius said. "This summer, I'll be passing through this village with eighty, blood thirsty, heavy infantrymen. If anything happens to Alerio or the Sisera farm, I'll bring my Century to your estate and guess what?"

"Is this another choice?" sniffled the man as he coughed up a mouth full of blood.

"Not this time," Optio Egidius promised dropping his voice. For the first time, he sounded threatening. "I'll come to your farm. I'll kill you and your entire family. Your slaves and your livestock. And as your villa burns to the ground, I'll drink your best wine in salute."

"You can't," the man began but Egidius buried his knuckles wrist deep in the man's stomach.

"I can and I will," the Optio stated. "Now get out of my sight before I change my mind about waiting till summer."

The man supported by the boys limped away.

"Thank you, Optio," Alerio acknowledged.

"What did you learn?" inquired the Optio.

"Stay calm, think ahead, keep your enemy off balance and use economy of motion," Alerio replied. "Did I miss anything?"

"Overwhelming violence," Egidius added. "Don't give the enemy a chance to attack or counter."

The Sergeant walked to the corner of the grain storage building and plucked a carved stick from between the boards. With a smile on his face, he took the trail back towards the Sisera farm. Alerio watched the Legion NCO for a long time before he turned and headed to the school house.

Chapter 9 - The Collection Town

Four years later, Alerio Sisera's frame hadn't grown much taller. All the growth was horizontal. Where his back had been slender and boyish, it now pushed his tunic out as if he were hiding wings under the fabric. His arms and legs, once thin and reedy, were thick with no fat to hide the underlying muscles. After several long harvesting seasons, Centurion Efrem and Optio Egidius had trained the farm lad to be an expert with the gladius and a talented tactician. On top of the skills, he was fast, athletic and had a short fuse.

Last year, he'd invited the three tormentors to a duel. Three against one with swords, knives, or javelins, whichever weapon they chose. Wisely, none of the three young men showed up at the appointed time or place.

Alerio Sisera and four friends hitched a ride on the community's grain wagons. It was a four-day trip to the nearest major collection town. While the commission would sell the farmers' grain, Alerio and his companions would do some gambling and drinking. And maybe take in a show, if they got around to it. The grain wagons were scheduled to return to the village after a three-day layover. They'd be filled with goods for the homesteads and five hungover teens.

Day one was spent at the better pubs. By day two, the quality of drinking establishments had gone downhill drastically. Sometime in the early hours of day three, Alerio and friends staggered into a less than savory pub.

The desperate came in two varieties: the dangerous or the despondent. The despondent were all huddled like sheep, clustered in the center of the common room, or crowded around games of chance. All drugged or drunk, not all present except for their pathetic bodies. Their will gone and their minds broken.

The solo dangerous lurked around the edges to the rear of the gamblers, seeking a loose pouch or an easy mark. The more ambitious of the dangerous stayed in the shadows along the walls waiting and watching for wealthier victims. They had banded together in gangs and preferred planning and scheming their crimes. Unless an obvious target wandered into their territory.

When the five country lads walked in, one gang took note. The boys were singing a drinking song they'd picked up at a better place.

Can the Magistrate grant me an audience?

Said the old woman, on the gallows' door

For the Judge is all blind

My old man, all the time

Drinks the darkest red wine

And that's why, he's dead on the floor…

Can the Magistrate grant me an audience?

Said the old woman, on the gallows' door

For the Judge, should relent

My old man, never paid rent

Our coin on drink he spent

And that's why, he's dead on the floor…

Can the Magistrate grant me an audience?

Said the old woman, on the gallows' door

For the Judge should be sacked

My old man, knifed in the back

Cause' he winked at a lass

And that's why, he's dead on the floor…

Can the Magistrate grant me an audience?

Said the old woman, on the gallows' door

For the Judge, failed to note

My old man, gambled our goat

And lost my wool red coat

And that's why, he's dead on the floor…

Easy laughter and a slight stagger signaled to the gang the farm boys' state of drunkenness. As Alerio's group leaned on the rough wooden bar, the gang emerged from the shadows.

"See here, this is a fine establishment," a man said in greeting. "There's a fee for first time visitors and bad singing." Behind the man, seven members of his crime syndicate spread out to trap the prey between their knives and the ale stained oak bar.

"I don't see a sign," Alerio replied with a smile. "But I'll buy you a drink."

Alerio's vision was tunneling due to the quantity of ale and wine he'd consumed over two days of hard partying. The man was standing in the tunnel so he was in focus. His seven associates were not.

"Ah, my friend," the man said smiling and displaying chipped teeth. "The fee is two Republic Silvers, each, for me and my friends."

It took a few seconds for the words to develop in Alerio's mind. Once the thoughts were formed, he scanned the men standing behind the talker. They all had knives cuffed in their palms. This wasn't a brawl where everyone walked away with black eyes and bruising. This was a knife fight.

"How many sweethearts have you brought to the dance?" Alerio said loudly. He continued so his friends could hear, "Let me count the darlings."

The man tilted his head out of confusion. What, he wondered was the big lad from the boondocks talking about?

"I see you, you, and you there in the back. Hello," Alerio was animated as he pointed out and waved a friendly greeting to each member of the gang. "And you there with the two big knives. Come closer, yes, let me buy you a drink."

While Alerio blathered as if he was a village idiot, two of his friends managed to slip away. The other two moved closer pretending to enjoy the show. In fact, they positioned themselves to guard Alerio's left side.

The rogue holding the two long knives began to push forward. Anyone who flaunted two weapons was either an experienced fighter or overcompensating. Alerio wasn't thinking of that, he wasn't thinking at all. He was on automatic.

The gang's mouth piece was the closer target. Alerio lifted a foot and powered it into the man's knee cap. The leg snapped. As the man fell, Alerio caught him and flipped his body into the semicircle of thugs.

Two knives tripped as the body rolled into his lower legs. He was forced to lean forward, his weapons still up in a guard position. Alerio plucked the knives from the unbalanced man's hands and head butted him. The man fell away and disappeared in the tangle of men on the dirty floor.

Two of the gang were still on their feet. They rushed forward. In their experience, most victims went on the defense when faced with two attackers. Alerio simultaneously drove his left knife through one's neck while slashing open the other's belly with his right knife. The thugs fell, one holding his guts in his hands, and the other gagging on his own blood.

At this point, Alerio and his two remaining friends could have circled around the downed gang and left the seedy establishment. But, Alerio wasn't thinking. He'd slipped into battle mode and the first rule was to never let the enemy counterattack.

"You lads go now," he ordered his friends. He was grinning and his eyes were sparkling. "I've got to have a conversation with these guys. Run along now."

They left as Alerio flipped one of the long knives into the air and caught it. Then he flipped the other. The knives were off balance, more ground down meat cleavers than proper cutlery. Nevertheless, they would do for this job.

"Who wants to dance?" Alerio announced to the room. Everyone in the pub had stopped and was staring at the big youth standing at the bar flipping the knives.

It started with a few but soon became a stream as the bar's patrons rushed for the exit.

Alerio ignored the fleeing customers. He scanned the gang members as he sang.

"Can the Magistrate grant me an audience?

Said the old woman, on the gallows' door

For the Judge, should relent

My old man, never paid rent

Our coin on drink he spent

And that's why, They're dead on the floor…

One of the thugs began to stand. Alerio stepped to the man and with an underhanded swing, split the man's face from chin to forehead. Another pushed to his knees and Alerio reached out and caressed his neck with a knife. Blood spurted as the blade sliced the artery. Before the man had time to bleed to death, Alerio jumped at another member who was scrambling to his feet. He received a foot to the face, and a stab to the heart as he fell on his back.

As a symbolic end, Alerio pulled the original owner of the two knives to his feet and drove both blades into the man's stomach. Then, still holding the man upright, reached back and snatched a mug of ale from the bar.

"I offered to buy you a drink," Alerio said as he drizzled the liquid over the dying man's face. "You and your friends should have accepted the offer."

The body dropped to the floor and Alerio took a long pull from the mug. Before he could set it back on the bar, four Legionnaires accompanied by a Decanus, and a Tesserarius, acting as Optio of the City Guard, flowed into the near empty pub.

Chapter 10 - The Dangerous Pub

They saw a blood splattered country boy leaning against the bar and singing out of tune.

"And that's why..., They're dead on the floor..."

On the rough plank flooring, eight bodies lay in a semicircle around the lad's feet. The first thing that saved the boy's life: he was unarmed.

In a small trading town, the city guard was composed of Legion units on temporary assignment. A larger city would have a permanent city guard. They might be less prone to chopping down a criminal as he might be a neighbor or related to a wealthy family.

The Legionnaires who entered the bar didn't know the boy or particularly care whom he knew. They held no compunction about taking down a murderer and the boy was certainly guilty of it, many times over.

The second thing that saved Alerio Sisera's life was the acting Sergeant of the Guard. As a Corporal standing in for a senior NCO, he wanted to get everything done legally and proper. It's why he'd accompanied the patrol when someone had called for help at the pub in this unsavory part of town.

While the patrol with drawn gladii prepared to overwhelm the criminal, the Tesserarius put a hand on the arm of the Decanus.

"Hold," ordered the Lance Corporal in response to his Corporal's signal. The four veterans stopped but held their gladii pointed at the boy.

"Put the mug down lad or die," the Tesserarius ordered. "I don't really care which."

Alerio turned his head slowly and tried to bring the troopers into focus. Then he did the third thing that saved his life.

He set the heavy clay mug on the bar, braced at attention as Optio Egidius had shown him, and announced, "Tesserarius, Lance Corporal, good morning."

The two NCOs exchanged glances at the recognition of their rank. It wasn't uncommon for someone to know military ranks, but it was unusual for them to assume the position of attention.

"What's your name lad?" the Corporal asked.

"Alerio. Tesserarius," the country boy replied.

Now the Corporal was really confused. His position in the Century was that of the unit's treasurer. The boy's military knowledge and fighting skills didn't jive with his farmer's clothing or his youth.

"Turn around and put your hands behind your back," the Corporal ordered.

As the Decanus secured a leather strap around his wrists, Alerio leaned forward and added a flood of vomit to the blood and guts on the pub's flooring. He didn't remember being led out of the establishment, through the streets, or being shoved into a holding cell.

Chapter 11 - The Town's Guard

"His name's Alerio and he single handedly took out eight members of the Cruor gang," reported the Tesserarius.

"Eight of the Spilled Bloods?" the City Guard's Centurion asked. "What did he use a heavy infantry shield and a gladius?"

"According to witnesses, he disarmed one and used the man's knives to kill them. Looks like a case of self-defense to me," the Corporal said. "Odd thing though, he knows military ranks. And he's obviously had some weapon's training."

"Well, the training won't do him any good when the rest of the Cruor find him," the Officer of the Guard stated. "Alerio you said. What's his family name?"

"I didn't get that," admitted the Tesserarius. "Between his vomiting and mumbling, I didn't have the chance to question him."

"Go find out," the Centurion ordered. "Oh, and move him to a private cell until we get this straightened out. I imagine the Cruor leadership has already put out a bounty on him. Better he died on the streets than in one of our cells."

"Yes, sir," the Tesserarius said while saluting and backing towards the door.

Alerio had picked himself up from the cold floor and stumbled to an open space on a stone bench. On either side of him, drunks, thieves, and brawlers sat hunched over waiting for morning court. They ignored the country boy in the blood soaked clothing. A commotion outside the cell drew their attention.

Everyone, sober enough to notice, sat upright when the cell door swung open. Four armed Legionaries stepped in followed by a Corporal.

"Him," the Tesserarius directed.

While two Legionaries moved forward to take the farm lad, the other two stood ready to put down any acts of rebellion from the prisoners. Alerio was dragged out. Before the door closed, a thin man was tossed into the holding cell. Then the two Legionaries on security duty backed out. Once they were gone, the thin man jumped to his feet.

"The Cruor are looking for a farm lad," he whispered looking around at the prisoners. "They're offering five Republic golds, dead or alive."

"Your timing sucks little man," a large brutish guy offered. "They just took him out." He was hunched over alone on the end of the bench. After a long pause he added, "When they bring him back, the lad and the coin are mine. Any arguments?"

No one disagreed that the big brute should have the bounty. Although a few did think, if the farm lad was returned, they might take a shot at the prize.

Chapter 12 - The Officer of the Day

"His full name is Alerio Sisera," the Corporal reported. "His family has a small homestead a few days west of here."

"Sisera, a farm," the Centurion repeated. "Did he happen to say anything about his father?"

"He mumbled something about an Optio Sisera being upset with him," the Tesserarius replied. "Does the name mean anything to you?"

"Corporal, if Alerio is retired Optio Sisera's son, we have a small issue," the Centurion said while slowly rubbing the bridge of his nose in irritation. "If the Cruor kill, said the son of retired Optio Sisera, we have a huge problem."

"Why is that, sir?" the Tesserarius inquired.

"Because, there are three Centuries of Legionaries two day's march from here who owe their lives to Sergeant Sisera," the troubled Centurion replied. "If his son is killed in our town, the Optio will march on this miserable piece of merda and burn it to the ground."

"A farmer and retired Legion NCO," the Corporal stated. "How much damage could he do?"

"Oh, it's not him alone," the Centurion said while gritting his teeth. "It's the three Centuries of heavy infantry who'll be more than happy to help former Optio Sisera level this fleapit."

"We could simply release the boy and send him home," volunteered the Tesserarius.

"Same problem. The Cruor hunt him down and the Optio comes seeking revenge," the officer replied. "Right now, I wish I was on the other side of the Republic."

The NCO and the officer stared at each other for a few heartbeats before the Corporal cleared his throat.

"Ah sir, suppose the lad was on the other side of the Republic?" he asked.

"Explain, please," urged the Centurion.

"We have a courier chariot leaving at dawn. There's room among the mail sacks for the driver and another body," the NCO said. "If the lad was a Recruit, he could easily get passage from the Capitol to the Eastern Legion."

"Sober him up enough to sign his name to the enlistment papers," the Centurion ordered. "I'll send a letter to his father. Thank you, Tesserarius. Dismissed."

Act 2

Chapter 13 - The Road to the Capital

Alerio Sisera woke up when the Courier shoved a heal of bread and a lump of cheese into his hands.

"Are we home yet?" the confused teen asked.

"Recruit Sisera, by order of the Consuls, you are hereby commanded to report to the Eastern Legion for recruit training," the Courier read from a scroll.

"But I'm a farmer. My father depends on me," Alerio pleaded. "He's expecting me to come home."

"No, he isn't. My Centurion sent a letter explaining the need to get you out of the western sector," the Legionary explained. "Seems you have a five Republic gold bounty on your head - payable by the Cruor gang, dead or alive. So, you enlisted in the Legion."

"I enlisted?" Alerio asked.

The Courier handed him a folded piece of parchment and said, "These are your travel papers. They'll get you passage on a ship from the Capital to the Eastern Legion."

Alerio unfolded the parchment and read down to the end of the document. There he found his name scrawled unmistakably in his own handwriting.

"Where are we?" Alerio asked.

"You slept through the two way-stations. This is an inn so we're fourteen miles from the trading town," the Courier informed him pointing out the single-story building with an attached stable. "We'll be here long enough to eat and change ponies. So, eat and do your business rapidly, the Legion's messages can't wait. We have another four pony changes before we sleep for a few hours."

"How many days to the Capital?" Alerio asked.

He'd studied maps of the Republic and knew his father's farm was over two hundred miles from the Republic's seat of government and the Consuls' and Senate's Government building. Even deducting the distance traveled to the collection town and the courier's progress, he figured they had about one hundred twenty miles to go.

"We should arrive at the military post outside the Capital," explained the Courier as he checked the harness on the two-pony rig. "Around mid-watch in two and a half days."

"How much sleep do we get each night?" Alerio asked realizing this wasn't a leisure trip. His head hurt and his stomach was sour.

"Sleep? As in stretch out, snuggle down in a feather bed with a fleece filled pillow? A warm blanket and letting the rooster's crow you awake sometime after daybreak?" the Courier asked. Alerio knew where this was going even if he hadn't seen the sneer on the Legionary's face. "We nap beside the chariot for an hour or so. A full night's sleep? No Recruit, that's not going to happen."

Chapter 14 - The Capital's Wall

Alerio saw the Capital for the first time two days later. The sun was low in the East and the morning light cast a halo over the hills of the city. The biggest of buildings, backlit by the rays, stood out as they glowed white.

"First time seeing the Capital City?" asked the Courier.

Alerio was standing beside the driver. His mouth hanging open while his eyes shifted rapidly in an attempt to take in every inch of the scene.

"Is it that obvious?" he replied when the driver nudged him in the ribs.

"Everyone acts the same when they see it for the first time," the Courier said. "The Capital is an awe-inspiring site."

They crossed a bridge as torrents of water cascaded down the river below them. Once across, the chariot dropped to the valley floor and pulled into the next to last way station. Far across the flatland, the city walls appeared no higher than three fingers' width in height. The perspective would change over the last fourteen miles of the trip.

Chapter 15 - The Legion Transfer Post

Alerio handed his orders to a Tesserarius at the Legion Transfer Post. His eyes looked beyond the tall NCO. Brick walls thirty feet high surrounded the city. Behind the ramparts, the city loomed higher with tightly packed buildings crowding every inch. On the highest hills, he could see narrow streets twisting and turning between structures.

"Eastern Legion," the Corporal said as he glanced at the travel orders. "You'll need to report in at the docks."

From the Western side, there didn't seem to be any bodies of water deep enough for a pier. Alerio looked back towards the river some twelve miles away.

"At the river?" he asked.

"No Recruit. The docks are two day's travel around the city," he explained. "We have a shipment of slaves from the northern campaign leaving the day after tomorrow. You can be part of the security detail."

"Yes, sir," he acknowledged.

"It's Tesserarius Gratian or Treasurer, only Officers and training NCOs are sir," the Corporal replied. "Take your orders to the quartermaster's office and they'll get you armed and outfitted. Can't have you dressed like a farmer in a Legion unit."

Chapter 16 - The Old Gear

The armor was old and cracked from age. Deep slices attested to the battles where the armor had protected a Legionary. A lack of oil and cleaning made the leather stiff and covered its metal fittings in rust spots and tarnish. The delight in having been issued his first gladius was dampened by the layer of rust and the dull-notched blade.

With the equipment slung over his shoulder, Alerio ate at the mess tent and went to find his rack for the night. Once he knew where he'd sleep, he went in search of supplies.

The Tesserarius he'd spoken with when he arrived strolled up. After watching as the farm lad scrubbed briskly at rust spots on the gladius, the NCO glanced at the rest of the Recruit's equipment. Beside the farm boy, a well-used set of armor, covered in a thick layer of goat grease, lay soaking in the fading light.

"You know, they'll take that set from you at the docks," advised the NCO. "There's no reason to waste time on it."

"It's good leather. Maybe the next man will appreciate having it in better condition," Alerio said as he scooped up a handful of sand and drew the blade through the abrasive material. The steel gleamed except where the notches marred the cutting edges. As he inspected the weapon he added. "The gladius is made of good metal. It'd be a shame to let it rust away."

"Do you know how to use that?" asked the NCO looking at the thick arms and broad chest of the farm lad. An idea was forming and he wondered if the Recruit could be useful.

"I've trained with a gladius," admitted Alerio.

"There's a camp competition tomorrow," Corporal Gratian said. "Winner gets five Republic silvers and a share of the gambling wages placed against him."

The Tesserarius wasn't looking for a champion. He already had a favorite in the competition. But betting on the early rounds was chancy. If the big farm boy could win the first two elimination rounds, the NCO could make a nice profit before the better fighters entered the final matches.

Alerio reached out and poked the armor's chest piece. It compressed under his fingers and reformed swiftly when he released the leather. Then, he studied the gladius. He knew from his father a blade with notches was inefficient. In combat, it would catch on another blade at odd and unpredictable angles.

"The leather and plates are as good as I can get them," Alerio said. "But the blade needs grinding and I haven't the coin to afford a metalworker's fee."

Corporal Gratian was taken by surprise. Not only was the Recruit big enough to last several rounds, he seemed to know his equipment. After thinking for a moment, he made a decision.

"I'll front you the cost of grinding," the NCO explained. There was a blacksmith who owed him a favor so there was no cost. He didn't tell the farm lad. Instead, he added, "But I want twenty-five percent of your winnings."

Alerio stood up and gripped the hilt with his right hand. After a few slices with the blade, he spun the gladius into the air and over his head. He skillfully caught the spinning hilt with his left hand. After checking the balance by demonstrating sword drills with both hands, he lowered the weapon.

"I'll take you up on the offer Tesserarius Gratian," he announced. "Where's the metalworker?

Chapter 17 - The Corral

The Legion Post was a transfer station and didn't have a proper arena. They had cleaned out a corral, spread a layer of sand, and stacked boxes and barrels around it for seating. Legionaries from nearby Posts, Stations, and units assigned to the Capital were flocking in for the entertainment. The camp's normal compliment was more than quadrupled for the competition.

Vendors set up tents and soon the air was filled with the aroma of roasting meats and baking bread. Voices bragging about the quality of their wines and ales competed with the noise of the crowd for attention.

Alerio wandered through the throng looking at the elements of the festival. He'd never seen this much activity in one place before. As much as he hated to admit it, he was intimidated and distracted by the activity.

In order to separate himself from the mayhem, Alerio sought out the Marshal of the competition.

"Recruit Sisera. Is this where I sign up for the tournament?" he asked a Sergeant.

The NCO was sitting at a table with pieces of parchment spread out in front of him. He studied the young man and after taking in the well-used but supple armor and the physique of the lad, he selected a page from the top of a short pile. "What's your record?" asked the Marshal gruffly.

"Record, Optio?" Alerio inquired.

"Your number of wins or second place finishes in recent competitions," the NCO explained in frustration. "I need to place you in a bracket. We don't want top competitors wasting time on rookies. It's not fair and the gamblers will have a fit if I put an experienced fighter against a nobody. So, record?"

Alerio was at a loss. He'd seen a few sword competitions when he and his father had visited the collection town. There had only been a few competitors. He had no idea what a bracket was or where he should be placed in it.

Corporal Gratian arrived and saved him.

"Optio, Recruit Sisera is in transit to the Eastern Legion," he explained. "He has no prior experience in competition. Put him in the first round."

"His gear looks well used. Plus, it's in superb shape," the Optio voiced, his meaning clear. "You better have not brought in a ringer, Gratian."

"He just arrived yesterday from the western region," the Tesserarius explained. "The gear's old and on loan from our quartermaster. He's definitely a first rounder."

The Marshal of the competition moved his hand from the short stack to a taller stack of parchment.

"What's your name again?" he asked as he picked up a quill.

Chapter 18 - The Tournament

Recruit Sisera watched the first three fights. All the competitors used basic Legion fighting moves. The difference between the winners and losers were simply strength and endurance. When his name was called, he fitted the helmet on his head and drew his gladius.

The man was short and thick through the shoulders. Although he delivered powerful strikes, he lacked foot work. Alerio shuffled in and out and from side to side. The powerful strikes soon became weak taps as the man wasted his energy in the first few flurries. Alerio parried the man's blade and drove the point of his gladius into the man's midsection. The armor prevented physical damage but didn't stop the embarrassment of him being pushed down on his butt.

The Marshal stepped in and declared Recruit Sisera the winner. Some of the crowd groaned while others cheered halfheartedly.

At the entrance to the corral, Alerio was met by Corporal Gratian. To his surprise and delight, the NCO handed him a roasted goose leg and a pouch of coins.

"Thought you'd like the money and you looked hungry," came the explanation.

"Who's next?" asked Alerio as he ripped off a section of the bird with his teeth.

"There are seven more matches in the first round," the Tesserarius explained. "The Marshal will select the matches for the second-round from the winners."

"Where are the competitors for the top brackets," Alerio inquired.

"They won't fight for another three rounds," the NCO replied. "They're over behind the supply tent."

"I'm going to take a look at them," declared Alerio.

He strolled away as the next fight started. Behind him, he recognized the rhythm of basic sword strikes. In his mind, he matched the clash of blades with the moves required to deliver them. It was all basic.

On the far side of the supply tent, an expanse had been roped off. In the area, camps had been set up for the top swordsmen. Alerio walked to the rope and glanced from camp to camp. At one, two men were sparring. One left-handed battled against a right hander.

They didn't restrict their moves to basic sword strikes. They leaped and danced while fainting and parring in fluid motions. Their blades blurred and flashed so rapidly, Alerio couldn't follow the path until the blade tip stopped on an opponent's chest.

He walked back towards the makeshift arena knowing his short career as a competitor was doomed to end. Though, a positive thought crept into the negative idea. He turned it over in his mind.

His name was called and he faced off against a thin, quick man. While his footwork made Alerio's seem as if he were dragging his feet in the sand, the man didn't have enough strength to power through Alerio's blocks. On the third pass, Alerio hooked the man's blade and sent it flying across the corral.

The Marshal rushed out and declared Recruit Sisera the winner. Around them, the boos had more venom while the cheers grew in intensity.

As he marched from the corral, Alerio took the purse and the meat pie from a grinning Corporal Gratian.

"Make it through one more round, and you'll walk away with a tidy profit," the NCO informed him.

"Suppose I make it to the fourth round?" Alerio asked. "And win?"

"What makes you think you can win against an experienced swordsman," the NCO asked puzzled by the farm lad's confidence.

"That depends on the Marshal's selection," Alerio explained. "If he matches me against the left-handed swordsman, I think I can win."

"You want to fight Daedalus?" the Tesserarius asked in horror. "He's with the City Guard and, on occasion, he fights in competitions. Nobody wants to fight Daedalus."

"I do. If the Marshal sets it up," Alerio said.

He and Corporal Gratian wandered around looking at the items for sale while munching on baked goods. Finally, the NCO stopped and faced Alerio.

"What makes you think you can beat Daedalus?" he asked looking to see if the teen was drunk or had a head injury.

"He's left-handed but practices against right-handed sparring partners," Alerio said. "What he's doing is reinforcing his advantage. Take that away, and he's handicapped."

"And you can counter this, ah, his advantage?" inquired the NCO.

"I believe I can," Alerio confirmed. "If the Marshal gives me the opportunity."

"No one wants to fight him anyway. I can't imagine the Marshal getting merda from the gamblers for setting up the match," the Tesserarius said softly as if he were thinking out loud. He stared at the farm lad for a few intense seconds before speaking, "I'll set it up. You win the next round and you'll have your match."

Chapter 19 - The Arena

Round three was easier than Alerio anticipated. His opponent possessed good skills with the gladius and adequate footwork. But he'd fought two long battles and he was exhausted. With no stamina, it wasn't long before Alerio trapped the man's blade. Once stationary, Alerio drove a knee into his chest. A backhand strike with the flat of his blade sent the man to the sand.

The Marshal strolled out with his arms extended playing to the crowd. A hush fell over the spectators as the Optio turned from one fighter to the other.

When a murmur of impatience ran through the audience, the Marshal shouted, "The winner of round three, Recruit Sisera!"

This time the cheers drowned out the boos. Recruit Sisera had picked up a following. There were five winners who'd survived the first three rounds. These five amateurs would face off against five ranked fighters in round-four.

To encourage betting, the competitors for the round four battles were paraded into the corral. Corporal Daedalus of the City Guard led the procession of ranked fighters and the Marshal placed Recruit Sisera at the head of the amateurs. No cheering greeted the procession; the spectators sat in weighted silence.

Starting at the rear, the Marshal pulled the last man from each line. He guided them to the center of the arena and announced the contestants. The crowd cheered. As he continued to make his way up the line, pulling out men and calling out the match ups, the cheering grew louder.

When the Marshal stood between the last two fighters, the audience knew the final matchup of round four.

"Tesserarius Daedalus, of the City Guard, five wins and ten second places, plus six appearances in the city arena." the Sergeant shouted over the screaming crowd. "versus Recruit Sisera, of the Eastern Legion, no record."

Most of the time round-four was a formality. The amateurs would lose rapidly and the ranked fighters would move on to face people more in their class. Even the gamblers knew the odds so, betting was usually light.

Chapter 20 - The Betting

Corporal Gratian wandered through the crowd trying to get a read on where the money flowed. People discussed the matches, mostly discounting the amateurs, yet, there were a few who seemed pro Recruit Sisera.

He had coins from the first three rounds and was confident the Recruit would lose in round four. Yet, the more he heard and the more he thought about the lad's confidence, the less sure he was about betting on Daedalus.

The gamblers were sitting quietly having taken all the bets before the start of round-four. Despite the attractive odds, few had placed coins on any of the amateurs. Recruit Sisera was different and a few people had bet on him. But the bookies ignored the bets figuring his backers were simply caught up in the hype of three lucky wins.

Tesserarius Gratian strolled casually up to the bookies.

"This hurts," he admitted. "but I've got to place a few coins on my guy. Support the home team, you know."

The six bookies understood a Legion Corporal tossing away coin to show backing for one of his men. His bet was more for morale than a chance to win. Five turned away while the sixth bookie held out his hand for the few coins he expected.

Tesserarius Gratian swallowed hard, creased his brow and, hesitantly, pulled a full purse from his belt. The bookie's eyes shot up when the heavy pouch landed in his hand.

"Recruit Sisera for the win against Daedalus," Gratian whispered so people in the passing crowd wouldn't hear.

A piece of parchment with the odds and the amount of the bet was passed to the Corporal. He walked away feeling like a fool for throwing away his money.

Chapter 21 - The Conspiracy

There had been little blood spilled during the first three rounds of fighting. When round four started, the ranked fighters needed to put on a show so they intentionally wounded the amateurs. The crowd loved it and the cheering reached a high pitch as each amateur fell to the more experienced swordsmen.

After each bout, Medics escorted or carried the injured from the corral. Then, Legionaries rushed out to throw sand over the red spots and rake the arena smooth.

"They're being especially brutal," Tesserarius Gratian explained. "Usually, the ranked fighters are satisfied with a display of swordsmanship. But this, this is butchery."

"What's different?" Alerio asked.

"I don't know," the Corporal admitted. "Let me go ask around."

He left Sisera at the corral and disappeared into the crowd.

Gratian avoided the usual gambling circles and moved to the edges of the spectators. He spoke with a few of his Legionaries asking them to mingle to see why the fighters were drawing blood in every match. His men spread out and he waited at a central location for their reports.

A short while later, two of his men returned and both looked troubled.

"There's a bounty on Sisera," one reported.

"Five Republic golds, dead or alive," the other added. "The fighters are drawing blood so when Sisera falls, it'll look like an accident during a rough tournament."

Tesserarius Gratian was troubled for two reasons. A Legionary was about to be executed legally. As a Corporal, he couldn't abide losing a man. The other reason was the large bet he'd placed on a targeted fighter. Both thoughts turned his stomach, as neither outcome was satisfactory.

He raced back to the makeshift arena and approached the Recruit.

"Sisera. Don't fight him," the NCO ordered. "There's a bounty on you and Daedalus plans on collecting it."

"Who did you bet on?" Alerio asked. The teen was running a grinding stone down the blade of his gladius.

"As much as I hate to admit it, I bet on you," Gratian informed him. "It's only coin and not worth your life. Forfeit and we'll get you out of here."

The big farm lad smiled and shook his head, "Can't do that to you, Tesserarius. I'm going to fight him."

Just then the crowd erupted in cheers as an amateur gushed blood and fell to the sand. In the deafening roar, Gratian motioned sharply for them to leave the arena. Sisera shook his head no and continued sharpening the blade.

Chapter 22 - The Corral Fight

Corporal Daedalus of the City Guard had thin legs, long arms, and the beginnings of a gut. With his left hand, he spun the gladius putting on a show for the audience. A few knee bends while the blade whirled brought applause and a few cheers. There was no doubt he was an expert swordsman and a crowd favorite. During the exhibition, he never looked at his opponent.

He didn't have to as he'd received reports on the lad's fighting style. Better than average foot work, strong defense, but basic striking skills. And he was decidedly right-handed. Overall, Sisera shouldn't have a chance against a left-handed attack.

Daedalus had resisted when the gang member approached him. Still, he was City Guard and had to live with all elements of the Capital's population. Not only would he receive the five Republic golds, the gang would owe him a favor. In a crowded city having friends in the underworld would prove useful. So, when the other fighters began to bleed the amateurs as cover, he agreed to kill the lad.

Alerio watched the swordsman preen for the crowd. His response was a few swings of his gladius and a shrug of his shoulders.

The Marshal walked to the center of the corral waving his arms to silence the spectators.

"This is the final match of round four," he announced. "Tesserarius Daedalus and Recruit Sisera will fight to see who moves on to round five. Gentlemen, are you ready?"

Daedalus raised his gladius and bounced the hilt off his chest. Sisera copied the salute and the Marshal backed away while motioning for the fighters to begin.

Alerio assumed a guard stance as Daedalus raised his blade and moved to the lad's left. The movement was designed to entice a right-handed fighter into taking a swing at the blade.

Two right-handed fighters would face a mirrored foe. With one being left-handed, his opponent couldn't deliver a powerful sweeping blow. It would leave the lefty's blade inside his guard, opening a path to the righty's side. This was Daedalus' advantage. He continued to circle.

Alerio ignored the opening and moved counter to his opponent. The crowd groaned as the fighters circled but didn't engage. They didn't realize the duel wasn't a tournament competition. It was a life and death sword fight.

Daedalus attacked first. He came in hard with swift strokes designed to confuse Alerio. Their blades connected time and time again. Alerio used only defense as he backed away from the expertly delivered strikes. Stepping back and to the side, allowed him to stay away from the blade while moving around the corral. Daedalus grew weary of the flurry and let Alerio put distance between them.

"For a tall man, you have small hands," Alerio teased. "You know what they say about small hands."

"What?" Daedalus asked. He'd been taunted and threatened many times over the years but no one had ever commented on his physical attributes.

"I bet you have a huge set of cōleī," Alerio said as he raised his blade. "The gods are kind like that. Compensation for a small mentula." Then he relaxed his guard and looking confused asked, "Is that the correct wording? Or did I get it wrong?"

Daedalus went from amused, to angry, to feeling the need to reply. For a second the lad's quizzical look and stupid ramblings exposed him for the amateur he was. To confirm it, Sisera lower his guard.

Daedalus lunged and stabbed for the Recruit's lower stomach.

Alerio circled his blade inside Daedalus' low thrust and knocked the man's gladius to the side. For a brief moment, he had a clear path to the Corporal's unguarded chest. He brought the blade back using the power of his body and just as the tip reach Daedalus, the experienced fighter leaned back. A deep scratch appeared on his torso plate and the blade moved far to the side.

Taking advantage of the wide swing, Daedalus reached out and ran the tip of his gladius through Alerio's old leather armor and into his deltoid muscle. He was aiming for the shoulder joint to cripple the lad, but Alerio rolled the shoulder forward. The blade only skewed the meat of his shoulder cap.

Daedalus was incensed. The blow was supposed to be a double move. One to cripple the shoulder, then as he withdrew the blade, he'd angle it to cut the lad's throat. A simple one, two and this fiasco would be over. But the inexperienced Recruit rotated inward instead of exposing his neck by leaning away from the blade.

The crowd screamed and howled as blood began running down Alerio's right arm.

Above the roar, Alerio heard Corporal Gratian yelling, "Walk away! Walk away!"

All the Tesserarius could see was the lad's blood-soaked right arm dropping seemly unable to support the weight of his gladius and the Recruit's eyes looking down at the sand. Daedalus also noted the weakness and lack of focus.

Instead of waiting for the muscle to fully cramp and for more blood lose from the shoulder injury, Daedalus stepped in close to the lad. Three inches closer and he'd have the lad's right arm trapped. There was a problem with the maneuver as he couldn't use his own gladius. He'd have to shove the lad away in order to finish him off.

Alerio noticed the foot as it snaked between his feet. Coming in from his right, the foot would hook his heel and send him tumbling helplessly to the ground. Just as Daedalus' foot reached the point where he could trip him, Alerio moved.

He clamped his legs together trapping Daedalus' leg. Then, he jumped and twisted. The rotation forced the experienced fighter off balance and he found himself slammed into the sand on his left arm. While Alerio spun in the air, he reached across and grabbed the gladius from his injured right arm.

Both men ended up on the sand, their legs intertwined. Daedalus began to roll away, confident he could gain his footing, and kill the injured lad. He never made it.

Alerio flexed his stomach muscles and twisted to a sitting position. With his strong and able left arm, he struck Daedalus in the head. The fighter collapsed. But Alerio didn't notice or care, he continued to pound the unconscious man's helmet until the Marshal pulled him away.

Unfortunately, the lad's shoulders were slick with blood. The Marshal lost his grip. The gladius began to swing towards the off balanced and unarmored Optio. It was half a body's distance from the man when Corporal Gratian tackled Alerio.

"At ease Recruit Sisera," he said while twisting Alerio's head around so he could look into the lad's eyes. "Stand down. It's over. Steady."

"Am I dead?" Alerio asked looking up at the Tesserarius. "Because you're the ugliest Valkyrie I've ever heard of."

"If you are done trying to kill people," the Corporal said as he stood and offered a hand to help the lad up. "The Medics need to stitch you up and I have an appointment with an angry bookie."

As Alerio stumbled into the arms of a waiting Medic, three of Tesserarius Gratian's Century closed in protectively around them.

Fifteen more of the Corporal's Legionnaires were holding discussions with the fighters who'd injured the amateurs to cover for the attempted assassination. None of the fighters would be competing again until their bones mended.

One of the bookies decided he'd had enough action for one day. Just as he finished packing up his money chest, four Legionaries and a Centurion marched up to his booth.

"Your gambling license requires you to stay open for the entire competition," the officer informed the bookie.

"I have a family emergency back in the city," the sweating and nervous man explained.

"I understand," the officer replied. "Let me have a look at your slate to be sure you've cleared all your debts and you can be on your way."

Hesitantly, the man handed over a scroll. All the bets from the day were marked paid or profit. There was only one wager still open.

"Excuse me, sir," Tesserarius Gratian said interrupting the Centurion. "I'm holding a chit for Recruit Sisera for a share of all bets placed against him. Also, I have a betting slip from this merchant."

The bookie plopped down on his seat and began to slowly unstrap his money chest.

Chapter 23 - Flight from the Transfer Post

Corporal Gratian found Alerio and the three escorts sitting down to eat in the mess hall.

"Recruit Sisera. I believe it's unwise for you to stay here any longer," he said. "If I were you, I'd rent four horses and pay these Legionaries to show you the way to the docks."

"With what coin?" Alerio asked pointing to the small pouch attached to his belt.

Tesserarius Gratian pulled out a small pouch and a large pouch. He dropped them on the table.

"A lot of people bet against you," Gratian said pushing the large one towards Alerio. He next pushed the small one over saying. "And you and I have a twenty-five percent agreement; this is your share."

As darkness fell, four riders left the Legion Transfer Post heading East around the Capital. They were armored and carried a complete load of javelins. No one interfered with them.

Chapter 24 - The Docks at the Capital

At a gate in the wall, a City Guard questioned them about the competition. Specifically, he was interested in where Corporal Daedalus had placed. Alerio remained silent as one of the Legionaries explained they had been on patrol, and sadly, had missed the contest.

Alerio and his three escorts were passed through the city gate by a disappointed guard. They went from the night with only a starlit sky for light to streets and buildings identifiable in spots of lantern light. Dark, long warehouse buildings bracketed the docks and piers of the harbor.

His escorts rode by the harbor and at a dark small building, they dismounted. Pulling out bed rolls, they settled in for the night outside the building's front door.

***

"Good morning Optio," the last man on guard duty said loudly enough to waken Alerio and the other two Legionaries.

"You're one of Corporal Gratian's men," the NCO stated.

"We're on assignment for the Tesserarius," the Legionary replied and explained. "We had a little trouble at the Transfer Post during the sword competition. Gratian wanted the Recruit separated from any fallout. He sent us to be sure Recruit Sisera got off okay."

"Trouble? Anything I should know about?" asked the NCO.

"No Optio," another of the Legionaries reported as he walked over from his bedroll. He pulled a pouch from his belt and handed it to the Optio. "Corporal Gratian appreciates your discretion in the matter of the Recruit and asked if you could stash him on a ship until it sails."

The NCO looked down at the pouch and smiled. He had dealings with the Tesserarius before and every time he walked away with a few extra coins and no repercussions. He couldn't see this time being any different.

"My Lance Corporal of transit won't be along until later," the NCO said as he opened the office door. "So, I'll handle this myself."

Recruit Sisera was escorted to the ramp of the Republic warship by the three Legionaries. Once he was safely aboard and as directed, hidden on the rowers walk, the escorts relaxed. Although, they didn't leave the dock area.

They sat on the dock for two days until the ship hoisted anchor, cast off their lines, and rowed to mid channel. The last time they looked the warship was heading down the Tiber river towards open water. Only then did they mount up for the trip back to the Transfer Post.

Corporal Gratian had been implicit in his instructions. The Recruit was to be watched until the ship sailed. If anything happened to him, their days would be spent digging latrines. Promotion papers and transfer requests would be perpetually lost. On the other hand, if the ship sailed and the Recruit was alive and on board, they'd receive a nice bonus and be excused from latrine duty for a year.

Chapter 25 - Warship Sailing Towards the Massina Strait

Alerio was bunked in the Legion quarters on the quinquereme. Due to lack of space, the slung beds occupied spaces between shields, javelins, bows and the Marines' gladii. To get around the space, he had to navigate barrels of arrows along the rowers walk. The only escape from the claustrophobic and cluttered space was the upper deck.

On the second day of the voyage, out of boredom, Alerio carried a gladius to the deck. With his left arm, he went through the sword drills. An Optio wandered over.

"You can't use your left hand in a shield wall," he stated. "It'll interfere with the man on your left."

"I don't have much choice, Sergeant," Alerio replied. He set the gladius down and pulled aside the sleeve of his tunic.

Two distinct lines of stitches ran down his deltoid muscle. The one to the front was a little longer than the rear line.

"Those are wounds from a gladius," the NCO declared. "Entrance and exit wounds. Care to explain how you got them?"

"Sword competition that got out of hand," replied Alerio letting the fabric fall.

"No dueling on my ship," the Optio warned. "But I've got four rowers who need to improve their sword work. This ship doesn't have a weapon's training officer and I'm too busy. Care to work with them?"

"Optio, I'm at your service," Alerio said.

The four Legionaries were from the Southwestern edge of the Republic where slings spears were preferred over swords. While they could knock down a bird in full flight with a stone, they had only managed to master the rudiments of the gladius.

Alerio began by having them spar. Right away he saw their problem. As slingers, they thought in speed, trajectory, and angles. Translated to a blade, it made the

Legionaries slow as they processed each swing. In short, they were focused on where the blade was going rather than how the blade traveled. He stopped the sparring.

Looking around the deck, he spotted long poles used to shove off attacking vessels. He gave each of the men one of the fifteen-foot poles and instructed them to hold it upright in one hand.

"Now, your first drill, go," he said. "Focus on your hand movement. Two strikes and one backhand just like you learned in training."

Of course, they could only manage to move their wrist slightly or the pole would tip over and fall to the deck. Three did and Alerio had them pick up the poles and resume the practice.

The Optio climbed onto the deck and watched for a few minutes.

"Recruit Sisera. The Legion doesn't have much use for circus balancing acts," the NCO advised.

"Look at their hands, Sergeant," Alerio suggested. "Their doing the first drill."

"It doesn't look like the first drill," the NCO stated. Before he could say anything else, a Private came rushing up and spoke to the Optio. "Duty calls. Carry on," the NCO ordered as he left the training deck.

Alerio went from one pole balancer to the other. To each man, he showed where the balance point for a gladius would be compared to the tall pole. After a while, the four left to do their shipboard duties.

The next day, the four reported for training and again he had them run the tiny movement drill with the long poles. Once satisfied the oarsmen had mastered the pole drill, he had them put the sticks away.

"Pull your gladii and hold them upright," Alerio instructed. "Now, do the small movements and feel the balance point on the blade."

From the tall unwieldly poles to the short gladii, they began to get a sense of where the power needed to be applied for the weapon to be useful. When he paired them up to spar, they swung with authority. The center of their blades connecting at the sweet spot. Their swings solid and delivered with confidence.

The Optio climbed the ladder and stopped before coming all the way to the deck. He stood there astonished at the loud and rhythmic clinging as blades met, parried and swung back to collide again in a steady cadence. His Legionaries were sweat soaked and grinning as they attacked each other.

"Time," Alerio announced when the ship's bell sounded the end of watch. "Dismissed."

The Optio climbed onto the deck and stepped out of the way as the four excited Legionaries descended the ladder.

"Recruit Sisera. That's one of the best and most efficient training lessons I've ever seen. Why aren't you a Centurion?" inquired the NCO.

"Sergeant. I barely know how I ended up in the Legion," admitted Alerio. "Let alone how I would become an officer."

"Money mostly. Enough personal wealth to outfit a Century," the Optio explained. "Or, if you have a patron with lots of money."

"I don't have either," Alerio observed. "I'm a simple Legionary."

"Not yet Recruit Sisera, you still need to complete the training," the NCO said as he walked to the ladder. "But I don't think you'll have a problem with it."

The weather changed as the ship sailed south and once through the straits of Messina tracked Northward. From the mild fall in the center of the Republic, the further South they traveled, the hotter each day became. Soon the men were sweating day and night from the humidity.

Ten days after leaving the Capital on a mild morning, the warship rowed into the broad harbor of Crotone. Alerio got his first look at the shoreline of the Eastern part of the Republic.

Act 3

Chapter 26 - Main Harbor of the Eastern Providences

The buildings were white, blindingly so, in the mid-morning light. Alerio blinked as he walked down the ramp. Other than crews loading supplies and unloading cargo, the dock was empty of military personnel. He dodged between porters pulling carts and made his way to a broad boulevard facing the harbor.

Up close the buildings were smooth with high arched windows. Civilians in loose robes hustled by and Alerio had to step to the side to avoid colliding with them. He studied the entrances of the buildings up and down the wide walkway. On his third pass, he saw a Legion flag hanging limp in the hot, humid air. Pushed his way into the moving mass of people, he angled for the flag.

"Recruit Sisera reporting in, Decanus," he said to the Legionary sitting behind a table. He followed up the greeting by handing over his travel orders.

The Legionary opened the parchment and studied it.

"There's a supply train leaving for the fort this afternoon," he said. "You can catch it if you hurry. Behind this building is a road, follow it to the fountain. Turn left there and look for the Legion Post."

"Thank you, Lance Corporal," Alerio said as he shouldered his few personal items. The armor and gladius he'd surrendered at the dock before leaving the Capital.

What he did carry came from purchases made while on the ship.

Alerio jogged out of the office, around the building, and by the time he started down the road, he was covered in sweat. A long-forced march later he located the fountain, it was dry. He took the left-hand road and picked up his pace. The road wasn't a straight Republic build. It wandered back and forth as if it were constructed by following a drunken goat.

Even longer from the fountain then from the town, the road began to solidify into a gentle curve. It started to lead back towards the harbor town. Eventually shapes appeared in the distance. Alerio spied a Legion flag and the tops of tents. He was almost back to the harbor, by the time he reached the gate of the Legion Post.

"Recruit Sisera reporting in," he said to the guard at the entrance.

The Private looked at him, at the long road he came down, and back at Alerio.

"Where did you come from?" the guard asked.

"The harbor," Alerio replied.

The guard lifted an arm and pointed between two buildings. Alerio saw a section of the harbor side boulevard and across the harbor the warship he took from the Capital. Apparently, the Lance Corporal had given him directions for the long way around.

Chapter 27 - The Harbor Transfer Post

"Welcome to the Eastern Legion Recruit Sisera," the Optio said looking up from where he sat.

The NCO laid the parchment on his desk and studied the big farm lad. He was dressed in bleached out woolen pants and a pullover. Washing clothes in ocean water took out the color and most recruits arrived after a sea voyage looking the same. Their clothing bleached out and their bodies out of shape.

Not being a Legionary and having no assigned duties, many recruits arrived weak from lack of activity. His training NCOs called it Civilian Malaise and they had a cure for it. The farm lad appeared to have trained every day as would any active duty Legionary.

"What's your story Sisera?" the Optio asked.

"My father has a farm in the Western Province, sir," Alerio explained. "I have two sisters and…"

"Shut up Recruit," the NCO ordered. "The proper response is I want to be a Legionary."

"I want to be a Legionary, sir," Alerio responded.

"Go find the supply tent and have them issue you recruit equipment," the NCO ordered. "Dismissed."

The Optio was pleasantly surprised when the farm lad slammed his right fist into his chest. He returned the salute and waved the lad away. Almost no recruits knew about saluting. He'd keep an eye on this one he thought. But a Legionary pushed into his tent with a stack of papers and he promptly forgot about the Recruit.

Alerio wandered around the straight roads between the perfectly aligned tents. As the Transfer Post for the Eastern Legion, all shipped in supplies, transferring Legionnaires and Recruits, passed through here. Command tents were behind the Optio's quarters and closer to the center of the compound. Further out, near the earthen walls, sat the larger supply tents. He took a walkway toward one of them.

"Recruit Sisera, reporting for my recruit equipment," Alerio said as he stepped out of the sun and into the shade of a supply tent.

A Private looked over from where he was stacking bundles of wrapped supplies.

"Four tents over," he said pointing to his right.

Alerio left the tent. As he walked, he peered into the open tents on either side of the road. In each, men were sorting and stacking items into separate piles. Some were handling bundles, others barrels, and in other tents, they rolled amphorae into groupings.

"Is this the right supply tent?" Alerio asked as he stepped into the indicated structure.

"These are all supply tents," a Legionary replied waving an arm to indicate their surroundings. He had a scroll in his other hand and half of the long document dangled all the way to the hard-packed sand floor.

Remembering himself, Alerio said, "Recruit Sisera reporting for my recruit equipment."

"Oh, those supplies," the Legionary said then over his shoulder shouted. "Tesserarius. You have a recruit in need of gear."

The Legionary went back to counting bundles and checking them against the scroll. An arm appeared between rows of stacked goods and motioned to Alerio.

"Recruit, come back here," a voice ordered.

Alerio made his way deeper into the tent and noticed the temperature rise the further back in he traveled. A Corporal stood holding a tightly wrapped bundle of gear. The bundle was dropped to the ground and the NCO reached onto a shelf and pulled down a backpack. It was thrust into Alerio's arms.

"Put this on Recruit," the Tesserarius ordered.

Once Alerio had adjusted the pack he felt items being placed in it. The first three items hit the bottom of the pack and jarred his shoulders. Other items didn't weigh nearly as much.

"Pick up your gear and report to the armory," the Corporal said as he held out a scroll. "You are responsible for the equipment. Every item. Lose any item and you will be charged. Break an item and you will be charged a replacement fee. Sign or make your mark here."

"But Tesserarius, I haven't inventoried the gear," Alerio explained.

The NCO stood in the hot humid interior of the tent glaring at the recruit. The tension lasted until Alerio signed the receipt and struggled out of the tent.

The backpack straps cut into his shoulders and the bundle in his arms was so large, he had to lean around it to see where he was going. Where he ended up was halfway around the compound at the armory.

Unlike the rest of the Post, part of the Armory was a block walled building with a goat skin roof. Not so much a roof, the cover was there just to block the sun and allow for air flow. Alerio stepped into the shade of the building and was hit by a wave of hot air.

To the rear of the building, a forge was flaring as ironworkers pounded on glowing lengths of metal. One of the muscular men pointed to a side doorway with his hammer. Alerio nodded in understanding and stepped to the door.

The metalworker laughed. The Recruit had to turn sideways to squeeze his body and, the equipment he carried, through the opening.

There was a slight drop in temperature in the tent attached to the forge area. Just slightly, it seemed to Alerio as he trudged with the unbalanced load across the tent.

"Recruit Sisera reporting for recruit equipment," he announced as he set the bundle on a thick board suspended between two barrels.

"Your merda is touching my counter, cūlus," a man growled. He was standing deep in the shadows between shelves of gladii and shields, "Who said you could use my space recruit?"

"My apologies, sir," Alerio replied as he hurriedly lifted the bundle, "Recruit Sisera reporting for recruit equipment."

"I heard you the first time," the Legionary said. He plucked items from shelves as he walked towards Alerio.

A large wicker shield was placed on the bundle along with three javelins. A heavy wooden practice sword was thrust into one hand and a dull metal knife into the other.

"Name?" asked the man.

"Recruit Alerio Sisera," Alerio answered.

"You are responsible for the equipment. Every item. Lose any item and you will be charged. Break an item and you will be charged a replacement fee," the man announced. "Now get out of my armory."

There was no way Alerio could navigate the doorway with all the equipment. Hesitantly, he squatted and placed the bundle and equipment on the floor near the door. After checking to see if the Legionary would complain about the placement of his gear, Alerio carried the shield, javelins, and sword through the doorway, the forge building and out to the street. He set the items down and rushed back to retrieve the bundle.

It was difficult, but he managed to balance all the gear in his arms. Standing on the street, it suddenly occurred to him. He didn't know where he was supposed to go next.

A Decanus, his chest armor oiled to a brilliant shine, his hobnailed boots polished and a buffed helmet tucked under an arm came from around a tent.

"You, on me!" the NCO announced.

He spun and marched away. Alerio stumbled after him while trying to hold and balance the pile of equipment. They walked between supply tents and onto an open field. Across the field and near the earth wall sat a ten-man field tent. On the sand beside the erect tent lay seven large bundles.

As Alerio tugged through the sand, he noted sword training posts and marked off lanes for foot races. They approached the tent.

"Drop your gear and stand by your tent," the Lance Corporal directed.

Alerio shuffled to the tent entrance and set the equipment down. He braced stiffly. The NCO stared at him for an uncomfortably long time.

"That's not your tent Recruit," the Decanus sneered. "That's my tent. Your tent is over there."

He was pointing towards one of the large bundles lying on the sand.

"Do you want my tent?" asked the NCO.

"No, sir," Alerio replied.

"Don't call me Sir!" the NCO screamed. "I'm a Decanus of the Legion. I've worked long and hard and earned the title. You, you haven't earned anything. Now, move your gear away from my tent. Now!"

Alerio scrambled to collect his equipment. He had it balanced and began to walk away when the heavy wicker shield slipped and fell to the sand.

"Did you just lose your shield?" asked the Lance Corporal. "If you drop your shield in combat you die, people die, I die. Do you want to kill me Recruit?"

"No sir," Alerio said as he lowered the equipment to the sand and began stacking it, again.

"Cur! Did you just call me cur?" the Legionary asked. "Do I look like a dog to you? Do you want to pat my head and scratch me behind my ear?"

"No, Decanus," Alerio said as he finally got the stack balanced and stood up. "I'm moving my equipment to my tent."

Recruit Sisera stood by his pile of equipment and the bundled tent. He stood until the sun past its zenith and slowly moved towards the flat hazy horizon. The Lance Corporal had long ago disappeared into his tent.

Eventually, four Privates appeared from between the supply tents and came towards Alerio. As they approached, he expected more harassment. Instead, they greeted him.

"We're here to teach you how to set up a tent," one explained.

The four instructed him in unfolding the ten-man tent. They had him refold it so he learned the proper way to stow it. They even took turns pounding in the stakes for the guide ropes. Finally, the big tent was erected and the four Legionaries stepped back to admire their work.

"Good luck Recruit," they said. Alerio watched as they crossed the field and didn't notice the Lance Corporal emerge from his tent.

"Attention Recruit," he barked. "Let me inspect your tent."

The NCO circled the tent, jerking on each guide rope and thumping on the tent sides. When he arrived back in front of Alerio, he pointed to the stack of equipment.

"The javelins can be strapped to the backpack," he said grabbing the weapons and tying them in place. He went on to explain how each piece of equipment could be layered for marching. Or strapped on for fighting. After the comprehensive lecture, Alerio had a grip on how to wear his equipment.

"Are you my instructor?" Alerio asked.

"No Recruit. I'm a Decanus in Headquarters Century," he explained. "We run security for the Post and for the baggage trains going out to the forts."

"Can I ask why the harsh words and attitude earlier?" Alerio inquired.

"It was a test," explained the Lance Corporal. "If you had pushed back or attacked me, my Squad would have made sure you were too broken up to be a Legionary."

"I assume I passed the test?" Alerio guessed.

"If you hadn't, you'd be sleeping out in the open. On the sand with the spiders and scorpions," the Lance Corporal said. "Your training class doesn't start for four days. Instructors will be here from six Centuries to do the training. That way they can select the Recruits they want for their units."

Chapter 28 - The Acting SOG

Alerio, as all farm lads do, was up before the sun rose. After getting a bowl of mushy corn from the mess hall, he wandered back to the empty training area. With no assignment or duties, he went to the tent and retrieved the practice gladius.

He was going through the sword drills on a post when the Decanus walked up.

"For a recruit, you're pretty good with the wooden gladius," the NCO said. He walked by the recruit and went into the NCO tent. When he returned, he pulled his gladius and handed a second to Alerio, "Let's see how you do against a living opponent."

They started with basic drills then the NCO slipped in an advance move. Alerio easily blocked the strike and countered. Then, he dipped his blade and grabbed his shoulder. A trickle of blood ran down his arm.

"Oh Hades, I've torn the stitches," the Recruit explained.

"I guess you've had enough," the Decanus said.

"No, let's continue," Alerio offered as he shifted the gladius to his left hand.

They ran through all the drills until both were soaked in sweat. When a horn blew, the Lance Corporal pointed towards a road heading away from the Post. Soon lines of Legionaries appeared with a wagon train following. Behind the long string of supply wagons marched several rows of Legionaries.

"That's a lot of security," observed Alerio.

Having grown up in a relatively tame province of the Republic, the thought of having to guard supplies didn't occur to him. A few armed men to protect against highwaymen was all he'd ever seen. Here, there was a Century and a half of heavy infantrymen accompanying the supplies.

Nine years ago, the Legion of the Republic had forced the ruling tribes to sign treaties. While the major cities and towns were under Legion control, the surrounding area wasn't.

"It's necessary. The local renegades would kill to get those supplies," the Decanus explained. "Heck, they'd kill for less. But mostly, they'd kill to prevent the goods from reaching our forts. The problem is, it leaves me shorthanded for Post security. I'm acting Sergeant of the Guard tonight and I need to fill guard slots. Thanks for the workout."

The NCO was three steps away when Alerio called out, "Lance Corporal. I'd like to volunteer for guard duty."

Chapter 29 - Guard Post Fifteen

Alerio shifted his shoulders. It was the first time he'd worn the recruit armor. Without time to rub in conditioning oil, the old leather was stiff and scratchy. The helmet flopped as he hadn't had time to line it with fur for fit. And the gladius and scabbard were on loan from the Post guard command. Despite the uncomfortable armor and the cold of early morning, Alerio was proud to walk Guard Post Fifteen.

The Lance Corporal assured him it wasn't likely to be attacked by rebels. In the near distance, lights from the harbor town glowed and overhead a multitude of stars seemed so close, Alerio felt as if he could reach up and grab a handful. Thirty paces along the wall, wave to the other Legionary and march back thirty paces. Wait and acknowledge the guard on the other section and repeat. The NCO had been by three times while making the rounds as Optio of the Guard. On each circuit, he reported all was quiet along the walls of the Transfer Post.

Alerio counted twenty-eight, twenty-nine and thirty. He stopped and stared into the night. Apparently, the guard on the other post was late in getting to the end of his route. Suddenly, a shape emerged on the earthen wall, an arm waved and the man turned and vanished into the dark.

All seemed well, except the shape was wrong, and there was no creaking of leather as the man moved. Alerio froze. If he called out and it was only his inexperience, he'd look like a fool. If he deserted his post and went to investigate, he could be tossed out of the Legion before actually becoming a Legionary.

He hesitated for a few seconds before racing along the dirt top. The man shape had vanished. Alerio slowed and bent to lower his profile. As he crept along the wall, voices in a strange sing song accent drifted on the still air. Alerio's foot caught on something. He knelt down and felt a foot. It was a hobnailed boot attached to the body of a Legionary.

Alerio cried out, "Sergeant of the Guard, Attack! Attack!"

Guards along the wall began sounding off that the action was to their left or to their right. This allowed the SOG and four reserve Legionaries to locate the trouble. They raced for a spot between Guard Post Fourteen and Fifteen.

The Decanus was upset but not worried. Putting a Recruit on regular guard duty was frowned upon unless you stacked them up and had an instructor nearby. Now the entire guard force, no, the entire Transfer Post, was awake and on alert.

After his second round of yelling, Alerio heard the sound of feet scraping as people climbed the wall from outside the fort. He drew his gladius.

The shapes, backlit by the lights from the city of Crotone, came level with the top of the wall. Long curved knives reflected the starlight but dark robes hid the men wielding the weapons. There was no hesitation, the four dissents rushed silently at the Legionary Guard.

Alerio arched his gladius up and over. On the downward sweep, it chopped into the leading man's forearm. The knife fell and Alerio kicked him over the wall and into the compound. The gladius continued to spin. In its up sweep, the blade cut into the second assailant's elbow.

The final two separated and came at Alerio from the sides. At knife distance, Alerio dropped to a knee and reached out. His blade tip ripped a gash in a renegade's side. But the maneuver caused the loose helmet to rocked and it tumbled from Alerio's head.

The other attacker planned to drive his knife into the Legionary's ear and into his brain. One second the helmet was level with his knife and he stabbed at the ear hole. But, Alerio had leaned away to deliver the strike and lost his helmet. The rebel's knife extended out and carved a slice of the Recruit's scalp.

With blood flowing into his eyes, and only partial vision, Alerio brought the gladius across his body and opened the knifeman's gut. The man collapsed and Alerio remained on his knees.

The acting Sergeant of the Guard found one of his Legionary guards dead and another kneeling with his hands over his head. It wasn't until later when he spoke with the Doctor, he learned how close he'd come to losing two men that night.

In short order, the men on guard duty and all off duty Legionaries were sweeping through the compound and supply tents. Small clusters of heavy infantrymen guarded any exits. Four renegades were captured and questioned. By dawn, command knew the rebels planned to start fires, burn supplies, and kill as many Legionaries as possible before escaping.

The only other deaths that day were from the Officer of the Day's blade. The Centurion executed the four rebels, then went to breakfast.

Chapter 30 - The Medical Tent

Alerio was propped up on a cot. Thick bandages spotted with leaking blood were wrapped around his head. He listened as the Doctor talked with the Lance Corporal, his Corporal, and his Optio.

"The Legionary's lucky he ducked when he did," the Doctor explained. "It took thirty-five stitches to secure the scalp. Even now, it's bleeding under the bandages. Nothing to worry about, head wounds do bleed a lot."

"Doctor, he's a Recruit and he didn't duck. He was stabbed as he killed four attackers," the Decanus reported.

"He's an extraordinary Recruit," the Doctor observed as he collected his instruments.

"I want him," the Optio said remembering the sharp salute from the Recruit. "Get him through training and claim him."

"We don't have an opening," the Corporal replied. Then remembering the dead Legionary corrected himself, "Oh, I guess we do."

"There's no one from our Century assigned as an instructor," the Lance Corporal said. "I've got a squad committed to assisting in the training but we don't have an instructor slotted."

"Corporal Thornernus, you've just been slotted as an instructor for this Recruit class," the Sergeant ordered. "I'll clear it with the Centurion."

"Yes Optio," the burley Corporal replied.

"I want him," the Senior NCO said again while pointing to Alerio. "Get him through training and claim him."

The Optio and Corporal walked out talking about other Century issues. As they left, the Decanus strolled over to Alerio.

"Recruit Sisera. I've something for you," he said pulling out a curved sheath. From the sheath, he drew a long-curved dagger with a hilt imbedded with pearls. "As near as I can figure, it's the one used to almost scalp you."

"It's beautiful, Lance Corporal," Alerio replied as he examined the exotic weapon. "But shouldn't you keep it? You were the Sergeant of the Guard."

"Thankfully Corporal Thornernus doesn't go for shiny things," the Decanus stated. "I've got one as does the Sergeant and the Centurion. So, this one belongs to you. The four apparently were professional assassins. They were coming in to kill Legionaries as a distraction for the renegades charged with lighting fires. It was a good plan except for you, Recruit Sisera."

Chapter 31 - The Training Century

Over the next three days, groups of civilians arrived and a squad from Headquarters Century escorted them through supply and taught them to erect the ten-man tents. They also instructed them in the proper way to carry their gear and how to dress for battle. Most were confused by the straps and necessity of hauling all the equipment. The squad assured them it was important.

While the recruits were settling in, five Optios wandered into the Transfer Post. The five were from the three Forts. With the largest garrisons, they were in constant need of fresh troops. Corporal Thornernus met with them and showed them to their quarters. Late at night on the day before training started, the sixth of the original instructors reported to the front gate.

"Halt, advance and be recognized," the Private on the main gate challenged.

A Legionary strolled towards the circles of light cast by the braziers. Even in the low light, the guard could see the man was dirty from traveling. Yet, he walked like a panther, measured steps with a powerful roll to his shoulders as he moved into the light.

"Optio Horus of the Legion Raiders," he stated.

"Sergeant of the Guard," the Private yelled. "Visitor at the main gate."

A short time later, the SOG and four Legionaries joined the Private. It took a few moments as the Sergeant of the Guard studied the visitor before he ordered the gate opened.

"Optio Horus. I thought you were dead," the SOG said as the man approached.

"So did they, Sergeant," Horus related. "Fortunately for me, they were wrong."

In the morning, the last Recruit to join the civilians was a big farm lad with bandages wrapped around his head.

Chapter 32 - Recruit Training

"Good morning Recruits. I am Corporal Thornernus," the NCO announced. "These are your training instructors. Impress them and you'll be invited to join their unit. Disappoint the instructors and you'll be here in training until you are dead."

Beside the Corporal, six Optios stood studying the civilian recruits. They were making initial judgements, sizing up the raw recruits, and already deciding who would fit in with their Centuries. All except for one. Sergeant Horus was yawning and seemed bored.

"We'll start with a conditioning run," the Corporal announced. "Just to loosen everybody up. Century, attention, right face."

Some of the seventy civilians knew to come to attention and fewer yet understood the right face command. Most stood looking lost and confused.

"Oh, pardon me," sneered an Optio as he stepped towards the lined-up Recruits. "Please stand with your backs straight, chest out, stomach in, thumbs along your sides, chin up and your feet at a forty-five-degree angle. Attention!"

Most of the recruits got it and assumed the position. Some still stood as if they were in the wrong place. In a sense they were.

Another Optio began wandering through the ranks. With a punch, a stomp and a sharp word or two, he taught the dazed to stand at attention.

"Right face," yelled another Sergeant.

Now the group who had originally faced to the right turned again. Some of the rest, who hadn't moved the first time turned to face right. And still, some remained facing the instructors. The training Century ended up facing in three different directions.

"Corporal. How many of these will make it?" another Sergeant asked.

"None Optio. We might as well take them to the harbor and drown the lot," Thornernus replied loudly.

"I agree. Any of you, who can understand me, raise your right hand," the Sergeant ordered.

Amazingly enough, all the Recruits raised a hand. Unfortunately, some raised their left arm.

"Everyone turn towards the sound of my voice," another Sergeant ordered. "Good. Now follow me."

He began to walk away and the Recruits like an accordion stretched out as the mob followed him.

They rushed to keep up with the Optio as he guided the Recruits out of the main gate and around the Transfer Post. He was setting a good pace so only the best conditioned Recruits stayed near him. The rest were strung out. These Recruits received help from the other instructors.

"Do you enjoy being last?"

"How about we find you a pony so you can keep up?"

"Do they have flying carpets where you come from? Because, I swear you don't know how to use your legs?"

As they neared the harbor, Corporal Thornernus jogged up and replaced the lead Optio. He continued jogging onto an old wooden pier and the herd followed. Near the end, he stopped. The training Century staggered up and filled the pier as he watched.

"Century, Attention!" shouted Thornernus. "Left Face."

Sergeants walked up and down the line adjusting each Recruit and turning many in the proper direction. Below them, waves slapped the pilings of the pier and the water appeared frothy and deep.

The Corporal looked over the fastest of the Recruits. They were standing in front of him near the end of the pier. Fresh blood leaked through the head bandage of one Recruit.

"Who are you eyeballing Recruit Sisera?" Thornernus shouted into Alerio's face. "I am not your girlfriend. I will not suffer silent insolence. I want to see you run fat boy. To the training camp and back. Move it, now."

"Yes Corporal," Alerio replied.

He snapped a left face move and ran down the line of puzzled Recruits. Mostly puzzled was Optio Horus. The big lad had managed all the instructions and certainly wasn't slacking off during the march to the pier.

"Optios. Are any of these goats worth saving?" the Corporal asked.

All the Sergeants sadly shook their heads indicating no.

"Then we drown them and go get another bunch," Thornernus announced. "Everybody, in the water."

Those who were strong swimmers jumped off the pier. Others, not sure of their abilities were pushed by the Sergeants. As the waves crashed over them, the training Century struggled until first one then another got a foot down and realized the water was only waist deep.

"Swimmers. Work your way around the pier," shouted Corporal Thornernus. "Non-swimmers walk to the beach."

As the Century divided, the Sergeants stripped and jumped into the water. They began teaching basic strokes to the non-swimmers or improving the motions of the swimmers. Water would become a weekly discipline as every Legionary was required to pass a swimming test in order to graduate.

By the time Sisera got back, the Century was standing on the pier dripping sea water. He ran up and joined the end of the line.

"Century, left face," an Optio commanded.

After a little shoving by the other instructors, they were all facing in the proper direction.

"Step off with your left foot and stomp with your right," another Optio shouted." Ready! Left, Stomp, Left, Stomp."

The stomps rippled along the line as the training Century attempted to march as a unit. During the movement, Optio Horus drifted back to where the Corporal was herding the slackers.

"Corporal. A moment of your time?" Horus asked.

The two NCOs slowed and let some distance grow between them and the rear of the recruit formation.

"The big lad. Why did you send him off?" Horus inquired.

"Recruit Sisera tangled with some rebels the other night," Thornernus explained. "He probably saved a few Legionaries' lives and for sure a lot of supplies. I figured the salt water would have been bad for a scalp and a shoulder wound. Funny thing though?"

"What's that?" asked Horus.

"I believe he would have been one of the first to dive in," Thornernus said. Then he noticed the rear of the formation was completely out of step. "Left, stomp, left, stomp."

Suddenly, Sergeant Horus wasn't bored any longer.

Chapter 33 - Gladius Drills

They spent the rest of the first day fitting armor and showing the recruits how to dress for combat. After a quick meal, they ran them through calisthenics. The exercises ended at sundown and the recruits were instructed to clean up their equipment, their bodies and get some sleep.

Before the sun's rays touched the Eastern horizon and while the stars shone brightly in the night sky, a voice called out.

"Training Century. Fall in," the voice didn't yell. It was spoken in a conversational tone without inflection.

No one appeared from the Recruit tents. The six Sergeants, the Corporal and a Lance Corporal entered the tents. Kicking, yelling, tossing of items across the tent, soon had all the Recruits standing in the cold predawn.

"It's my throat," an Optio said so softly the Recruits had to lean in to hear him. "I can't yell so, when I call, I expect everyone to repeat my words. I appreciate the help."

The Recruits relaxed. All the yelling was simply a misunderstanding.

"Get on your faces," the soft-spoken Sergeant whispered.

A few repeated, "Get on your faces."

"Get on your faces," insisted the Optio.

This time, every Recruit yelled and dove to the sandy ground as they repeated. "Get on your faces."

"On your feet," whispered the Optio.

"On your feet," the Recruits shouted as they jump to their feet.

"On your faces," the Optio ordered.

What seemed to be a long while later, the Recruits were sweaty, hoarse from yelling, and covered in sand. The Sergeant walked off silently and another Sergeant came from behind the instructors' tent.

"What are you people doing?" he asked as the sun brightened the horizon. "You are filthy. Bad enough you're dirty, you're not in the uniform of the day."

The recruits glanced around at each other. A universal what is the uniform of the day passed through their minds.

The silhouette of Corporal Thornernus came strutting out from between the supply tents. As the sun cast the first weak light of the day, he patted his stomach and stood picking his teeth with a straw.

"Breakfast was excellent this morning, Sergeant," Thornernus announced. "Are the men ready?"

"Corporal. Would you be seen in the mess hall with these goats?" inquired the Optio.

"What?" asked the shocked Corporal. "Not a uniform of the day in the entire Century?"

"What are we going to do?" questioned the Optio.

"Give me a second to figure this out," Thornernus begged. After a few heartbeats he announced, "Alright people, the uniform of the day is chest armor and your left boot. Go, you're wasting time."

The Recruits ran back into their tents and lit lanterns. Moments of panic later, they were back on the practice field. Some had on both boots, some had shirts under their armor and a few were completely dressed for battle.

"Optio. Your opinion?" Thornernus asked.

"Corporal. I don't see any uniformity in their dress," stated the Sergeant. "Let's try this again."

After changing uniforms of the day six times, the training Century was dressed in tunics and their boots.

"Corporal. I believe they are dressed in the uniform of the day," announced the Sergeant. "You are free to march them to the mess hall."

"Optio. The mess hall closed at the end of the watch," confessed Corporal Thornernus.

"That can't be right," challenged the Sergeant.

The two NCOs began bickering and, as they argued, they wandered away until they were swallowed by the supply tents. Every Recruit looked at the man next to him looking for an answer. The answer arrived in the form of Optio Horus.

"Collect your training gladii and form up at the poles," he ordered.

It wasn't his gruff voice that drove the Recruits into action. It was the deep scars covering the man's arms and legs. And the look in his eyes. As if Sergeant Horus could kill you with his bare hands and not break a sweat.

A short while later, the training Century was formed up around the Sergeant. They all held wooden training swords.

"This is a gladius," the Optio said holding up a wooden sword. "It's heavier than its metal cousin. But it is a gladius." He pointed the practice sword at a heavyset Recruit. "You attack me."

The Recruit took some urging but eventually, he swung at Horus. In two moves the Recruit was on his back with the point of the wooden sword at his throat. Horus picked out five more Recruits and demonstrated how dangerous the wooden weapon was before stepping back.

"This is a gladius," he repeated. "I can kill you with it as easily as I can with its metal cousin."

The squad of Legionaries who helped the instructors appeared. Two of them at each practice pole soon had the Recruits running the first drill against the air. Optio Horus walked from group to group until he saw one recruit practicing left-handed. It was the big farm lad.

"You. Come here," he growled.

Alerio jogged over holding the sword in his left hand.

"You can't defend a shield with your left hand," Horus explained. "It'll throw off the entire unit. What's your name?"

"Recruit Sisera, Optio. I understand," Alerio replied. "I was favoring my right arm but if you insist, I'll use my right."

"Do it," ordered Horus. He watched as the lad switched hands. He was as fluid in the drills with his right as he'd been with his left.

After all the Recruits had proven rudimentary skills, he directed them to begin striking the poles. A line of Recruits was queued up at each pole. On his signal, the Recruits near the poles began the first drill.

He didn't have to look to see who was doing it correctly. He listened to the tone of the wood striking the poles, the rhythm of the strokes, and the speed of the assault. None of the recruits had it right.

They went through almost an entire rotation before a pattern emerged. Some Recruit at one of the poles had the blade singing a battle song. As the practice gladius beat out an almost perfect tempo, Horus turned. Recruit Sisera's wooden blade was dancing and smashing the pole. But the Sergeant became alarmed.

Blood was pouring down the Recruit's right arm, streaks of red appeared on his wrapped head and blood drops dribbled onto his ear. Yet, the lad wouldn't let up until Horus called for a change. Recruit Sisera staggered away from the pole and shook off one of the training squad members.

"You. Come here," Horus called to the Recruit.

"Yes, Sergeant?" Alerio responded.

"Get to the medical tent," the Optio ordered. "That's an order."

"Yes, sir," Alerio replied. "But really, I'm fine."

Horus squinted at the farm lad. One of the Optio's eyes quivered and the veins in his neck plumped up. Alerio recognized the danger signs. He spun on his heels and headed for the medical tent.

Chapter 34 - A Little Jog

The morning passed with the training Century rotating through sessions on the striking posts. Most of the Recruits could barely lift their training gladii or their right arms after hours of wielding the heavy swords. They were ordered to stow the gladii in the tents and report back to the practice field. To a man, they were hungry and tired, and it was only mid-morning.

"Good morning Recruits," another of the Sergeant said. "I trust you all had a good night's sleep. I did, but I need a little exercise. Let's go for a jog. Shall we?"

As if by magic, Corporal Thornernus, and the other Sergeants appeared. They adjusted the lines so the Recruits were in even rows. Next, they positioned themselves at the sides and behind the Recruits.

"Attention! Right Face," called the Optio. "Forward march. Left, stomp, left stomp."

The training Century stepped off heading for the main gate. Before the first row reached the exit to the Post, Recruit Sisera jogged up and fell in to the rear. His head was wrapped in a fresh bandage and the sleeve over his right shoulder displayed the bulge of another wrap.

Optio Horus observed the farm lad.

"Quick time march," shouted the Sergeant. The Recruits went from marching to a slow jog.

They didn't mind the run until mile five. At that distance, a few fell back holding their sides and gasping for breath. As the column moved forward, more Recruits slowed and drifted back. Recruit Sisera on the last row offered encouragement and physically pulled two men along with him. Regardless of Alerio's help, the trail behind the unit was soon littered with walking and limping Recruits.

The non-hackers weren't alone. Sergeants talked to them, offering assistance at a high volume and directly into their ears.

"Does it hurt you to run? The enemy runs all day. Are you weaker than our enemies?"

"Do you want to die? If you can't run away, the enemy will kill you first?"

"It only hurts until you die."

Some responded to the motivation and jogged to catch up. Others were lost in their misery and couldn't respond.

At mile six, the column made a U-turn and headed back to the Transfer Post. In the weeks to come, the distance would increase until every recruit could run twenty miles in under five hours. Those failing to meet the time and distance, wouldn't graduate.

As the column reach the main gate, the Optio called, "Unit, march. Left foot. Stomp. Hold up your heads, you are Recruit Legionaries. Be proud."

Stragglers stretched out behind the column as if it had a long tail. Because Alerio had pulled two recruits along, he was separated from the main column by a few steps. As the unit began to march, he kept running and pulling to close the distance. Before he could reach the last row, a Sergeant stepped in front of him.

"The order was to march," the Sergeant growled. "Half rations for those not keeping up."

Further back, where those truly suffering staggered in, another Optio shouted, "Quarter rations for the non-hackers."

They were halted at the mess hall. As announced, the first group got a full meal. Recruit Sisera and his companions received half a meal. The remaining Recruits had only a quarter of a bowl of stew. In the Legion, performance was rewarded.

Chapter 35 - Hand Launched Missiles

The rest of the day was spent having the Recruits dress in their armor. Straps were tightened and pieces adjusted for fit. Optio Horus walked among them striking them with the flat of a wooden gladius.

"Tighten the shoulder strap," he'd say as a Recruit jerked back from the strike.

It was the first time any of them had seen him smile. Bruised and bone weary, the Recruits were ordered to clean their gear, their bodies, and get some sleep.

***

"Recruit Training Century, on the road for chow," the Sergeant said softly.

It was still dark and the exhausted Recruits were sound asleep. Yet a few heard and repeated the order. Soon, the Recruits were dressed and piling out of their tents. They marched as a unit to the mess hall for a quick meal then back to the practice field.

They were greeted by the training squad and lines of measured off rows.

"Javelins and shields," ordered the Optio.

Once the recruits had their equipment, they were lined up at marked off areas. The areas started about a shoulder's width wide and angled out until they were ten yards wide and forty yards deep. A bale of straw was laid every ten yards down the center of each range.

With the heavy wooden shield and a javelin, the recruits took turns launching the missiles. Most had an issue balancing the shield while throwing the javelin. A few understood the benefit of counterbalancing the shield and using the momentum to aid their throw. Recruit Sisera was one of them. Sergeant Horus took notice.

After assessing their abilities, some recruits were pulled out for extra javelin training. Others were lined up and instructed to touch the edges of their shields together. They were split in half and turned to face each other. For the rest of the morning, the recruits jabbed at the other's shields with the javelin.

"You can only throw a javelin once and kill one enemy," an Optio explained. "Or you can stab over your shield a hundred times and kill a hundred of the enemy."

For the rest of the day, the recruits were rotated between the shield wall and the range. At the end of the day, the entire training Century was queued up at the range.

"Recruits. You have four targets on the range," Corporal Thornernus announced while pointing at the straw bales. "Hit the fourth bale and you get full rations. Miss it and you'll receive three quarters rations. Hit the third target and you'll also receive three quarters rations. Miss three and you earn half rations. You have three javelins to earn your food."

Recruit Sisera was fifth in line. Along the range, fifteen of the recruits had managed to reach the fourth target. Five had hit it twice while the other ten had only hit it with one of their three javelins. Alerio stepped up and rocked his shield up while dropping his right arm back. He rocked transferring the power of the dropping shield through his shoulders and into his right arm. The javelin launched high into the air and arched over. Its point drove into the back edge of the fourth target.

"Full ration," announced a Sergeant. "Two more throws."

But, Alerio didn't pay attention. He was bent over with his right shoulder tucked into his shield. Behind the shield, he held the painful shoulder in his left hand. Sergeant Horus saw the agony displayed on the Recruit's face and walked over.

"Can you do that left-handed?" he asked.

"Yes, Optio," Alerio replied. "I believe I can."

"Do it," Horus ordered.

With the shield on his right arm and the javelin in his left, Recruit Sisera dropped the next two javelins on either end of the fourth straw bale. Sargent Horus strolled away as if he wasn't impressed.

Chapter 36 - Every Recruit Has a Weakness

After two weeks of gladii and javelin practice with the shields. Running until the distance became twenty miles and weekly swimming, the recruits returned from the mess hall.

The range had been adjusted. Stacks of straw bales were staggered downrange and armorers stood by a wagon.

"Recruits with archery experience step out," a Sergeant ordered. "The rest of you break into squads."

Every Legionary was trained on the bow. However, it was a specialty and, only those with true talent would be assigned to a Bowmen Century. Recruit Sisera stayed with the non-archers.

The experienced archers gathered at the armorer's wagon and selected bows. After stringing them, they tested the pull. Many returned the original bow and selected another. Once they held bows that met their personal preference, they marched to the range.

Sergeant Horus pointed to Recruit Sisera and waved him over.

"What? No left-handed archery?" asked the Sergeant.

"The bow has never been my friend," Alerio admitted.

The future archers pulled and soon every target bristled with arrows. As they notched and fired, the inexperienced Recruits were instructed on the finer points of archery.

Over the next several weeks, all the Recruits became proficient with the bow. While they could earn full rations some of the time, the experienced archers earned double rations. The Legion valued and rewarded their specialists.

Chapter 37 - Recruit Guard Duty

Along with the running, swimming and weapons practice, the Recruits were instructed in proper military procedures. After learning ranks and the rules governing military orders, the Recruits were assigned guard duty.

Throughout the day and night, recruits were assigned to walk circuits around the recruit camp. The Century had been issued their metal gladii, bows, and iron tipped javelins. Besides the weapons, their armor had been changed out for new issues. Guarding was more than an exercise. Now it was necessary to protect the valuable equipment.

While training continued, the Recruits began to work more and more in specialized groups. Archers practiced with their bows, and future infantrymen with shields, javelins, and gladii. They all joined in for marching and tactical maneuvering.

As the training progressed, five of the Optios and Corporal Thornernus discussed the merits of each Recruit. Thornernus expressed his interest in Sisera and asked the others to pass on him. They had begun the selection process and one Recruit wouldn't make a difference. All the instructors expressed interest in groups of Recruits, except for Optio Horus. He kept his own counsel.

Recruit Sisera and a Recruit from another tent had the overnight guard duty. As the sun rose, their relief marched up and the two sentries retired to their tents. They would be allowed to sleep in before joining the day's training.

Corporal Thornernus didn't have to teach a class until later in the day so he lounged in the instructor's tent. Growing bored with the inactivity, he decided to check on the progress of some Recruits who were lagging in their swordsmanship. The NCO tossed aside the tent flap and noticed a Recruit sneaking between the tents.

The Recruit was bent over to keep a low profile. Thornernus observed him vanishing from sight before reappearing on the other side of a structure. A Recruit avoiding training wasn't unusual but this one had a knife in his hand. When the man ducked into a specific tent, Thornernus ran over to question the Recruit.

Alerio Sisera was sleeping in his bedroll at the back of his tent. He'd pulled the blanket over his head in an attempt to ignore the fact it was late in the morning. When the knifeman entered, he was temporarily blind. Once the tent flap fell his eyes began to adjust to the dark interior.

He located the sleeping Recruit and was two steps towards his target when the tent flap opened.

Corporal Thornernus stepped in and demanded, "What's going on here?"

The Corporal was also partially blinded in the dim light, but he was an experienced fighter. When the knife swung in his direction, he read the body language and leaned back. Unfortunately, his hand came up in a defensive reflex and the knife edge sliced his palm open.

Alerio heard the Corporal's question and grunt from being slashed. Still wrapped in his blanket, he sat up to explain why he was in bed while his squad was out training. Suddenly, a shape hurled itself across the tent. Alerio swung his legs up, caught the attacking knifeman in the midsection, and vaulted the man up and over. The taut side of the tent gave way from the man's weight, a little, before rebounding.

The knifeman bounced off the goatskin leather side and landed partially tangled in Alerio's blanket. That's when Alerio noticed the knife. From under the crumpled blanket, the blade jabbed out. Alerio rolled away and his hand landed on his pearl handled knife. Drawing the long-curved blade, he stabbed at the moving blanket trying to defend himself from the knifeman.

A man rose, tossed off the blanket, and stooped in a fighting stance. Before he could attack, a big fist connected with his head. He crumpled to the floor of the tent. Corporal Thornernus added a swift kick to be sure the man would stay down.

"The cūlus cut me," he complained. "Recruit Sisera drag, this piece of merda outside and let's have a talk with him."

Chapter 38 - Five, No Seven Republic Golds

The man woke to bright sunlight and four men standing over him. He attempted to move an arm but it was stretched out. As was the other arm and both of his legs. He realized he was staked out, spread eagle on the hot sand.

"Do you recognize him?" Optio Horus asked.

"He was one of the late arriving recruits," replied Corporal Thornernus. His left hand was wrapped in a bloody bandage, "From the Western provinces, I believe."

"Recruit Sisera. You're from the West. Do you know him?" another Sergeant inquired.

"No Optio. I've seen him during training but we've never exchanged words," Alerio reported.

"Optio. Corporal. I have to ask you to leave the area," Sergeant Horus said as he pulled a curved knife from his hip. The dagger was the same shape as Alerio's pearl inlaid weapon except it was sans any fancy decorations. Horus added as Alerio began to leave with the NCOs, "Sisera, you stay."

The Legion Raider knelt beside the staked-out man and asked a simple question, "Why?"

"Why what?" the man replied defiantly.

"In spite of the training you're still a civilian at heart," Horus explained. "Let me enlighten you about military field justice. I am a Sergeant and I asked a question. Why?"

The man spit at the Optio. Without a word, Horus nicked the side of the bridge of the man's nose. Drops of blood began running into the eye on that side.

"If I had my gang here you wouldn't be able to lay a hand on me," the man blustered, but the effect was diminished by his attempt to dump the pooling blood from his eye socket. "Back home I'm important."

"Why?" asked the Sergeant.

"There's a seven Republic gold reward on him, dead or alive," the man stated.

"The bounty has gone up. It was five gold," Alerio said. Horus looked at Alerio and tilted his head as if listening for more, "It was in a pub and I got mixed up in a knife fight with some members of the Cruor gang."

"I understand revenge and a bounty," Horus replied. "but just how many of the gang?"

"Seven or eight, I can't remember," admitted Alerio.

"You butchered them all," the man screamed. "The Cruor want you dead."

An evil grin crept over Horus' face before he started laughing. The laughter was so out of character for the drab Sergeant, that Alerio pulled back a few steps.

"Seven or eight," the Raider Optio mumbled as he cut the straps from the man's arms and legs.

He helped the failed assassin to his feet and took a cloth from a pouch and dabbed away the blood from the side of the man's nose. Then, he offered the man a drink from his water bag. A gentle shove and the Optio guided the man towards the practice field. Alerio followed.

Chapter 39 - Graduation Day

Corporal Thornernus saw the three men approaching and noticed the Sergeant's hand on the knifeman's shoulder. They walked towards the sword practice area. The Corporal called the other Recruits over and had them form a semicircle so they could watch.

The would-be murderer was handed a gladius and Horus drew his.

"I'm not going to fight you, Optio," the man announced.

"This is a gladius," Horus said as if delivering a lecture. He walked around the knifeman as he spoke to the assembled Recruits. "We teach you to hack and chop because, in a shield wall, things get messy."

He strolled back and forth, with his back to the assassin, as he lectured.

"In truth, the gladius is an elegant weapon," he said finally stopping and standing still. "The blade is perfect for…"

The knifeman charged at Horus' unprotected back. His blade swung level with the Sergeant's head to deliver a killing blow.

Alerio was too far away to help. He watched, horrified, expecting to see the Raider NCO die.

Horus dropped to a knee. The blade of his gladius extended backwards from under his arm. It skewed the surprised knifeman. A man could recover from a puncture wound if treated quickly. But, as Alerio observed, when the gladius was twisted in a man's gut, his intestines get wrapped around the blade and were pulled out when the sword was removed.

The knifeman sank to his knees. His hands attempting to hold in his intestines.

"The gladius is an elegant weapon," Horus explained as he stood up. "The blade is perfect for stabbing. As such, one must be aware and try to prevent training accidents."

"You. Run and fetch a Medic," Corporal Thornernus ordered. He had selected a notoriously slow Recruit for the task.

Act 4

Chapter 40 - The Selection Process

Corporal Thornernus stood in front of his Optio's desk. Beside him were Sergeant Horus and Recruit Sisera.

"I agree, Sisera can't be stationed at the Transfer Post," the Sergeant stated. "It's too much temptation for gang assassins and bounty hunters. Has he completed training? Should he? Or should we discharge him for the good of the Legion?"

"As one of his instructors, I'd graduate him today," Thornernus offered. "But I don't know of any unit that wants to be saddled with a wanted man."

Horus who had been silent, spoke up, "The Raiders will take him."

The Post Transfer Optio spun a piece of parchment around and shoved it across his desk.

"Recruit Sisera sign here," he ordered while pointing to the bottom of the form.

Alerio leaned down and jotted his name on the paper. Next, the Corporal Thornernus and the Sergeant Horus, as his instructors, signed off on the Recruit's fitness. The Post's Sergeant studied the signatures. After checking to be sure it was signed properly, he stood and offered his hand to Alerio.

"Private Sisera," he said while gripping Alerio's wrist. "Let me be the first to congratulate you. Welcome to the Legion."

Corporal Thornernus and Optio Horus both added their congratulations while Alerio thanked them for the hours of instruction. Finally, the Post's Sergeant had enough.

"Out, get out of my office," he said with a smile. "I have real work to do. Not babysitting a bunch of glad-handing Legionaries."

Outside of the Optio's office, Horus turned to the Corporal, "Thornernus, I need Sisera's gear brought to my quarters."

"I'll arrange it," the Corporal replied. "When do you leave?"

"Tonight, after dark," the Raider explained.

"You know most people like to travel during the day," offered Thornernus.

A rare smile crossed the Raider NCO's face. "Most people don't have a price on their head," Horus replied.

Private Sisera opened his mouth, but Horus spoke first, "Not on you Private. The bounty is on me. The rebels are offering ten Republic golds for me, dead or alive."

Chapter 41 - Traveling Raider Style

Shortly after dark, two figures marched out of the Transfer Post. They headed straight down the Republic road. The guard and Corporal Thornernus watched them until the men vanished into the dark.

"Dangerous for only two men to travel at night," the Private observed.

"Not if they're Raiders," the Corporal replied as he stepped back. "Secure the gate."

"Securing the gate, Corporal," the guard stated as he swung the doors closed.

In the black of night, Horus angled off the road and looped back towards the harbor. Alerio followed silently in the footsteps of his Sergeant. They wandered back and forth as if lost until the Optio stopped.

"Over there," he whispered.

Placing a hand on Alerio's shoulder, he guided them to a small shrub tree. The Optio dropped to his knees and began to dig. Soon his hands touched a leather bag and he changed from digging down to digging around. Finally, with a grunt, he pulled the satchel free.

From the sack, he pulled two sets of rough woolen clothing and two hooded robes.

"Take off your uniform and stow it and your armor in here," Horus directed as he shoved the workmen's clothing into Alerio's arms. "Keep your gladius but hide it under the cloak."

Once dressed, the Legionaries each grabbed a side of the bag and continued walking towards the lights of the harbor town. A long trudge over the sand and rocks later, they stopped at the rear of a single-story warehouse. Horus dropped his side of the bag and jumped for the edge of the roof. With a powerful pull, he disappeared over the edge.

Seconds later, he leaned over the roof.

"Hand me the equipment bag," he whispered.

Alerio jerked the bag to his chest and pressed it overhead. The weight lifted and the bag vanished. A moment later, Horus dropped from the roof.

"Let's go see about a ride," the Sergeant suggested. "And, I could use a drink after all the military stuff."

They took an alleyway and emerged at the wide boulevard facing the harbor. Horus flipped the hood up and stooped so he appeared shorter and less threatening. Alerio flipped up his hood and stooped as well.

As far as anyone could tell, the two nondescript workmen entering the pub were there for a drink after a hard day's labor. They took seats in the back and the thin one ordered two ales. The ale arrived and the two sat drinking quietly.

"Are we looking for a ride?" Alerio asked as he took another sip of the malty brew.

"We're gathering information," explained Horus. "That group in the corner are local thugs. They're planning a robbery. Not our concern."

"How do you know that?" Alerio inquired. "I've been sitting on the bench for as long as you. All I know about the pub's patrons is a guy near the door likes the waitress a little too much."

"Listen and watch their body language," Horus instructed. "Most people say important things three or more times. Mostly to impress themselves. But also, to be sure everyone understands the issue. When one person leans forward again and again and says the same thing over and over, you can collect a little of the story with each telling. Soon, you'll know the complete tale."

"If not for law enforcement, why are we gathering information?" Alerio asked.

The pub door opened and two men entered. They examined the room before one stuck his head outside. Four more men came in and while three stood, three sat and huddled together.

"Them," replied the Raider Sergeant. "Watch and tell me later what you learn."

Of the three, one was fat and animated. He would lean in and speak softly. The two other men were very attentive and never took their eyes off the speaker. Four times he engaged one, but only once did he single out the other man. After a round of wine, the three stood and the six men left the pub.

"It was a scolding," Alerio reported. "Both men messed up, but one really bad. The other not badly enough for a chewing out, but not good enough to be praised. The three standing were bodyguards. I noticed the swords and long knives. Care to tell me who they are?"

"The fat one is Speckled Pheasant, a Captain with the renegades," Horus related. "The other two are his Lieutenants. I don't know what they did but I agree with your analysis. Their mission didn't go as planned. Time to go home."

They set down their mugs, dropped a few coins on the table, and left the pub. Horus guided them along the boulevard passed the big piers where the merchant vessels lay tied to the docks.

"Optio. If they're rebels," asked Alerio as they walked. "Why don't you bring them in?"

"Revolutionaries in name only here in Crotone," Horus replied. "Until they do or say something rebellious, we can't. Out at the Legion Forts, they cause trouble. Here, it's mostly a protection racket. They extract funds from merchants to support the Cause. When the merchants get fed up, they'll call for the Legion. In the meanwhile, we keep an eye on the renegades."

Further down, fishing boats were anchored in the shallows. The two Legionaries stepped off the walkway and onto a rocky beach.

A campfire glowed in the distance and they angled up the beach towards the flames. As they approached, Alerio could see a man sitting and tending the fire.

"It's a good night for a stroll," Horus said to the man poking the fire.

"Not good for fishing," replied the man. He didn't look up.

"Still, I'd like to see your boat," Horus insisted.

"If you're going to be like that Sergeant," the man said standing and reaching out to grasp Horus's wrist. "We can be gone as soon as your gear arrives."

There was a noise further up the incline and Alerio reached for his gladius.

"Steady there, Private," Horus said. "It's only our gear."

Two men hiked into sight hauling their equipment bag. The man at the fire walked to the shoreline and began pulling on a rope. At the end of the line, rested a midsized fishing boat. It slowly came towards them.

Chapter 42 - Raider Post Eastern Province

Two men rowed and the third handled the rudder. At the entrance to the harbor, the men hoisted a sail and the fishing boat tracked into the wind. Horus curled up in his robe and went to sleep. Alerio, on the other hand, sat watching the dark shoreline race by. As they traveled, the land shifted from flat to hills. As the moon rose, the shore's profile grew taller until the hills loomed over the water.

Someone shoved a piece of bread and a wedge of cheese into his hand. He ate as he marveled at the waves and the illumination of the moon reflecting off the water.

Later as the sun touched the smooth horizon, the boat turned and entered the mouth of a river. Steep cliffs loomed over both sides of the waterway. Horus stood, stretched and yawned.

"Introductions," he announced as two men pulled down the sail. "This is Private Alerio Sisera. He's good with a gladius and has a price on his head."

Alerio was shocked the Optio would reveal information about the bounty.

"How much?" the man on the till asked.

"Private Sisera, this is Decanus Remigius," Horus said. "It's seven Republic golds."

"Ba, I'm up to nine," Remigius bragged. "Welcome to the Raiders, Sisera."

"The two rowing are Lance Corporal Wido and Private Ireneus," Horus said before turning to the pilot. "Remigius. We overheard our favorite rebel Captain, Speckled Pheasant, chewing out two of his Lieutenants. Can you find out what they were discussing?"

"Absolutely Sergeant," the Decanus replied. "After we do a little fishing. We have to maintain our cover."

"Just get me the information," Horus ordered as the fishing boat bumped against a rough pier.

While the Raider Sergeant jumped to the dock, Wido and Ireneus hoisted the equipment bag and tossed it onto the rickety boards. Alerio jumped next.

"Private Sisera bring the bag," Horus ordered as he started up a narrow trail.

Alerio looked up to the top of the hill looming over the river. The trail was no more than a winding footpath carved into the side of the towering knoll. He lifted the bag and placed a foot on the track. It slipped on the small pebbles scattered over the risers.

"Careful there Private," Lance Corporal Remigius shouted as the crew dipped the oars and moved the fishing boat down the river.

High above, Optio Horus reached the top and vanished over the crest. Alerio adjusted the load on his shoulders and gently placed his foot. Behind him, laughter rolled across the water from the retreating fishing boat.

Chapter 43 - Legion Raider Camp

Alerio struggled to the top. The land flattened and stretched for about twenty yards before dipping off. He traipsed to the other edge and happily found a set of steps carved into the hill side. Below him, Legion tents were neatly arranged in a wide valley. On the far side of the valley, the slope rose until it was higher than his plateau.

Off to his right, three Legionaries stood watch on a peak at a large tube of leather. They had their backs to him looking away from the valley. To his left, a range was organized. Legionaries and men in robes performed weapons training. Behind the range, a small well-traveled ravine marked the exit to the encampment.

He was three stepped down when a Corporal and a Decanus jogged up. They waited for him at the bottom of the stairs.

"Private Sisera. I'll take Optio Horus' gear," the Corporal said. "This is Lance Corporal Velius. He's your squad leader. I'll get with you later."

The Corporal opened the bag and grabbed the Sergeant's gear. He jogged off without another word.

"Is he always so talkative?" Alerio asked Decanus Velius.

"Centurion Stylianus is off Post and Corporal Manfredus has been running the show, solo," Velius replied. "He has a lot to discuss with Horus. Follow me."

They strolled between evenly placed tents on straight walkways. On the last row before a range, Velius turned towards a tent. Men were sitting outside watching the action on the range while sharpening gladii, mending armor, or patching big heavy infantry shields.

"Private Sisera is our new guy," Velius announced. "Show him the ropes. I've got an NCO meeting."

The Lance Corporal spun on his heels and rushed off.

"Alerio Sisera," Alerio said introducing himself to the seven Legionaries.

None looked up. After an uncomfortable length of time, one stopped and jerked as if just noticing Alerio.

"Wow, where did you come from?" the Legionary asked. "You shouldn't sneak up on a man like that. Bad for the nerves, you know."

Another stopped honing his blade with a stone and studied Alerio from toes to head.

"He's a big lad," he observed. "They must feed them good in recruit training these days. When I graduated, I was nothing but skin and bones."

A rock flew over and struck the man in the shoulder.

"That's because you were on quarter rations the whole time," another squad member teased.

"Because you are uncoordinated," the rock thrower added.

"I'm not uncoordinated," pleaded the Legionary. "It's just the instructors didn't like me."

"Don't mind them Alerio. Their mothers dropped them on their heads when they were babies," another Legionary said as he stood. "Name's Didacus. Let me show you to your bunk."

Didacus ushered Alerio into the tent and pointed out a wooden pallet next to the entrance.

"We slept on the ground in training. This is much better than being a Recruit," Alerio stated.

"Mountain spiders and scorpions," Didacus replied flatly. "They like the body's warmth so we sleep off the ground."

Before Alerio could say more, shouting came from outside the tent. They stepped out to find a bowman standing nose to nose with one of their Legionaries.

"If you think you can do better, unknot your coin purse and lay a few down," the Archer challenged.

Didacus looked at another squad member, "What now?"

"Pholus said the targets were too close. Said, he could hit those targets with his javelin," he recounted. "Seems the Veles heard him and took offense."

"Come on big mouth," the skirmisher challenged. "Let's see what you and your javelin can do."

"Not only me," Pholus bragged. "My whole squad can hit those targets."

Didacus slapped a palm to his forehead and exclaimed, "This is going to be expensive."

"Why is that?" Alerio asked.

"We are Second Squad, heavy infantry, Raider Century," Didacus said with pride. "You take on one of us, you get all of us."

"Hold on a second," Alerio said loudly. The Archer and Pholus turned to look at him. "How about we go javelins against bows, then double or nothing, gladii against gladii," he suggested feeling proud about maybe saving his new squad some coin.

"No, javelin against bow," the light infantryman offered. "Then we switch to bow against javelin."

"Done," Pholus shouted. "Five coppers each."

Alerio was shaken. He'd meant to tilt the competition in his favor. Now, with the bow as the second weapon, he worried about letting his new squad down.

The eight heavy infantrymen grabbed their three javelins and walked to the range.

"Three javelins at the targets and we'll shoot three arrows.," the Veles explained. "Then we switch and the archers will throw three javelins. Afterwards, we'll sit back and count our money."

Every Light Infantryman laughed knowing they were proficient with the javelin; the Heavy Infantrymen probably not so much with the bow.

Didacus, Pholus and the other five threw their three javelins. The targets bristled with spears near the center point. Alerio stepped up and one after the other of his javelins hit center mass. His new squad mates pounded his back and taunted the Archers.

The skirmishers released three arrows each and their arrows matched the javelins. Bows were brought out for the Infantrymen and javelins for the Velites. The bowmen threw first.

Only a few javelins landed center target, yet the skirmishers acquitted themselves nicely. The first seven Infantrymen shot arrows.

After the round, the Velites held an edge. Everyone stepped back as Alerio walked to the line.

Seeing as Alerio had saved the Infantrymen with his javelin throws, the squad expected their new guy to win the match.

"Just like you did with the javelins," encouraged Pholus.

Alerio's palms started to sweat. He had to inhale deeply several times while trying to steady his nerves. The first arrow hit the edge of the target. A groan erupted from the infantrymen. When his second hit the bottom of the target, they remained silent. On his third shot, they held their breath. It zoomed over the mound and stuck in the earthen embankment behind the range.

"Told you the instructors were getting soft in recruit training," complained Pholus. "With bow work that sad, he should have been on quarter rations."

None of the infantrymen would meet the new guy's eyes. They handed over their coins to the elated Light Infantrymen. Alerio surrendered the bow to an armorer.

"That's really bad archery," Horus called out.

The Optio, Corporal Manfredus, and Decanus Velius had arrived to watch the competition. They stood in a group on the slope by the tents. Behind them, a Legionary was positioned with his back to the NCOs. He wasn't watching the match; he was focused on the high hill with the spotting tube.

The Sergeant dug into a pouch and pulled out a coin. He flipped it into the air and the sunlight reflected off the spinning Republic Silver.

"Sword drills," he announced as he closed a fist around the coin. "Private Sisera will represent the Heavy Infantry. Velites, pick your two best swordsmen. Four touches for the win."

Alerio pulled his gladius and walked to a sandy pit. He swung the weapon a few times before letting it rest on his right thigh. The infantry squad had no idea if the new Private was any good with a gladius. Nevertheless, he was one of them so they reluctantly pulled out more coins. While bets were placed, two broad shouldered skirmishers joined Alerio in the pit.

"Private Didacus, loan Private Sisera your gladius," Optio Horus ordered.

Didacus drew his weapon and, with confusion on his face, walked to the pit.

"Is something wrong with your gladius?" he asked Alerio.

"I believe the Sergeant is going to redefine gladius drills," Alerio replied as he took the sword with his left hand.

"Now we know Velites are tough but they spend most of their time with the bow and javelin," Sergeant Horus stated. "It's not fair to pit them up against a heavy infantryman who practices daily with the gladius."

The light infantrymen nodded and murmured about the unfairness of the sword fight. Even if they had the advantage of rotating fighters against one infantryman, the gladius wasn't their primary weapon.

"So, for this fight, it'll be two against one," the Optio explained as he flipped the Republic Silver to the Legionary managing the bets. "Place that on Sisera."

Suddenly the Velites crowded around the Legionary shoving coins at the hurried man. Betting was heavy yet, only a few infantrymen added to their wagers. The Scouts, who had been watching from the hill sides, walked down to add their coin to the pile for the skirmishers. One hesitated and studied the young infantryman.

Corporal Ceyx Eolus of the Scouts watched as the infantryman's left hand grasped the gladius offered by Didacus. The grip was firm and the arm moved with no hesitation. He walked over, and to the surprise of his fellow Velites, tossed coins onto Alerio's pile.

"Private Sisera are you ready?" Horus asked. When Alerio slammed the hilt to his chest, the Optio turned to the two light infantrymen, "Velites. Are you ready?" They also saluted. "Begin," instructed Horus.

Rather than placing the blades in a high guard, Alerio held them down as if he were about to impale a charging bull. The skirmishers separated by four steps and shuffled forward.

The first to strike was the Veles facing Alerio's right gladius. His strike was designed to engage the blade and keep it occupied defending against the attack.

While the blades clashed, the skirmisher, facing the left gladius, delivered a powerful smash. It was designed to put the blade in the weaker arm out of position and open a path to the infantryman's chest. The ploy would have worked if Alerio's left arm was weaker.

Alerio dueled with his right gladius countering the skirmisher move for move. When his left blade was smashed down, he didn't resist. Instead, he used the power of the Veles' wallop to propel his gladius. The blade swung down and around. Before it arched higher than his shoulder, the light infantrymen stepped forward trying to score the first touch. Momentum carried the blade from the apex of the arc directly into the advancing skirmishers chest.

As the point of the left gladius stopped the advancing Veles, Alerio rotated his right wrist. The blades went from clashing against each other to Alerio's spinning around his opponent's blade. The effect halted the skirmisher's blade in mid attack. Alerio's gladius reached out and touched the man's shoulder.

"Two touches for Private Sisera," Horus announced as the fighters separated.

The Heavy Infantrymen were yelling and slapping each other on the backs. It didn't matter they'd been shy in betting on the young man. As one of their own, he'd get their full vocal support.

Corporal Eolus, the Light Infantryman, didn't display any outward emotion. His face was scrunched down as the Scout mentally went over each move of the first round.

The skirmishers saluted the heavy infantryman and brought their gladii up in a high guard. Alerio bowed to them, raised his gladii above his shoulders and held them wide apart. It seemed as if he was inviting the pair of Velites to go for his unguarded chest. They did.

As their blade tips dropped and thrust forward, Alerio rotated his blades inward. The four blades met. Alerio's were circling rapidly while the skirmishers were on a straight line held almost at arms' length. Private Sisera's gladii drove the attacking blades apart. Now it was a race to see which of the combatants could recover first and bring their weapons back to the line of attack.

Alerio let his blades continue to circle until they were inside his opponent's. He stepped forward and each blade touched a Veles' chest.

"Two more touches," Horus announced. "That's four and the winner is Private Sisera."

Didacus raced forward and took back his gladius. He inspected the blade before saying, "You're going to grind out the nicks. Oh, and nice sword work."

Alerio was halfway out of the pit when a voice cried out, "Signal! Alert Signal!"

The Legionary standing behind the NCOs was speaking to the Sergeant. On the high peak, one of the men at the scope was waving his arms.

"Go," he said to the Signalman. Then to the Lance Corporal. "Velius, have your squad stand by."

Decanus Velius shouted down to his men on the practice field, "Second Squad gear up."

While the infantrymen of Second Squad jogged to their tents, a Legionary from the spotting scope was fast roping from the high peak. He touched the valley floor as the duty Signalman reached the foot of the cliff. They exchanged words and, before any of Second Squad had time to strap on the rest of their armor, the Signalman was back speaking with the Sergeant.

"Lance Corporal Velius. Two wagons pulled by oxen teams. Plus, four guards are traveling from the North," Horus reported. "Get your squad to the pass. If they don't have contraband, collect a tax and let them go. And remember, it's easier to dispose of renegade bodies than to replace a Legionary."

Chapter 44 - The Eastern Pass

A squad of Light Infantry had led Second Squad out of the Legion Camp. Some went to reinforce the defensive positions guarding the approach to the valley. Others continued down the gullies and ravines making sure the way was clear for the men in heavy helmets, thick leather armor and carrying the large curved shields.

In battle formation, the Heavy Infantry formed a moveable and almost impenetrable wall. Conversely, in steep sided canyons, their movements were restricted by the terrain. The Light Infantry patrol went first to give the heavies warning of any ambush attempted by an enemy force.

Once on the flat land of the pass, the squad of heavy infantry was in its element. They went online blocking the center of the gap.

Alerio rested the edge of his shield on the ground. As an unproven Legionary, the Decanus had placed him third from the far right. This was the enemy's left side and traditionally the weakest point of an attacking line.

Private Pholus anchored the far-right side. Private Didacus anchored the opposite end of the eight-man line. Both ends were key to pivoting movements and both Legionaries were proven combat veterans.

Lance Corporal Velius paced behind the line talking to each Legionary. His job was command and control. If this was a Century formation, he would be looking to the Corporal or the Optio for guidance and orders. But this was a patrol stretched across a third of the narrow pass between the foothills. Here, his word was law and his orders unquestionable.

The Scout, who had gone into the hills for a better view, reported back.

"The two wagons are about a quarter of a mile out," he reported to Decanus Velius. "I couldn't see what they're hauling. But their guards are armed with bows and long swords."

"Might be a merchant guarding a valuable shipment," Velius replied. "Or Greek revolutionaries trying to bring in weapons. We'll see."

Alerio overheard the conversation and strained his eyes trying to see the caravan. There was a smidgen of dust in the distance, but rising against the flat range stretching north, he couldn't tell if it was small and close or, towering and far away. What he could make out in the hazy distance were the tops of ragged mountains. From the pass, they appeared to be no more than teeth on a saw.

The Light Infantryman faded back behind the shields and joined four others. The five Velites had baskets of javelins and would act as close in artillery if it came to a fight. Between the missiles and the moving wall bristling with steel, a reinforced squad of Legionaries was a formidable force. In this case, it proved to be unnecessary.

Two of the caravan's guards jogged ahead of the wagons. The Legionaries shields were up and only the tops of the heavy infantry's helmets and eyes were visible. Behind the shields, gladii were sheathed as each Legionary held an iron tipped javelin in their right hand.

The merchant guards stopped ten feet from the line. They grinned at the show of military might and raised their hands away from their curved long swords. As the oxen drawn wagons approached, Lance Corporal Velius and Private Didacus took a circular path to the side of the first wagon. Their route was designed so they wouldn't block the line of attack between the Legion Squad and the wagons.

"What are you hauling?" Velius asked as the oxen waddled to a stop.

The oxen herder pointed to one of the guards trailing the wagons. At the rear of the last wagon, a man, with soft footfalls and almost no movement to his shoulders, seemed to glide forward to the second wagon. His face was hidden behind a scarf and long sleeves hid most of his arms. With nimble fingers, he untied a strap and peeled back the cover.

He moved gracefully to the first wagon and repeated the procedure.

"What are you hauling?" Velius repeated.

"Honey from the Golden Valley," the man said in a sing song accent. Then he reached over the wagon's side and his arms disappeared.

Alerio and the rest of the squad flexed. Didacus shifted his shield to provide cover for himself and the Decanus if it came to a fight. The man didn't brandish a weapon when his arms reappeared.

He lifted out a polished wood box. With it balanced on a sideboard, he raised the top and extracted a pouch of coins and a scroll. He offered the items to Velius.

Ignoring the offerings, the Lance Corporal marched over to get a better look at the box. Inside, were more purses of coin and a stack of identical scrolls. He shifted his focus to the wagon and inspected the cargo. After carefully looking over the short, stubby amphorae, he moved to the second wagon. Once satisfied the wagons held nothing except jars of honey, he marched back to the man.

"There's a tax," Velius began to explain but the man ended the conversation by handing the Decanus a coin pouch.

"All right move along," the Lance Corporal ordered. "Second Squad, by fours, wheel left and wheel right."

The line of Legionaries broke as the four on the left pivoted as a unit until they were lined up along the pass instead of across it. The right three Legionaries mirrored the maneuver and were joined by Didacus as they lined up along the other side of the pass. If the caravan guards attacked, they would be trapped between the shields of the Legionaries. Smartly, they simply urged the oxen into motion.

As the wagon wheels began to turn, the man handed Velius the scroll.

"For your commanders," the man said as the second wagon rolled by. He fell in behind it and the caravan moved away.

The Decanus waited until the wagons were out of arrow shot distance before ordering the squad to stand down. He unrolled the surprisingly short scroll. Usually a scroll was used for long missives and parchment for short notes and letters. This had hardwood knobs and a thick center post but only a short section of parchment connected at the end.

He read from the odd scroll, 'Return the Nocte Apibus. Retribution is due. Heed this, the Dulce Pugno.'

The man said it was for his commanders and Velius would happily deliver the scroll. Any document signed, from the Dulce Pugno or Sweet Fist, was a document he'd gladly turn over to higher authorities.

Before he could return to the Raider Camp, his squad was required to patrol the areas on either side of the pass. A caravan was a good lure to draw out a squad. If an enemy wanted to attack, they could wait to see if the Legionaries relaxed after checking the merchant's vehicles. Second Squad wouldn't relax.

"Left and right units, forward march," the Lance Corporal ordered. The four men on the left and four on the right side began marching towards each other. When they were four steps apart, he commanded, "Squad, halt, one-two."

"Left flank, right face. Right flank, left face," Velius ordered. The two units performed the ninety degree turns and now the squad faced in one direction. "Second Squad, Raider Century, forward march, left, stomp, left stomp," he directed the squad. They marched Eastward, out of the pass, and onto the plain.

While the squad drilled and patrolled, the Light Infantrymen headed South following the caravan. Although they couldn't see its destination they could judge if the merchant's wagons halted or veered off the road leading to the trading town.

For decades, the trading town, some five miles from the pass, had been the resupply and preparation stop for caravans and travelers heading north. For those traveling south from across the plain, the trading town was the first civilized settlement they encountered in over a hundred and fifty miles. It was a major economic center due to its location. To avoid the trading town and the pass, travelers would need to journey hundreds of miles to the west and travel around the mountains or, set sail on the ocean to the east.

The squad marched, drilled, and patrolled on both sides of the pass until the sun hung low over the horizon.

"Second Squad, route step," commanded Velius. This directed the squad to break their uniformed steps and allowed each man to choose his own footing.

They angled off the pass, climbed into the ravine, and hiked upward towards the Raider Camp.

Chapter 45 - Quarters of Raider Optio Horus

Alerio sat cleaning his gear. As the junior member of the squad, he was forced to a position almost to the next tent in the row. Across the walkway, First Squad was cleaning their gear. They had been training or rotating to guard posts during the day while Second Squad patrolled. Insults and taunting were bantered back and forth across the walkway as both squads sat cleaning their gear.

Second Squad's Decanus Velius had continued on to the command tent. After reporting in, he would return to inspect the equipment. No one wanted to fail inspection as it meant extra guard duty, punishment, or latrine duty, which to everyone, was the worst punishment.

The latrines were downhill from the weapon's range and beside the trail leading out of the camp. In the view of most Legionaries, it was the perfect spot. An enemy who attempted to infiltrate the camp from that side of the trail would have to dodge the deep holes, half filled with merda.

Alerio's armor, shield, knife, and the pearl handled dagger were cleaned and laid out for inspection. He was honing Private Didacus' gladius and planned to start on his next. It had been a good first day with the new squad. The heat of the day passed and it was turning into a pleasant evening. Even though he would draw third shift guard duty, Alerio was happy.

Lance Corporal Ceyx Eolus climbed the hill from the range after a visit to the latrine. He was preoccupied with planning evening patrols and guard posts for his Light Infantry squad. As usual, he ignored the barrage of heavy infantrymen's barbs as he made his way to his tent on the second row.

Ceyx marched stoically between the flying insults and was almost to his tent when a glint from an Infantryman's display of equipment drew his attention. Ceyx stopped and his mouth dropped open in surprise and horror. Laying among the armor was a forbidden dagger.

The gear belonged to the young Infantryman who had defeated two skirmishers that morning.

"Where did you buy that?" the Decanus demanded while pointing to the pearl handled dagger.

"What, this?" Alerio asked as he leaned over and picked up the curved weapon. "I didn't buy it."

"Do you know what the inscription on the blade means?" inquired Eolus.

"No. I was presented the knife as a reward for killing four assailants," Alerio bragged as he twirled the dagger, showing off.

Ceyx stared at the young Legionary with a shocked look on his face. As he opened his mouth to speak, a Signalman ran up.

"Lance Corporal Eolus. Optio Horus wants you at the command tent right away," he said while still six steps from the Velites NCO. "He said to drop everything and double time."

Ceyx was torn. He needed to finish with the young Legionary but the summons sounded urgent.

"Put the dagger away," he ordered. "Hide it. Don't let anyone see it until we speak."

After making sure the Legionary stashed the pearl handled dagger out of sight, Decanus Eolus spun and ran for the command tent.

***

"Eolus. You're from the East," Horus said holding out the scroll. "Can you make sense of this?"

Eolus took the scroll and unrolled the short piece of parchment. For longer than it took to read it, he gazed at the words.

'Return the Nocte Apibus. Retribution is due. Heed this, the Dulce Pugno.'

His hands shook as he returned the scroll to the Sergeant.

"Bring the young Legionary here. The new swordsman with Second Squad," he said softly as if it were a secret. "Have him bring the dagger."

"I don't understand," pleaded Horus. "What does Private Sisera have to do with the message?"

"Please Optio. I'll explain, but I need the Private and his dagger," Ceyx begged. "It's important."

"Bring me Private Sisera. He's with Second Squad, heavy infantry," Horus ordered to the duty Signalman. "Ask him to bring the dagger."

Corporal Manfredus was at his desk jotting numbers in his log book. As the Century's treasurer, he was responsible for their burial money, pay and any taxes they collected for the Republic. As well, he was the second most senior NCO in the Legion unit.

He looked up from the ledger, "What's with the hush, hush Lance Corporal Eolus? It's just a message. So, tell us what you know."

"If it was just a message, I'd gladly give you my interpretation," stated Ceyx Eolus. "But its meaning goes deeper and the ramifications deadlier. Please, let's wait for the Private."

Chapter 46 - Nocte Apibus / Night Bees

"Private Sisera, reporting as ordered," announced Alerio as he stepped into the command tent.

"Show them the dagger," ordered Decanus Eolus.

Alerio reached into his tunic and took out a package. He unwrapped the soft leather wrapping to reveal an ornate sheath. When he pulled the pearl handled dagger, Eolus held out his hand.

"This is a Nocte Apis as referred to in the message," Eolus explained as he displayed the weapon to the occupants of the tent. "None may possess a Night Bee except a brother of the Dulce Pugno, or in laymen's terms, an assassin of the Sweet Fist."

"For this, they threaten retribution?" asked Sergeant Horus. "Many of us have bounties on our heads. What's different about a bounty from the Dulce Pugno?"

"The bounties on our heads are from alley rats," Lance Corporal Eolus replied. "They're too cowardly to attack us themselves. So, they offer money hoping someone else will do the killing for them. Sometimes people try but mostly, no one takes them up on the offer."

"True enough," admitted Horus. "The Greek renegades talk a lot but never actually follow through unless they catch one of us alone. So again, what makes the Sweet Fist's threat different?"

"Let me tell you a story," Eolus said as he handed the long, curved knife back to Alerio. "I'm from East of the mountains and the legend is told around the evening fires as a cautionary tale."

Chapter 47 - Dulce Pugno / Sweet Fist

"Centuries ago, a wandering troop of families decided to head West," began Eolus. "Their lands had been confiscated by the King's tax collectors. Rather than become destitute, they went searching for a new home. The East was crowded with towns and farms, and also under control of the King. Their only escape was to cross over the Western mountains. Now, few had braved the high peaks, mostly hunters and trappers, but no group with entire families had attempted the passage."

"They left the flat land in the Fall after their harvest and lands had been taken," Eolus explained. "Before leaving, they stole back their own ponies. With twelve wagons of possessions and twelve families including babes in arms, the families rushed for the foothills. The King's men were furious at the missing ponies and gave chase."

"They caught up with the families just as the hills transcended to the steep slopes of the mountains. Two wagons were trampled and the families slaughtered. It was late in the evening and the Captain of the King's horsemen was pleased with the day's butchery. He ordered his men to make camp and make merry on the spoils from the dead families. Drunken, loud and bragging the King's men celebrated late into the evening before laying down to rest."

"In the still of early morning, twenty men from the ten remaining families slipped into the horsemen's camp. They silently slit the throats of all but one of the horsemen. The Captain's life was spared. However, the tendons and muscles around his knees were sliced with his own knife. His wounds were bandaged and he was tied to a horse. It was the last time he would ride as the injuries made him a cripple. The families placed a note of independence on his chest and the horse was set free to find its way home."

"That's the first of the Dulce Pugno?" ventured Corporal Manfredus.

"Not as we know them today," Eolus said. "The Captain's pearl handled knife was presented to the youngest of the family's raiders. After stopping their tormentors, the families climbed higher into the mountains. Weeks later, they were lost in the snow of the high peaks. Many had died, yet the survivors pushed on. There was no guide, no path, just an unbroken trail of snow. The lead wagon climbed a steep rise and many of the members complained while pointing to a flatter stretch. By then, the lead wagon had reached the top of the rise and its herder yelled back that the way was flat. Because they had come so far together, the other families made the steep climb."

"Desperation set in after a week of struggling across the plateau. The mountains were closing in on both sides and the trees thinned. Little game could be found and hunger was piled on top of their many woes. Yet they pushed on."

"The land seemed to rise and they feared another mountain peak to circle. But, it proved worse. The mountains closed in and they were stopped by a wall of snow. Many fell to the cold, white ground in exhaustion and despair. Only the hardiest of the families rose again."

"It was decided to send a group of their youngest and strongest over the snowy barricade. In the morning, as small fires, barely alive enough to fend off the cold, glowed five young men and three women climbed from the camp. The last the families saw were the eight vanishing over the edge. Those left behind huddled and waited for death to claim them."

"A day later, fifteen fish fell from the sky. Many called to the gods in thanks for the gifts of food. But it wasn't the gods unless you were a believer. It was the young people. One made the climb down the snow wall and told the tale of a wondrous mountain valley."

"They rigged lines of cloth and one by one, the families deserted their wagons and scaled the wall. Some fell, being too weak to go on but most scrambled or were pulled up the face of the snow cliff. On the other side of the blockade of snow, the sun shone across a broad valley. A light blanket of snow lay from end to end. A wide creek flowed down the center, trees grew in abundance giving promise of good soil, and game tracks were obvious even from the heights of the pass."

"Trees were downed and shelters constructed. Between the wild game and abundant fish, starvation was averted. During the long first Winter, all of the men who had participated in the raid told their stories and explained the lessons they learned while defending the families. The young people listened and were in awe of the Captain's pearl handled knife when it was displayed."

"In the Spring, as the snow melted and plants blossomed, swarms of bees awakened from hibernation. Their hives were discovered and the families collected the honey. Soon they had so much, they stopped collecting it.

And they began to move queen bees to domestic hives so the families could attend to the hives. The families began to call their new home the Golden Valley."

"The next Spring, a group was sent forth with rough clay jars of honey. Not knowing any other direction, they headed down to the East and the King's land. In the first two villages, they exchanged honey for seeds. Rapidly, they returned to the Golden Valley. Fields were planted and crops grown. Another winter passed and, in the Spring, another trading party was organized. They were at the second village when a patrol of King's men caught them. Along with their jars of honey, the four men were taken to see the King."

"Now the Queen and King had two daughters and a taste for the finer things in life. But this was centuries ago and securing finer things was difficult. It was before the days of trading between regions so the King and Queen developed the habit of taking the best from their kingdom. The fattest livestock for their herds and coops, the hardiest of grains for their bread and the most handsome young men for their personal guard. All that was superior, the royal family took for their own. When the Queen tasted the captured honey, she demanded her husband claim all the honey from the Golden Valley."

"One of the men was released to deliver the King's proclamation. It was a long march through the mountains and back. In the meantime, the King grew tired of feeding and housing the three captives. As they were related to the men who had crippled his Captain, a cousin of the royal family, the King deemed them outlaws and hanged the three."

"Later in the year, four wagons of honey rolled into the royal stockade. When asked about the three captives, the men and women escorting the honey were hanged. All except one man. He was sent back to the mountains with the King's demand for more of the exquisite honey."

"That winter, the original family raiders gathered. Again, they spoke of their experiences and the lessons they learned defending the families against the horsemen. While they analyzed their tactics and taught the best to their young men, a blacksmith smelted iron and added carbon to the mix. He hammered and folded the hot metal, and hammered and folded some more, until the blades were steel. Using the Captain's curved blade as a guide, he duplicated it many times over. Families dug through their possessions and produced pearls which were embedded in the handles. These were the first Night Bees."

"Before spring, while frost still lay upon the fields, ten men snaked down the mountain. They traveled by night and lay hidden during the day. At the royal stockade, they didn't go to the gate and announce themselves. Rather, they scaled the wall at night."

"The King and Queen were supping with their daughters. Fat fowl lay upon the table and delicate wine filled their goblets. Servants hovered at their elbows, salivating and hungry, yet ready to fulfill any of the royal wishes. As the King burped, ten men entered the royal hall. While the servants backed away, ten men with scarves wrapped around their faces and wielding exactly the same curved blade, slit the royal throats. Honey was drizzled over the royal bodies. After finishing dispatching the royal family, the assassins melted into the night."

"Over the Centuries, rich people have hired the Dulce Pugno to solve problems," Eolus said. "In cases where the assassins were killed, the Nocte Apibus were returned to the Golden Valley. A few men thought to keep a Nocte Apis as a trophy. All the trophy collectors were killed. You ask why their threat is different from a bounty offered by a gang of thugs?"

Decanus Eolus paused and held out his palm for the curved dagger. Alerio lay the weapon in the outstretched hand.

"Because to have this," Eolus turned the weapon over so light reflected off the blade. He then exhibited the Nocte Apis to everyone in the room before saying. "To possess this, is to be next in line for centuries of honor killings by the Dulce Pugno."

Everyone watched as Eolus gently presented the knife to Alerio as if it were a snake likely to come to life and strike.

"Hold on," Optio Horus ordered as he reached for the scroll. He snatched it from his desk and unrolled the parchment. "The message says Nocte Apibus. There's more than one missing?" he asked.

Alerio coughed to clear his throat and said, "There are three more. The Centurion and Sergeant at the Harbor Post and a Lance Corporal of the Guard all have one."

Horus sat down heavily in his field chair. "Where is Centurion Stylianus?" he asked. "I'd like an officer in on this."

"He's still in the trading town," Corporal Manfredus said. "Working his contacts for information about the rebels."

"Decanus Eolus. Thank you for the information. You are dismissed. There's nothing the rest of us can do tonight," Horus stated. "Sisera. You're bunking in here. Lance Corporal Velius, I want guards around this tent until morning. Have the first shift bring his gear. We'll sort this out tomorrow."

***

In the early morning, while the moon was still visible in the western sky, the guards outside the tent issued a challenge. Moments later, a Scout was ushered into the command tent. He was met by four drawn gladii.

"Stand down," ordered Optio Horus. He recognized the Scout. While shoving his sword into its sheath, he demanded, "Report."

Manfredus, Alerio and the Duty Signalman also put away their blades.

"Centurion Stylianus has been taken," the Scout announced. "We were gathering information. Something has the revolutionaries stirred up so we split up to cover more ground. When Centurion Stylianus didn't show at the appointed time, I waited 'til sundown. When he still didn't report in, I started asking around."

"What do you mean, taken?" Horus asked softly. The veins in his neck were bulging and his eye was twitching yet he remained otherwise calm.

"At the stables, I learned five rebel sympathizers had rented ponies. They had Centurion Stylianus with them," the Scout reported. "The stableman said they headed out on the road towards Crotone. I figured you'd want to know. At this point, they have half the night's head start."

"Guard," Horus called out. When a sentry stuck his head in the tent, Horus ordered, "I want a man on the dock. As soon as Decanus Remigius returns bring him directly to me. Go!"

"Do you think the Dulce Pugno have something to do with them taking our officer?" asked Corporal Manfredus.

"I don't see a connection," admitted the Optio.

"There might be," Alerio ventured. "When I killed the assassins, they were supporting a renegade attack on our supplies. If the rebel's hired the Dulce Pugno for the killing, it would explain the connection."

"And the mission failed," surmised Corporal Manfredus. "Now the Sweet Fist want their Night Bees and some payback. They're leaning on the leader of the rebels for a solution."

"And you think Centurion Stylianus was taken as a bargaining chip?" asked Horus.

"Unless there's another explanation," Manfredus replied.

The Sergeant sent the Signalman to fetch Lance Corporal Ceyx Eolus and his gear. Later, Eolus shouldered his way into the tent and set his armor down in a corner.

"You seem to know more about this Night Bee stuff than anybody else," Horus explained to the Light Infantryman. "I may require your advice."

"Whatever you need Sergeant," Eolus assured the NCO as he sat on the ground beside Alerio.

Optio Horus paced until dawn. His rapid strolling bothered Manfredus so much the Corporal left the command tent to check on the Raider Camp. While Ceyx Eolus and Alerio Sisera were restricted to the tent, dawn gave the Signalman an excuse to leave. He stepped outside and began his vigil of the team on the peak with the sighting roll.

Act 5

Chapter 48 - A Troubling Report

The Sun was well over the horizon when Decanus Remigius walked into the command tent. His eyes were red rimmed from lack of sleep and he stunk of fish.

"Optio. You wanted to see me?" he asked with a salute that seemed out of place with his rough fisherman's clothing.

"Centurion Stylianus has been kidnapped," Horus stated. "Any idea where he was taken?"

"No idea, Optio," the Lance Corporal replied. "But Speckled Pheasant has gone to ground. He's holding up in a warehouse and has the place surrounded by thugs."

"It's as good an idea as any for where they've taken our Centurion," Horus said. "What about the disagreement between the rebel Captain and his Lieutenants? Anything come of that?"

"Everyone's pretty tight lipped about the issue," Remigius admitted. "But it concerns something they lost. They've been asking a lot of obscure questions but none that'll give us a clue to what they're looking for."

"I hate to do this to you and your crew," the Sergeant said as he grabbed his armor. "But Private Sisera, Decanus Eolus, and I need to get to the Harbor Transfer Post."

"As a great sailor once said," Remigius exclaimed. "Not high winds, or heavy swells, nor lack of sleep, shall keep the weary Mariner on shore when duty calls."

"What great sailor said that?" Horus asked.

"Me," Remigius replied with a smile.

"Who said you were a great sailor?" the Sergeant challenged.

"You Optio. Because I'll be navigating with one eye closed," the Lance Corporal answered as he yawned, "If I'm not great, you'll be steering the fishing boat yourself."

"Decanus Remigius," pronounced the Sergeant. "Have I told you lately, you are a great sailor."

"Why, I'm blushing," Remigius replied. "Thank you, Optio Horus. Shall we go?"

Chapter 49 - The Harbor Transfer Post

Remigius masterfully tacked the fishing boat into the wind until noon. Around midday, the wind shifted and the craft went from a time killing zigzag and began running with the wind. Even so, the vessel wasn't a sloop or a yacht, it was a wide beamed working vessel. It took the day to reach their destination.

The sun had long ago set when the lights of the Harbor of Crotone appeared.

"As close to the Legion Post as you can get us," Horus reminded the pilot.

"I'll run her up beside the old pier the training instructors use," replied Remigius.

It seemed as if the lights from the harbor town barely moved as they sailed by the lighted buildings and the ends of the big docks. Eventually, Remigius shoved the rudder over hard and the fishing boat leaned until water splashed over the gunwale. A short while later, the boat shimmied as it ground on the sandy bottom. Then, it jerked to a stop.

Horus, Alerio, and Eolus jumped to the pier and raced towards the Legion Transfer Post.

Remigius collapsed on the rear oar while Lance Corporal Wido and Private Ireneus dove into the water. Once they had rocked the boat enough to refloat it. They secured the boat and ran off to join their Sergeant at the Post. Remigius stayed on board to catch up on his sleep.

Chapter 50 - Centurion Quarters at the Transfer Post

A Doctor and a Medic were bent over the Post's Centurion. While they sewed, he swore and thundered. Horus, Alerio, and Eolus heard the officer as a bandaged Corporal Thornernus escorted them towards the tent.

"They rushed the guards on the perimeter," Thornernus explained as he ushered them towards the Centurion's quarters. "At first I thought it an all-out attack. But they made straight away for the NCOs' and officer's tents."

"How's the leg?" Horus inquired pointing to the field dressing around the Corporal's thigh.

"Five of them, it wasn't a fair fight," the burley NCO replied with a smile. "Poor lads, next time they'll know not to mess with a Legion Tesserarius." He pivoted and shoved aside the tent flap. Speaking towards the officer's bed, Thornernus announced. "Sir, Optio Horus may have information about the attack."

An arm appeared between the Doctor and the Medic. The Medic was shoved aside and the Centurion's raised his head.

"Horus. Talk to me," demanded the wounded Centurion.

"Alerio. Hand me the Nocte Apis," the Sergeant ordered. Once he held the curved knife, he showed it to the Centurion and explained. "They were looking for this."

The Centurion shook his head to focus as the Doctor pulled a stitch tighter. After inhaling a ragged breath, the officer replied, "I have one as well. It's in my trunk. Are you telling me the attackers were looking for a perfututum knife?"

"It's a symbol of an assassin's sect called the Dulce Pugno," Horus related. "They are very possessive about their knives. In your own word's sir, anyone holding a Nocte Apis is perfututum."

"Well the attackers weren't trained assassins," the Centurion observed. "They were barely efficient at all. Well, except for the one who sliced my chest open. If Corporal Thornernus hadn't interceded, they'd have done real damage."

"You handled yourself well, sir," Corporal Thornernus added. Everyone understood a little sucking up wouldn't hurt when the next promotion board convened.

"Those weren't the Dulce Pugno," Horus explained. "They were revolutionaries commanded by Speckled Pheasant. That leads me to another issue. Centurion Stylianus had been taken by the rebels. I believe the Captain hired the assassins and is feeling pressure from the Dulce Pugno to get the four Nocte Apibus back. I think they'll approach us to trade Centurion Stylianus for the knives."

"What's wrong with that?" challenged the Centurion.

"If we bargain once for a hostage, the renegades will expect us to do it again," Sergeant Horus replied. "It'll open a flood gate for kidnappings and demands."

"Well-spoken Optio," the Centurion said. "What's your plan to retrieve Stylianus and to appease the Dulce Pugno. And, to punish the rebels."

"First, I need to collect all the Night Bees," Horus said listing the steps. "Then, I'll need two squads of heavy infantry and." The Sergeant stopped and looked around at Decanus Eolus. "How long to sneak into the warehouse and secure the Centurion. You'll need to guard him until the heavies arrive and butcher the renegades?"

"Private Sisera and I will need time to slip in and secure the Centurion," Eolus replied. "We'll enter, pull the officer to a defensive location, and guard him. It'll be close once we stir up the rebels. Don't be late Sergeant."

Alerio was shocked to be included in the rescue. He'd expected to be among the heavy infantrymen, but to be part of the entry team was a complete surprise. It apparently caught Horus off guard as well.

"Why Private Sisera?" asked the Optio. "Wouldn't you rather have a team of Light Infantrymen?"

"It's going to be bloody gladius work in the warehouse," Eolus admitted. "Sure, I'd like a squad with me but only two men can slip in silently. Once it gets hot, I'll need a swordsman with me."

Chapter 51 - Preparation, The Hallmark of Legion Raiders

Alerio followed Ceyx Eolus to the armory. When the Armorer bulked at Ceyx's request, Lance Corporal Eolus reached across the counter, grabbed the man, and shoved his chin into the wooden counter top.

"Armorer. My Centurion is being held captive," Ceyx said between clinched teeth. "Your Centurion is wounded and being treated by a Doctor. Assassins are hunting your Optio and a Decanus of the Guard. I've had an extremely long day and I still have to pay a social call on a warehouse full of blood thirsty agitators."

The Armorer mumbled something, but Ceyx wasn't done. "All I require is for you to tool together two sword belts so they fit the broad back of Private Sisera," he said. "I haven't the time to run over and ask Corporal Thornernus to come and ask you nicely. He's rather busy organizing two squads of heavy infantry. So, will you make the rig? Or do I knock your teeth out and go find someone more willing to help?"

Despite the beefy arms and the weathered hands on the big man, the Armorer seemed intimidated by the lean, Light Infantryman. 'Was it the overwhelming force and the steady flow of words?' pondered Alerio. 'Or was the man convinced once he heard the entirety of the situation?'

He didn't have time to think further about the Armorer's motivation. Alerio was dragged to the back of the tent. While standing in the midst of hanging leather and metal armor pieces, shields, straps, and belts of all sorts, the Armorer snatched sword belts of different sizes and shapes and piled them at Alerio's feet.

When he produced a short, curved knife, Alerio was worried for a second. But the knife wasn't for him. The Armorer laid belts over Alerio's shoulders, adjusted them then carried the belts to a work bench. There, he sliced off sections until the straight edges of the belts had curves and notches.

After another fitting, the Armorer pounded in rivets to permanently join the two sword belts. When he finished, he slid two gladii in the sheaths and held up the finished cross harness.

"I don't see a reason for carrying two gladii," he said as he fitted it over Alerio's shoulders. "You can only use one at a time."

The hilts hovered just above Alerio shoulder blades. After knotting a strap across his chest to secure the harness,

Alerio reached back and easily drew both swords. He carefully inspected the blades.

"They're fresh from the metalworkers," the Armorer said with pride. "You'll not find a ding or a rough spot on those blades."

Alerio whipped both gladii in a circle before aiming the tips over his shoulders. One went in on the first attempt. Ceyx stepped up and helped guide the other into its sheath.

"Practice putting them away later," the Veles NCO instructed. "We've got business in town."

Private Ireneus met them outside the Armory. He had two dark colored, hooded cloaks draped over an arm.

"Wido is scouting the warehouse," he said as he placed a cloak over Eolus' shoulders. "We'll meet up with him three blocks from the building."

He laid the second cloak over Alerio's shoulders and commented, "A dual rig. Haven't seen anything like that before. Don't see the reason. You can only use one gladius at a time."

Private Alerio and Lance Corporal Eolus jogged after Private Ireneus. The three passed two squads of heavy infantrymen. As the left stomp, left stomp faded, they swept through the main gate and flipped up their hoods.

Chapter 52 - Three Blocks Out

"It's three blocks from here," Decanus Wido explained. "They've placed guards at the entrances, the corners of the warehouse, and on the roof patio."

"Do we fight our way in?" asked Alerio.

"Spoken like a true heavy infantryman," Wido teased. "No. The roof patio has an interior ladder. That means there's a landing above the warehouse floor. We don't know if it's a complete floor or just a landing. In either case, it's your best chance of gaining entry and surprising the renegades."

"And how, pray tell Lance Corporal Wido, do we get to the upper floor? Fly?" asked Ceyx.

"There's a street vender booth at the southwest corner," Wido explained. "The booth has a substantial roof built over the alley. From the roof, you can reach where the clay bricks are set back a course. Not much foot room but, it's claimable."

"What about the guard at the corner?" Ceyx asked. "If you start killing too early, you'll ruin our element of surprise."

"How many guards on the roof patio?" Alerio asked interrupting the skirmisher NCO.

"No more than two will bother you," Wido promised. "Optio Horus sent me two squads of Archers. They're hidden on the roofs of buildings across from the warehouse. Once you call out, the patio will become a kill zone. As far as the guard near the booth? I'll distract him."

Decanus Wido pulled a wine skin from his side, uncorked it and squeezed a spurt across his face. "Instant drunk," he announced. "Everybody needs to have a drink with a fun loving drunk. When you're ready Lance Corporal Eolus."

Chapter 53 - The Rebel Warehouse

Alerio watched as Decanus Wido staggered down the center of the street. A soft tune, unevenly whistled and slurred, emitted from his lips between squirts of vino.

"Yo, friend," he mumbled as he approached the guard. "It was a good catch and I'm celebrating. Have a drink with me."

"Go away," the guard whispered. Obviously, he didn't want to draw attention to himself or his duties.

While waving the wine skin around, Wido jingled a coin purse on his hip to show his earnings. Once he was sure the thug had seen the bulging coin pouch, he shrugged, spun too fast and almost fell. In order to keep his balance, he stumbled to the other side of the street. There, he leaned against the wall.

As the drunk with the heavy purse slumped, the guard looked around. It was too easy. He pulled his knife and deserted his post.

Ceyx tapped Alerio on the shoulder and the two men moved forward staying in the deep shadows. As Wido sank to the pavers, he rolled over on the coin purse and began snoring loudly. The guard leaned over and shook the drunk. As he busied himself with trying to roll over the large, passed out fisherman, Ceyx and Alerio reached the low roof of the booth.

The covering was only head height and the two-man entry team easily vaulted to the top. With cautious steps, they crossed to the corner of the warehouse. A hip high ledge created where the thick lower wall ended, left a one brick wide shelf.

Ceyx placed a hand on Alerio's shoulder and stepped up with his left foot. Slowly, he brought the right foot around and placed it on the ledge. Shuffling his feet and hugging the wall so closely he scraped his cheek, Ceyx inched along until the fingers on his right hand curved around a hole in the brick face.

There were three openings in the upper wall. These allowed air flow into the warehouse at night and released heat during the day. The cavities were circular with a diameter of thirty inches. Above the openings, the wall continued upward creating the retaining wall of the roof patio just a few feet above Ceyx.

While Ceyx could easily slip through the hole, he worried about two immediate issues. What if the big Legionary didn't fit? What if he couldn't cling to the shelf? If Private Sisera fell, it would tip their hand and their task of getting silently to the Centurion would fail. With his finger cupping the edge of the air hole, Eolus reached out with his left hand.

The second issue resolved itself. Ignoring the outstretched hand, Alerio stepped up on the ledge without assistance. He shuffled rapidly until Ceyx had to move further down so both men could use the opening as a hand hold.

When Alerio was too young to remove stones from the fields or to construct walls, his father would lift him to the top of a finished section.

"A well stacked wall will stand for centuries," the elder Sisera would say. "Just piling up loose rocks and it will fall in a season."

Alerio would walk each course and tell his father where a stone rocked or slid. His father would dutifully reset the stone so the wall rose solid and strong. When Alerio grew older and could participate in preparing the fields, he would lay a course of newly dug up stones, jump up on the wall, and walk it to test for stability. The brick wide shelf on the warehouse wasn't a problem for the surefooted farmer's son.

Ceyx pulled himself up and into the air passageway. He needed to get a view of the warehouse's interior. If required, they'd scoot to the next hole to find the second-floor landing. It was dangerous but not as dangerous as falling two stories to the warehouse floor. The plan was for him to peek and find out where the landing was located.

Alerio watched as the Veles set his hands on the passageway and pulled himself up. First one elbow vanished into the hole then the other. A kick of his legs for momentum and Ceyx shimmied into the air shaft. Suddenly, all of Ceyx's body was swallowed by the dark passageway.

Shuffling rapidly so he was directly under the hole, Alerio got a grip and pulled himself up. Where the NCO had fit easily, Alerio needed to place one elbow over the other. Raising up on his elbows, he lifted his torso high enough for his shoulders to slip into the round opening. Keeping the high profile, he walked with his forearms while dragging his lower half into the circular air vent.

The dual sword rig scraped against the upper section and his forearms left a trail of skin and blood on the rough clay bricks. A shout sent a charge through his spine and Alerio rushed to catch up with the Veles.

"For the Republic," Ceyx bellowed. "For the Republic."

Alerio, still in the tight round opening, repeated the yell to alert the Legionaries outside the warehouse. The assault on the storage building had commenced with one man in the building and another still in the air vent. It wasn't the plan.

Chapter 54 - A Rescue and a Prisoner

Lance Corporal Ceyx Eolus held his gladius and a curved dagger out at waist level. Three Greeks rushed towards him. The two bodies lying at his feet and the two behind him were the reasons for his hasty entrance.

When Ceyx reached the end of the passageway, he first noticed the solid wood flooring. A partial second floor extended from the wall and the legs of a ladder to the roof rested off to his left. The wood flooring extended out for fifteen feet and ended at a railing used for observing the storage space below. To his right and near another wall, an opening in the planking gave access to the warehouse floor below. The top of a ladder jutted through the hole.

Upon peering into the warehouse from the end of the vent, his first emotion was relief. He and Alerio wouldn't have to heel and toe it on the narrow ledge to reach the next air passageway. His second emotion was horror.

Speckled Pheasant, the rebel Captain, had a knife in one hand and was pulling on Centurion Stylianus' ear with the other. It was obvious the renegade leader was going to saw off the ear. Whether to show his resolve when he demanded the Night Bees or because he was a sadist, didn't matter. Ceyx reacted by yelling and jumping from the passageway.

The leader of the revolution released the ear and danced back. For a fat man, Speckled Pheasant moved fast. He avoided Ceyx's gladius but the two holding the unconscious Centurion were standing close to the wall with no room to retreat. Plus, their hands were busy holding up the limp Centurion. They weren't quick enough to drop the Legion officer and draw their weapons. Ceyx's blades slashed and stabbed. The men were still falling when Ceyx turned to face the rebel Captain.

The revolutionary commander was screaming for his guards and stepping back. One moment, he was upright, the next he tumbled over a chair. In four steps, Ceyx had the tip of his blade at the obese Rebel's throat. Encouraging the Captain to stand and move with the point of his knife, Ceyx guided Speckled Pheasant back to where the Centurion lay. The hilt of his gladius swung around and the pummel connected with the temple of the Renegade leader's head.

That's how two unconscious men ended up beside the Light Infantryman. The three rushing towards him had come from the roof patio. He'd have to have a talk with Lance Corporal Wido about his ineffective placement of the archers.

Right now, Ceyx faced three armed men, and from the sounds, more were climbing the ladder from the warehouse floor. And there was no sign of Private Sisera.

Alerio reached the end of the passageway and scanned the scene. Two men were down, and based on the amount of blood, dead. Two others were crumbled in a pile. One displayed bruising on his face, chest, and arms. The other was fat and wearing a gaudy vest encrusted with multicolored stones. Decanus Eolus was standing beside them with a gladius in one hand and a wicked looking knife in the other.

The three, armed men were five paces from Ceyx when Alerio launched himself from the passageway. It would have been heroic for him to land on his feet in front of the Greeks. It would have been, except, his heels collided with the top of the passageway. He was in mid jump when the bump flipped him over.

Ceyx crouched with weapons extended ready to meet the charge. At four paces and closing fast, it was going to be a short and deadly encounter. The Veles didn't have much hope of surviving. Then, the big body of Private Sisera flipped over his head and crashed, back first, into the three rebels.

The three men toppled over as if someone had tossed an oversized sack of grain at them. In this case, the sack was a dark cloak and it came up swinging elbows, fists and knees. Ceyx stepped forward and carefully stabbed between the flurry of flying limbs and took an agitator out of the fight. Alerio gained his footing and stood. One Greek's head received a Legion stomp. The other caught Private Sisera' weight in his sternum from a dropping knee. They wouldn't be getting up.

"Nice entrance," Ceyx teased while tilting his head and looking askew at the young Legionary. "Kind of reminds me of a circus tumbler I once saw. Except, he landed on his feet."

Before Alerio could reply, rebels began streaming up the ladder from the warehouse floor. He reached over his shoulders and pulled both gladii from his back.

"I'd love to stay and reminisce about the circus, Decanus Ceyx Eolus," Alerio said as he swung the swords to loosen up his shoulders. "But I've got to go and save your life again."

"What do you mean, again?" Ceyx replied. But he was speaking to the young swordsman's back. Alerio had already turned to face the ladder and the first of the rebel's reinforcements.

Chapter 55 - Fight in the Warehouse

Five thugs leaped from the ladder and spread out. It was a good strategy. One at a time and they'd be cut down.

Attacking in line would allow them to swarm the two Legionaries.

Ceyx was mid step in following Alerio towards the fight when Speckled Pheasant moaned. He couldn't leave an enemy combatant in his rear, so he stopped. Plus, he needed to guard the access from the roof.

While he rushed to cut lengths of cloth from his cloak, Ceyx watched in frustration as the young Legionary shuffled forward, alone, to face five armed assailants. Right away, he judged Sisera's opening move to be a mistake.

Alerio held his gladii together with bent arms as if he were preparing to offer the weapons to the Renegades. The Legionary slid his left leg far out-front putting him off balance if attacked from the side. And his flanks would certainly be attacked when the men enveloped him.

Ceyx's fingers fumbled with the knot as he bound Speckled Pheasant's hands. Once they were secured, he rushed to tie the Captain's legs.

The rebels faced a young man holding two swords outward with one foot extended out in front of the rear foot. His feet were a ridiculous distance apart with the front knee bent as if he were about to do calisthenics. Seeing the odd stance confused the five and they hesitated. When Alerio's swords parted at a less than impressive rate, the renegades simply leaned back to avoid the moving tips.

Ceyx watched the unorthodox stance and his heart sank at the halfhearted opening swings. Maybe, he thought, it had been wrong to bring such a young, inexperienced Legionary on the rescue operation.

Suddenly, Alerio's right leg whipped forward. As it passed the bent left knee, he flicked the swords an inch forward and nicked two of the gangsters. The right foot continued on its path and kicked the center rebel in the chest.

Air expelled from the man's lungs as he flew back. Another agitator at the top of the ladder only managed to see the arrangement of the fighters on the second story before the flying man landed in his arms. Both fell screaming to the warehouse floor below. Another, climbing the ladder lost his grip when the falling men clipped him. He ended up hanging precariously from the side of the ladder with one hand. The flow of reinforcements stopped as the man fought to regain his grip on the rungs.

Alerio finished the kick, slammed his right foot to the floor and pivoted on it. As he spun, his gladii acted as sickles slicing deeply into two of the thugs.

From either side, the renegades with the nicks dove at him. One received the end of a hilt to the back of his head. He landed unconscious against Alerio's foot. The other lost three teeth when his face connected with a knee before his arms could wrap around the swordsman's legs.

Dancing between the four downed men, Alerio skewed and sliced to be sure they were all permanently out of the fight. Then leisurely, he rolled one of the bodies to the top of the ladder. He kicked it. The body fell and landed on the man who was trying to regain his hand hold. The unbalanced rebel and another revolutionary from the ladder screamed as the two toppled with the dead body to the warehouse floor.

By the time Speckled Pheasant's gang reorganized and commenced climbing again, Alerio had stacked two more bodies at the opening for the ladder.

"Are you going to kick the other bodies down as well?" Ceyx inquired.

Lance Corporal Eolus leaned casually on the wall behind the hog-tied rebel and the unconscious Centurion.

"No. They'll learn to duck if I do it again," Alerio turned his head and replied. He snapped his head around and jammed his left gladius into the opening for the ladder. A thug screamed and others cursed as the wounded man fell into those attempting to climb up behind him. "The bodies will act as barricades in case they start shooting arrows," Alerio informed the NCO. Glancing over his shoulder, the Private winked at the Veles and apologized. "Excuse me."

He twisted around and slashed downward with his right gladius. The chorus of pain and complaining from below the floor level rose to a new volume.

On the warehouse floor, the renegades were crawling over each other trying to gain a place on the ladder. Behind the mob, Speckled Pheasant's Lieutenants urged them forward with kicks and threats. A banging noise drew their attention and they stopped shoving and spun their heads around.

One entire wall of the warehouse had tall doors set between columns of clay bricks. At the next bang, all the doors flew open.

Eolus and Sisera could hear two voices raised above the yelling of fighters and the screams of the dying. Both voices were calling out the same thing.

"Watch for our men," Corporal Thornernus and Sergeant Horus were shouting. "Watch for our men!"

The two-man rescue team agreed it was a grand idea. Still, they were glad they were on the second floor. Below them in the warehouse, the Legion's heavy infantrymen stabbed with their gladii, slammed with their shields, and stomped with their right feet. As taught in recruit training, the stomp was as much of a weapon as their javelins, gladii, and shields.

Anything under the hobnailed boots got smashed. Ankles, feet, legs, chests and heads, anything on the ground became neutralized pulp. In a fight, a Legionary's vision was restricted by the helmet and shield. They wouldn't necessarily recognize a Lance Corporal and a Private guarding a rescued Centurion. So being on the second floor was a stroke of luck. Below, all the revolutionaries in the warehouse were butchered by the partially blind meat grinder of the Legion.

Chapter 56 - Medic up, Medic up

It ended swiftly. Other than the heavy breathing of a warehouse full of Legionaries, the large space was quiet.

Sergeant Horus called out hopefully, "Eolus. Sisera. Decanus Eolus. Private Sisera. Report!" He looked around for a signal before lifting his eyes to the balcony on the second floor.

Ceyx and Alerio were peering over the railing and down at the carnage. When Horus spotted them, they waved casually to the Optio.

"Did you locate Centurion Stylianus?" the Optio called up to the smiling men. "Do you require medical assistance?"

"The Centurion needs looking at," Ceyx shouted. Before he could explain, the Sergeant began yelling, "Medic up! Medic up!"

The call was repeated by a squad's Decanus and by Corporal Thornernus, "Medic up. Medic up."

As if created by the bow of a ship at sea, the Legionaries parted and two medics rushed for the ladder.

"Let's dismantle your barricade before the Medics trip over the bodies," suggested Ceyx.

By the time the first Medic's head appeared in the ladder's opening, the bodies had been dragged to the side. Though the flooring in front of the opening was covered in slices of skin, bone, and an inch of blood. It resembled the aftermath of an epic battle.

"Hurry," the medic called down to his compatriot. "It's a blood bath."

He expected to find the rescue team cut and bleeding. Instead, he found a shaken and bruised Centurion and two grinning Legionaries. The only wounds were to Alerio's forearms. Red and raw as if a cheese grater had been employed, they oozed drops of blood.

Optio Horus climbed up next and he swore as his boots sloshed through the gore. Spying the medics surrounding the Centurion, he rushed to check on the Officer.

"We're fine Sergeant," Ceyx informed the NCO as he raced to the Centurion's side. "If anybody is interested?"

Chapter 57 - Cleaning Up and Clearing Out

Four Legionaries cleared the ladder and Lance Corporal Eolus directed them to the roof ladder.

"Not sure what's left on the roof," he said. "But no dissent should walk down. Understand?"

They didn't know the NCO, but, the Optio was occupied speaking to a man being attended to by a medic and ignoring them. They accepted the orders and hurried towards the roof ladder.

The second medic realized he wasn't needed to attend the Centurion. While looking around for something to do, he noticed Alerio's deep scrapes. After scolding the Legionary for not reporting the injuries, he opened a kit. A light dusting of sterilizing salt was sprinkled on the wounds and the medic proceeded to bandage Alerio's forearms.

"I assume that's Centurion Stylianus," guessed Alerio using his chin to indicate the direction. "I've seen the obese gentleman in the fancy vest before. Isn't he the dissent leader?"

"That, Private Sisera, is the illustrious rebel Captain, Speckled Pheasant," Eolus replied. The medic finished, accepted Alerio's thanks, and turned to repack his medical bag.

"Let's go pay our respects to Centurion Stylianus," Ceyx suggested.

As they approached the Centurion, Horus indicated for them to step closer.

"Sir, may I present Lanced Corporal Ceyx Eolus and Private Alerio Sisera," their Sergeant announced. "They were the entry team that protected you until the Infantry arrived."

Someone had placed Ceyx's tattered cloak over the Centurion's shoulder. His eyes were dull but alert.

"Lanced Corporal Eolus. I know you," Stylianus whispered through a sore throat. "But I don't recognize the Private. Is he one of ours, Sergeant?"

"He just joined the Raiders, sir. Fresh out of Recruit Training," the Optio replied.

"Just out of training and you picked him for the Raiders," Stylianus said hoarsely. "And you picked him for a rescue mission. He must have impressed you."

"I didn't choose him for the mission. That was Decanus Eolus' decision," Horus reported. "But you are correct sir, he is an impressive young Legionary."

The sound of screams reached them through the roof opening. Shortly after, the four Infantrymen climbed down the ladder.

"The roof is secure," one reported to Horus.

"Good. Pass your shields down to the men below," the Optio ordered. "You'll help the Centurion down the ladder. Then, come back for this fat cūlus. I need the rebel Captain alive for questioning, but don't be too gentle."

***

A cart hauled Centurion Stylianus and Speckled Pheasant back to the Legion Transfer Post. While Stylianus was taken to the Officer's tent and helped into a clean, soft bed, Speckled Pheasant was taken to a small, smelly wooden box and helped in by the bottom of a boot.

On the march back to the Post, Ceyx described the action in the warehouse to Wido and Ireneus. Alerio blushed at the praise from the Veles NCO. Happily, for the young Legionary, no one could see it in the dark hours of early morning. Still, he was pleased.

Horus waited for Ceyx to wash up. Once he was presentable, they went to consult with the Centurion. Alerio, with Wido and Ireneus in tow, strolled to the Armory.

"Private Sisera turning in equipment," Alerio reported as he laid the dual gladius harness on the counter. "You did a fine job of constructing it. Thank you."

The leather, just hours before, had been new with a freshly tanned aroma still clinging to the material. Now, it lay creased with flecks of dried blood peeling off and falling on the counter.

"I can't take that harness," the Armorer replied as he carefully poked the leather. Using only two fingers, he eased first one of the gladii and then the other out of the sheaths.

"Oh, excuse me. It's been a long night," Alerio offered. "Of course, it should have been cleaned before being turned it in."

"No, you misunderstand me," the Armorer explained. "I have no one who wants or needs a two gladii rig. I've already written it off as research and development. It's yours."

The Armorer reached back and pulled a leather pouch from a box. "But you're right," he stated handing Alerio the pouch. "The leather should be cleaned. Here's a bag of goose grease so you can do it right. It's better than the goat merda you were issued."

"Hold on," Lance Corporal Wido insisted. "What good is the harness without gladii?"

"Sorry, the Legion only issues one gladius per Legionary," the Armorer replied. "He already has one."

"How would he requisition another?" Wido asked. Then he studied the new gladii the Armorer had extracted from the harness and added, "More specifically, those two?

"He'd need a chit from a Centurion," answered the Armorer while pointing a thick, gnarly finger at Alerio. "Stating the requirement for equipment is for a Legionary specialist. Specifically, that Legionary."

"Don't put them away," Wido said as he pulled Alerio and Ireneus out of the Armory tent.

"How am I going to get a chit from the Centurion?" Alerio asked once they were outside.

The sun was peaking over the horizon casting soft shadows as the rays chased away the dark of night.

"Let's get you cleaned up and after breakfast," Wido explained. "We camp outside the officer's tent and wait for Sergeant Horus. He'll know. Meanwhile, Private, you need to clean your gear."

**

Optio Horus had spread the four Nocte Apibus out on a table beside the Centurion's bed.

"The assassins from the Golden Valley want their hog stickers back," he explained. "Apparently they were hired by Speckled Pheasant for the attack on the Transfer Post. Their part was the killing while the agitators lit the fires. Seeing as Speckled Pheasant hired them, the Sweet Fist hold him responsible for returning the Nocte Apibus. If the Dulce Pugno had to come and retrieve the knives themselves, they were going to kill whoever possessed the knives, as well as, Speckled Pheasant. Grabbing you was supposed to help him trade for the knives."

"Alright. We have two issues. One is what to do with the renegade? Slit his throat, or kill him slowly by crucifixion as an example," Centurion Stylianus pondered. "The other issue is how many Centuries we'll need to wipe out that nest of vipers in Golden Valley?"

His voice was low, rough and scratchy. His message, on the other hand, was clear. The Legion did not barter with or abide threats from dissents or terrorists.

"Excuse me, sir," Ceyx asked, "If I may?"

"Go ahead Decanus. I believe you've earned the right to voice your opinion," the Centurion assured him.

"The Dulce Pugno have defended the Golden Valley against their enemies for centuries. In all that time, only once have they punished an enemy beyond their mountains. It was a King and his family," Ceyx explained. "One story told by my people is about a greedy merchant group. The merchants grew weary of the restrictive distribution practices and the high price of the honey from the Golden Valley."

"They hired a Warlord to attack the mountain valley and claim it for the merchants," continued Ceyx. "The Warlord force marched his troops into the mountains. A half a day's march from the valley, the army set up camp. Three scouts were sent forward to run reconnaissance on the valley's defenses. As the sun set beyond the high peaks, extra sentries were posted. As darkness descended, the warriors settled in for the night."

"In the morning, the common soldiers awoke late. Confused by the lack of morning harassment and marching orders, they began searching for their Lieutenants and the Warlord," explained Ceyx. "The search ended in the command tent. There, they discovered the Warlord and his command staff laying in pools of honey and blood with their throats slit."

"As they milled around leaderless, the three scouts staggered down the rutted track from the direction of the Golden Valley. Each scout had a heavy yoke strapped across his shoulders. Hanging from the ends of the yokes were large buckets of honey," recounted Ceyx. "The men feasted on the delicious honey, broke camp, and marched from the mountain."

Sergeant Horus blustered and challenged, "You think a bunch of amateur assassins could sneak into a Legion camp and kill our command staff? I don't think so."

"Hold on Optio, while I agree with you, I have a few questions," Centurion Stylianus stated. "Did the Dulce Pugno murder the merchants?"

"No, sir. The merchants lived. Although for years they traveled with bodyguards," commented Ceyx. "After assassinating the Warlord and his staff, the Dulce Pugno extracted no additional retribution. It was as if the planned attack never happened."

"Curious. You mentioned something about the restricted distribution of the honey," Stylianus commented before asking. "Explain that?"

"Honey from the Golden Valley is handled by small trading houses," Ceyx further explained. "The honey is beyond the means of all but the wealthy. As such, the trading houses specialize in rare delicacies such as wines and teas, silks, exotic grains, and of course, the honey. Produce from the Golden Valley is transported to specialty houses located around the region. Always under guard and always under the protection of the Dulce Pugno."

"That's the answer," Centurion Stylianus announced. "The assassins have a reputation for non-intervention. Other than the paid killings, they don't leave their valley. I can't imagine we'd ever encounter them if a squad of our Legionaries hadn't killed four of their assassins and taken the Nocte Apibus."

He pointed to the table where the four knives were displayed.

"Excuse me, sir. It wasn't a squad," explained Optio Horus. "It was Private Sisera, before he started recruit training."

"Well, I guess he is a special young man," the Centurion said as he slowly closed his eyes. Horus and Ceyx, assuming their officer needed to rest, began backing out of the tent. Stylianus' eyes popped open and he said sleepily. "Before we go stomping all over what might be the Consuls' and the Senate's favorite honey farm, let's get more facts. Find the trading house. Question the merchant."

He snuggled his tortured body deeper under the blanket, rolled onto his side, and began snoring. Horus and Ceyx stepped softly out of the tent. They were met by a squad of heavy infantrymen in full kit. Three more Legionaries sat off to the side.

"Corporal Thornernus assigned us to guard the officer," reported the squad's Lance Corporal. "He said if anything happens to the Centurion, we'd have the worst merda duties he could invent until the day we died. That's if he didn't kill us first. The Centurion will be safe. I can assure you."

"Sound reasoning," Horus remarked to the squad leader before turning to the three sitting Legionaries. "Wido. We're going to speak with a merchant. Stay here and keep an eye on things."

"Sure Sergeant. But Private Sisera needs a favor," The Raider Decanus explained. "The Armorer wants a specialist chit to issue gladii for the dual rig."

The harness was splayed over Alerio's knee and he was vigorously rubbing the leather with geese oil. He looked up and nodded in agreement

"We'll take care of that later," Horus promised.

He and Ceyx strolled away. At the end of the tent, they turned towards the main gate.

Chapter 58 - Intelligence, the Rarest of Commodities

The trading house for rare goods was indeed a house. Sitting in the center of the warehouse district, it was out of sync with the surrounding buildings.

Horus and Ceyx passed the warehouse from last night's action. Circled three more long, low warehouses until they arrived. The out of place villa was surrounded by a high stone wall with a wide gate. To secure the gate, thick, iron reinforced doors hung open. Although open, the feeling as they walked through the gate was grave.

Maybe it was the silence in the courtyard compared to the shouting of men filling or unloading carts. Or, maybe it was the whinnies and hee-haws of mules waiting impatiently to haul the goods from the warehouses' loading bays. In any case, a sense of being stalked raised the hairs on the backs of their necks as they marched to the front door. Horus grabbed the knocker. Before he could rap on the door, it swung open.

"Legionaries. Please, enter," a young lad greeted them with a bow and an outstretched arm. He was pointing to a large but sparse office set just off a long corridor.

Doors to other rooms faced the hallway and where it ended, they could see short stacks of polished wooden boxes through a doorway. Obviously, the rear of the villa acted as the storage area for the expensive merchandise.

In the office, a slightly built man sat behind a large desk. Scrolls and parchments were neatly stacked in front of him. Although his body was hidden under a bulky robe, he appeared slender. When the man extended his arm to indicate two chairs for his visitors, the sleeve of the robe rode up displaying a thick forearm. The slight movement of pointing caused the muscles to ripple under the taut skin.

'Not the build of an ordinary merchant,' thought Horus. 'It would take hours of daily training to achieve those muscles.'

"Legionaries. Welcome to our humble trading house," the man said in the sing song accent of western Greece. "I am Bright Home or Hampus in your language. Call me whichever you favor. How may I be of service?"

Horus pulled the Dulce Pugno scroll from a pouch and passed it across the desk.

"What can you tell me about this?" he asked.

Hampus weighed the scroll in his hand while he thought. Then without unrolling it, placed the scroll on the desk.

"I am aware of the Dulce Pugno's warning," he admitted.

Hampus and Horus stared at each other. The Legionary waited for more information. The merchant, with a blank look on his face, not giving any. As the standoff stretched into an uncomfortable length of time, the veins in the Optio's neck began to bulge and his patience ran out.

"Look, I'm not here to verbally duel with you," Horus stated bluntly. "Before I gather a Legion and lay waste to the Golden Valley, I want answers. Give me an alternative or live with the consequences."

"I can assure you, we are a simple trading house," Hampus replied defensively. "The Golden Valley is one of our clients. A very loyal client but still just a supplier. I know nothing about the intensions of the Dulce Pugno."

Horus, out of frustration, shoved back his chair and jumped to his feet. "If that's the case, we're done here," he said taking a step towards the doorway. "I'll take the Nocte Apibus to the valley myself and shove the four of them up a Dulce Pugno's cūlus when I get there."

"Wait. You know about the Night Bees," Hampus stated. It wasn't a question. "Please return to your seat. I don't know about the Sweet Fist's plans. But possibly, I can give you some guidance as far as the Nocte Apibus are concerned."

Ceyx hesitated as his Sergeant sat back down. When Horus stood, the light infantryman had slipped from his chair and drifted back. His intention was to cover his Optio's back as he moved to the door. Something about Hampus made him leery. He remained behind the Sergeant's chair.

Hampus shifted his eyes from the Optio to Ceyx. "Please countryman. We are simply talking," the odd merchant said. Hampus held up his wrists while spreading his hands apart to show they were empty. "Sit and let's discuss this issue," he encouraged the light infantryman.

The movement of both arms caused the sleeves to slide up the arms allowing full view of the merchant's lower arms. Both were thickly muscled and crisscrossed with knife scars.

Ceyx shuffled around Horus and retook his seat. He never took his eyes off of the merchant.

"I apologize for the confusion," Hampus stated before continuing. "I truly don't know the intensions of the Dulce Pugno. If I were home in the Golden Valley, I would ask. But alas, I am here and cannot. What I can tell you is the Sweet Fist do not start blood feuds. Yes, they contract out assassins. That's business. They protect the honey shipments. That's also just business. People die. Those of the valley and those in the outlying world, that's also business. However, when a Nocte Apis, or worse yet, four Nocte Apibus are misplaced, it becomes a matter of pride."

"That confirms our suspicions," Sergeant Horus interjected. "The scroll mentioned retribution. We are prepared to return the Nocte Apibus. But we are concerned with the retribution comment. The Legion will not allow the murder of our people without taking vengeance of our own. So, do you have a suggestion as to how we avoid a bloody war?"

"It is tradition for one possessing a Night Bee to return it to the Golden Valley. Or pay the cost in blood," Hampus advised. "As for retribution, that would be for the Dulce Pugno to decide. I can tell you, most return. Say if the squad of Legionaries who killed the owners of the Night Bees returned them to the valley, they might also return."

"Why would I send men to their deaths?" challenged Horus. "Without a guarantee of safe passage?"

"In this life Optio, there are no guarantees," Hampus stated, "We are born, we do our duty, and we die. Nothing is promised. It is tradition that guides us along the way. As I said, traditionally, most return from the Golden Valley."

Horus and Ceyx stood and said their goodbyes. While Sergeant Horus marched out of the room, the Lance Corporal backed out never taking his eyes off the merchant. As he stepped into the hall and just before exiting the front door, Hampus jerked his arm. Suddenly, a gleaming knife appeared in his hand. The merchant pointed the blade at Ceyx and winked. The light infantryman didn't rush, nor did he hesitate, he simply backed out of the house.

They remained quiet while crossing the courtyard. Once through the gate, Horus glanced over at Ceyx, "They think a whole squad took down their assassins."

"You didn't correct him," Ceyx replied.

"Never tell all you know when negotiating," Horus advised, then asked. "How many men would you need to defend the villa?"

Ceyx glanced around at the compound, the wide clean streets, and the low single-story warehouses boarding the trading house.

"With a reinforced squad of light infantry on the walls and a squad of archers on the roof," the Decanus stated. "I could hold this place against a Century of heavy infantrymen for a week."

"From your answer, I can tell you are a light infantryman," laughed Horus. "But you're close. The villa is nothing short of a strong hold in the center of a defensive area. The only thing missing are barricades between the warehouses. From the roof of the villa, archers can shoot over the surrounding buildings."

As they reached the corner of the villa's perimeter wall, the wind rustled a pile of rags laying on the side of the street. In the warehouse district, packaging and wrappings were stacked for future use so, the pile went unnoticed.

"This place might rate some watching," suggested Ceyx.

"You might be right," Optio Horus said agreeing with the Veles squad leader.

As the Legionaries crossed the street and turned on a boulevard heading back across the district, the rags shifted. From the pile, the lad who had greeted them at the front door rose up. He collected the loose, tattered cloth and ran back through the villa's gates.

Chapter 59 - For the Specialist, a Chit

"We can send a squad to Golden Valley and probably get them killed," Sergeant Horus reported. "Or, there is an off chance, they come back alive. I don't like their odds."

"If I may?" asked Lance Corporal Eolus asked.

"Speak up Eolus," Stylianus commanded.

The Centurion was sitting in a chair putting on a good show. Still, they could tell he was fighting exhaustion and struggling just to stay upright.

"Private Sisera should go," Ceyx stated. "It was his blade that slew the assassins. So rightfully, he owns the Night Bees. The Sweet Fist might honor his prowess when he returns the Nocte Apibus."

"I'm not happy with sending one Private into a den of assassins," Horus stated. "I'd rather the Legion march in and pacify the whole nest of wasps."

"Bees, Optio, and it's a hive," Stylianus corrected. "As I suspected, and after some inquiries at the mess hall it's confirmed, honey from the Golden Valley is, in fact, the Consuls' favorite sweet treat. For political reasons, the General will never approve the assault."

"Consequently, we send an inexperienced Private to his death?" complained Horus. Then he remembered Wido's comment. As it was shaping up, it was the least he could do for Private Sisera.

He brought it to his Centurion's attention, "Sisera needs a chit to draw two additional gladii from the Armory. You might have noticed the dual harness he was wearing during your rescue, sir."

"I don't remember much except for Speckled Pheasant using me for a punching bag," Stylianus admitted. "Drawing two additional gladii means the chit goes to a specialist. Has Private Sisera mastered a skill? Is he an expert at something?"

Sergeant Horus rubbed his chin and pondered the question. A few months ago, Sisera was a farm boy. In his time in the Legion, he hadn't been to any schools or apprenticed with a master of anything.

"Weapon's Instructor," Ceyx blurted out. "He knows more about sword fighting than anyone I know. So, he is a specialist, a gladius instructor."

"Sisera. Get in here," Horus shouted.

Alerio pushed through the tent flap after a few words with the Infantrymen at the entrance. They had been aware of him as he conditioned the strange leather harness when they came on duty. Conversely, the guards hadn't spoken to him and didn't know him. It took a few heartbeats of convincing for the sentries to let the Private enter the tent.

"Optio. Alerio Sisera reporting as ordered," he said.

Horus pulled his gladius and struck a guard pose.

"What am I doing wrong?" the Sergeant asked.

Alerio walked behind his Optio and studied the posture.

"Your rear foot is twisted and you can't push off with any power," he explained while nudging the foot forward. "Stance is too wide."

Alerio adjusted the Sergeant's posture, his grip, the set of his shoulders and finally, he tapped under Horus' chin.

"Hold your head that low and you can't see through the helmet let alone over a shield," Alerio directed.

When he was finished, he stepped back. Optio Horus was posed in a perfect guard stance.

"Sir, your judgement?" Horus asked as he sheathed his gladius.

"He knows the stance," Stylianus admitted. "What about the gladius drills?"

"I can attest to his expertise," Horus stated.

"Well, here's the final issue," the Centurion said as he swayed trying to keep his balance. "A Private can't be a gladius instructor. Is there anything he'd done to earn a promotion?'

"Sir. I was going to put him in for a Legion medal," Ceyx announced. "for his actions in the warehouse. I expect, he'd trade an award for a promotion."

The Centurion uncorked an ink vase and dipped a pen. He wrote a short note before offering the quill to Horus. The Sergeant jotted his name at the bottom of the document.

"Optio. You handle the rest," Stylianus slurred as he raised an arm. "It seems I've used up my stamina. Decanus Eolus. If you wouldn't mind."

Ceyx dipped his shoulder under the outstretched arm and helped Stylianus stand. Together they shuffled to the Centurion's bed. The officer was asleep before Ceyx finished pulling the blanket over him.

"Sisera. I've got some good news and some bad news for you," Horus announced. "Good news, you are now a certified weapon's specialist. Bad news, you're going to the Golden Valley to return the Nocte Apibus. More good news. Congratulations, Lance Corporal Sisera on your promotion."

Ceyx gripped Alerio's wrist and congratulated the young Legionary. Meanwhile, Horus fretted. He had helped promote Sisera and was probably condemning him to his death on the same day.

"Enough of this," Horus ordered. "When do you want to leave, Lance Corporal Sisera?"

"We leave at day break from the Raider Post," asserted Ceyx. "And we're taking Speckled Pheasant with us."

"Alright, I'll bite," Horus said as he screwed down his eye brows as if facing an unsolvable puzzle. "Why the rebel? Why you? Go."

"Speckled Pheasant contracted for the assassins. It was on his assignment where they lost their men and the Nocte Apibus," Eolus replied. "Besides, he lied. It must have been his report to the Dulce Pugno that convinced them a squad of Legionaries killed the assassins. Seems to me, if the Dulce Pugno want retribution, it should be on Speckled Pheasant."

"Acceptable," the Sergeant declared. "Go on."

"One man can't watch a prisoner and guard the Nocte Apibus," offered Ceyx. "Plus, I know the mountain trails. The last thing you want is for Decanus Sisera to become lost. Imagine the legend of the lost Raider wandering in the mountains for thirty years. It would reflect badly on the Legion."

"Can't have that now can we," Horus said. Then to Sisera, he asked, "Are you okay with all this? We could put you on a ship and spirit you away."

"Optio, I will not refuse my duty," Alerio assured the NCO. "Besides, according to my instructors in recruit training, it only hurts until you die."

"Go. Do what you need to do," the Sergeant ordered Lance Corporals Ceyx Eolus and Private Alerio Sisera. "You'll sleep in here tonight, under guard, and near the Nocte Apibus. We sail at first light."

Chapter 60 - Raider Post

The fishing boat drifted on the last dip of the oars and nudged against the rickety pier. Horus jump first and jogged up the narrow trail. Eolus and Sisera formed a human chain and guided Speckled Pheasant off the deck, precariously over the short span above the water, and onto the dock. By the time the out of shape revolutionary placed both feet on the weather worn wood, he was gasping for breath.

"You expect me to climb that?" Speckled Pheasant asked while inhaling lungs full of air. He lifted one hand to his chest and pointed up the steep hill with the other.

Ceyx pulled his long-curved knife, laid the blade against the rebel's cheek, and explained, "You can climb. Or, you can feed the fish."

Reluctantly, Speckled Pheasant lifted a foot and carefully set it down on the first riser. He pushed on his knee with a hand and brought the trailing foot up beside the first. He stepped up again and repeated the motions.

"Decanus Eolus. This is going to take all day," commented Alerio. "And we have over a hundred and fifty miles to travel. How is he going to make it?"

"First, call me Ceyx. Next, I'm not so worried about crossing the high plains," Ceyx commented. "It's the mountain trails where he'll really slow us down."

"We could starve him and he'd lose weight," Alerio suggested. "It works in recruit training."

"Over five months maybe," Ceyx replied. "We only have a day. Starve a fat man and he'll get weak before his body adjusts to the short rations. No. We'll need to find a way to transport him."

At the top, a goodly portion of time later, the Legionaries stood watching as the rebel Captain sat down again to rest. High above, on the far side of the plateau, Corporal Manfredus also sat. Not because he was tired, because it was easier to watch Optio Horus pace from a fixed position.

"What's taking them so long?" demanded Horus.

"Well, based on your reports from the last four times you went over and checked," Manfredus replied. "I'd say Speckled Pheasant was the glitch in your perfectly planned agenda."

"We did learn something," admitted Horus. "They'll need a mule and a cart to haul the fat cūlus."

A long time later, the Nocte Apibus were stored in the command tent and Speckled Pheasant was in the care of Second Squad heavy infantry.

"He's rich and unethical," Manfredus warned the squad leader. "He may try to bribe your men."

"After what he did to Centurion Stylianus, I'm not worried about the men helping him," Lance Corporal Velius replied. "I'm worried about them murdering him."

"He's got to be alive and fit to travel," Manfredus said casually. "But there's no reason he has to be comfortable."

Over the last few years, Raiders had been killed or injured by the rebel Captain's men. So, he ended up naked and strapped to the tent's center pole. Happily, according to the men of Second Squad, it was going to be a cold night.

"How am I supposed to sleep with that in our tent," complained Private Pholus. "Just walking in, I was blinded by the pale, flabby flesh. I almost lost my dinner."

"He does resemble a toad," observed Private Didacus. "We could hide him under a blanket."

"It's too far to walk to the stables," Pholus said. "Besides, the blanket will keep him warm. I'll just pretend there's a full moon out tonight."

Act 6

Chapter 61 - A Small Caravan

After nudging an exhausted Speckled Pheasant through the gullies and ravines, a squad of light infantrymen delivered him to the pass. Alerio and Ceyx stood beside a two wheeled cart and a mule. They enjoyed the show as the Captain of the revolutionaries complained, cursed, and offered enormous sums of Republic coin to anyone who returned him to the harbor town. Between the tirades, he yelped as sharp rocks poked the bottoms of his city shoes.

"Should we have requisitioned him more appropriate footwear?" asked Alerio.

"He's riding, we're walking," Ceyx sneered. "His pretty, civilian slippers are fine."

The light infantry squad leader shoved the dissent at Ceyx.

"The loud mouth's all yours, Decanus Eolus," he said in disgust.

"Unfortunately, he is," Ceyx admitted as he took a firm grip on the rebel's arm. "Let me escort you to your coach, Princess."

"You'll be spitting blood out of your throat when my comrades catch up to us," threatened the Captain.

"What no bribe offers?" asked Ceyx. "Alerio and I are disappointed."

"Would you take a bribe?" Speckled Pheasant asked hopefully.

"Well, no. But it would have been a nice gesture," Ceyx replied as if his feelings were hurt.

Then, he shoved the fat rebel over the rear board of the cart. Speckled Pheasant ended up half in the low cart with his feet touching the ground.

"Move it out, Alerio," Ceyx shouted.

Speckled Pheasant's toes scraped and his feet kicked at the moving earth as he attempted to crawl fully into the cart. While the renegade clawed his way onto the Legionary gear, the food supplies and the amphorae of watered wine, the light infantry squad jogged ahead of the small caravan.

They would provide security for half a day before returning to the Raider Post. The caravan would be on its own afterward.

As Legionaries, Ceyx and Alerio could travel twenty miles in half a day. Then rest for a period and run another ten miles. At that rate, they could reach the mountains in a little over five days. The heavily loaded cart, unfortunately, moved much slower.

Miles from the pass as the sunlight extended their shadows, Alerio and Ceyx began to seek a camp site for the evening. Although the land appeared flat, it was rutted and had mounds swelling above the terrain.

"There, about fifty feet from the road," Ceyx suggested while pointing to a low rise.

"You call this a road?" Alerio asked while he nodded his head in approval of the camp site.

"Caravan trail, well beaten path, or animal track," replied Ceyx. "It's straight, relatively level, and leads in the direction we're traveling. By definition, it's a road."

The wheels of the cart bumped over stones and down and up ruts. As they approached the rise, Ceyx marched ahead to survey the area. Alerio pulled the mule to a stop. From the edge of the cart, he lifted a feed bag and strapped it to the mule's muzzle.

The dissent was sitting and gazing at the back trail.

"I'm going to clear rocks for the camp," Alerio explained to the Captain as he walked to the back of the cart.

The point of a dagger dug into the top of Alerio's right arm. Private Sisera jerked the hand and his body back as the dagger stabbed for his face. Speckled Pheasant swiped sideways with the dagger and struggled to climb out of the cart.

Alerio drew his gladius with the bleeding arm and passed it over to his left hand.

"Stay back or I'll gut you," the rebel said as his feet touched the ground.

For a second, Alerio was tempted to sever the man's knife hand. Speckled Pheasant had misread the pause as a sign of victory. Guessing the injury to the Legionary's right arm put him at a disadvantage, the Captain moved in close.

"You'll tell your boyfriend to stand down," the renegade leader ordered as he stepped up. "If you know what's good for you."

At first taken back by the swiftness of the fat man, Alerio tensed preparing to windmill his blade. The effect would be a handless Captain who probably would die on the plain and never reach the mountains. Before he could begin the maneuver, Ceyx's hand clamped over the hilt of his pummel.

"Step back," ordered the Light Infantryman and Alerio rolled to the side and away from the dagger.

They exchanged places so swiftly Speckled Pheasant was confused as to whom he was trying to intimidate. The blade shifted back and forth between the two Legionaries.

Alerio was a step away when he realized Ceyx hadn't drawn his gladius. He raised his blade and took a half step.

"Stay," Ceyx ordered.

The voice gave Speckled Pheasant a focus and he drove his dagger forward. Ceyx's wrist shot out and touched the wrist on Speckled Pheasant's knife hand. The blade veered off course. As the renegade attempted to bring the blade back to the attack, Ceyx's wrist stayed connected. When the agitator made a circle with his arm trying to dislodge the Legionary's wrist, Ceyx rotated his hand until his palm was touching the rebel's wrist.

It was as if the wrists were tied together. The Legionary's wrist, hand or palm redirected every move by the Captain. They remained in contact despite the rapid moves. Finally, Speckled Pheasant grabbed with his free hand.

Ceyx countered. He attached his other hand to that wrist. Now, both men seemed to be hand dancing. From a frontal attack, the miniature battle had dissolved into Speckled Pheasant stepping back in an attempt to free his wrists from the Legionary's hands.

"Get off me," Speckled Pheasant pleaded. He was rapidly shaking his hands as if to clean pony merda from them. Sometime during the moves, the dagger fell but Ceyx didn't relent.

The revolutionary shouted in frustration and clamped his hands behind his back. Ceyx drew back his head and smashed it into Speckled Pheasant's nose. Blood spurted as the fat man sank to the ground holding his face in his hands.

"What was that?" Alerio asked. He was awed by the movements of the other Legionary.

"Disarming an armed opponent without hurting him," Ceyx answered.

"He doesn't look uninjured," Alerio pointed out as Speckled Pheasant sniffed and dabbed at his nose trying to stop the bleeding.

"That is injured after being disarmed," Ceyx explained. "There's a difference."

Chapter 62 - Sticky Hands

They cleared rocks from the hill and used them to build a ring of stone around the camp site. Any enemy could easily walk over the barrier but in the dark, they hopefully would trip over the loose stones first.

Alerio started a fire and Ceyx cooked a corn meal mush. Once the corn had softened, he tossed in pieces of dried goat jerky.

"Smells wonderful," Alerio said as he took the clay bowl. Then glancing over towards Speckled Pheasant exclaimed. "Good Legion field cooking. Enjoy!"

The rebel mumbled something in response. Alerio and Ceyx couldn't understand as the sound was filtered by the mule's feed bag. It hung from his neck forcing him to used his bound hands to press the bottom of the bag so the food lifted to his mouth.

"What did he say?" Ceyx asked.

"He was complimenting you on the fine cuisine," Alerio explained between bites. "So, what were the hand movements you used to disarm Speckled Pheasant?"

"When I was a lad, an old Hoplite lived in our village," Ceyx replied. "One day, a bunch of us lads were playing war. We had chopped down bamboo poles."

"Bamboo?" asked Alerio.

"A utilitarian reed that can grow thicker around than your arm muscle," explained Ceyx.

"I'd like to see that," Alerio commented. "The reeds in the West grow in ponds and are only the size of your little finger, if that."

Speckled Pheasant began making muffled noises.

"Smells bad, doesn't it?" Alerio asked the dissent.

"Tastes bad as well," Ceyx commented. "As I was saying. The bamboo poles we cut were about as thick as a javelin. For a day, we chased and wacked each other until we ran by the old Hoplite's hut. He liked to take the afternoon sun and usually ignored the children. This day for some reason, he called us over."

"War is small, he said. Swords and sticks are big. You don't start big, you start small," Ceyx stopped the tale. Taking pity on the rebel, he walked over and removed the mule's feed bag. After sniffing it, he coughed and swore, "Ah, that's foul. You know Speckled Pheasant, if you hadn't gone all pit fighter on my fellow Lance Corporal, we could free your hands."

"I'm going to enjoy killing you Ceyx Eolus," the revolutionary leader stated. "And you, Alerio Sisera."

Ignoring the threats, Ceyx turned to Alerio and continued, "In order to fight and win big battles, explained the old warrior, you need to learn to fight small. He pointed to the biggest lad and ordered him to strike and strike hard. The lad brought the bamboo pole over his head and swung it down toward the old man's head. As the pole came down, the old Hoplite reached up with the palm of his left hand. He touched the lad's wrist. Seemly without any effort, the pole was guided out of its path and struck the ground. Totaling missing the old man."

"He ordered the lad to try again. This time, the old Hoplite reached up with his right hand, touched the lad's wrist and the pole missed the old man but struck the lad on his own knee," related Ceyx. "We begged him to teach us small warfare."

"He called it sticky hands. You make contact with your opponent's hands or wrists. Every movement they make you mirror. When they punch, you redirect it. When they try to grab, you rotate around their hands to avoid their fingers," Ceyx explained. "It's as if your hands and theirs were stuck together."

"Show me this sticky-hands," begged Alerio.

"What about the wound on your arm?" asked Ceyx.

"It's a scratch," Alerio stated. "The fat pig isn't much of a knifeman."

By the light of their camp fire, Alerio attempted to shove Ceyx. The energy was redirected harmlessly to the side. As Alerio brought his arms in, Ceyx's hands stayed with them.

Alerio attempted to strike, hit, shove and even just to touch Ceyx's torso. Each move was gently countered by the sticky hands.

In the morning as they broke camp, Ceyx had to suppress a laugh. After harnessing the mule, packing the cart with the night's equipment, and boosting in Speckled Pheasant, Alerio began making small movements with his hands and arms. The sight of the big Legionary making small gestures as he walked beside the mule was too much. Ceyx broke and the laughter erupted from his belly.

Alerio's only response was to cast a smile over his shoulders while continuing the small moves. The cart bumped on the road as the sun appeared over the high desert plains.

Chapter 63 - Rebels on the Trail

Three days of slow traveling brought them no closer to their destination as far as Alerio could tell. The mountains still resembled jagged saw teeth and the high desert plain remained mostly level.

They made camp at dusk and after dinner, Alerio and Ceyx stood pushing and shoving as they hand fought. Speckled Pheasant glanced down the trail, smiled, and lay down. While the stupid Legionaries played a children's game, his men were catching up. From his rear-facing seat in the cart, he had observed an occasional dust trail. After half a day, the signs of pursuit grew closer.

Alerio took first watch. He waited for the rebel Captain to begin snoring before walking away from camp. At the road, he backtracked their trail for a couple of hours before returning to wake Ceyx. The other Legionary would patrol ahead looking for any trouble they might encounter during the next day's travel. By the time Speckled Pheasant woke, one of them would be on watch and tending the fire.

They broke camp in the dim predawn light. All day Speckled Pheasant strained his eyes for signs of his men. Dust would rise before being blown away by the light breeze. Each time he wanted to yell out in triumph. Instead, he settled for chuckling to himself.

The sun was still up when Ceyx called a halt for the day. After dinner, Speckled Pheasant watched as Alerio cleaned their pans and dishes. He failed to notice Ceyx sneaking up behind him. The gag looped over his head and was snugged down before he could cry out. His hands and feet were bound and he was laid on the ground.

"Got work to do," Ceyx whispered as he pulled a blanket over the dissent. "Here, so you don't catch a chill."

Chapter 64 - Ambush in the Night

By the time Ceyx arrived at the cart, Alerio had finished strapping on his armor and the dual gladius rig.

"How far back?" Alerio asked. "Could it be a caravan?"

"About ten miles based on the dust," Ceyx replied as he pulled out his chest pieces. "They're closing too fast to be merchants."

"It's going to be a long night," proclaimed Alerio.

"A Legionary doesn't rest until the job is done," exclaimed Ceyx as he finished strapping down the last piece. "Ready?"

The standard run for a Legionary was twenty miles in less than half a day. Because the two had walked the road in the daylight and studied it as they traveled, they had a good idea where the holes and rocky obstacles lay. Armed with this knowledge, the Legionaries broke into a jog at the road.

Later, a candle sized light flickered in the distance. Further along the road, the light formed into a small yet identifiable campfire. They eased to a walk and continued on the trail. When voices reached them, the Legionaries left the wagon path and began to circle around the renegade's camp.

Ceyx reached out and tapped Alerio's arm six times. Alerio responded by confirming the presence of six dissents with six taps of his own. They were squatting behind the renegade's camp just out of the ring of light. One man stood by the fire obviously on guard duty. Luckily for the Legionaries, the sentry spent more time poking at the fire then looking out into the darkness for danger. Around the fire, another five men lay wrapped in blankets.

Legionaries, renegades, highwaymen, barbarians, and tribesmen hated fighting at night. You couldn't tell friends from foes as gladii and knives stabbed blindly in the dark. Then again, this was six on two and it was to Ceyx's and Alerio's advantage to initiate a night attack.

Ceyx traced a circle on Alerio's arm then completed the message by running a finger down the center of the circle. It was the simplest of plans; you take half the camp and I'll take the other.

Fighters disliked night attacks for another reason. You couldn't tell if your gladius struck a vital organ and actually fell the enemy. Or, if the jolt and surprise caused them to topple to the ground only to rise again and stab you in the back. The Legion's recruit instructors had an answer for this issue. Forget stabbing on the first round, the gladius was wide and heavy. It made a great club. You could always come back and dispatch the unconscious enemy at your leisure.

Ceyx stepped over a sleeping form while his blade rapped the side of the sentry's head. The blow should have driven the man to the side. It's an odd thing about the human head; it weighs a lot.

The sentry's head rocked and bounced off the man's shoulder. As it wobbled back the other way, the mass of the head turned the man. His body sprawled into the campfire. Suddenly, hot ashes and embers washed over the five sleeping men.

"Precision gladius work," Alerio teased. From the dark, he swung both gladii.

Two of the men rose cursing and brushing off the glowing embers. They dropped from Alerio's blades. Another went down as he sat up. Feeling good, Alerio skipped to the other side of the campsite and knocked out a fourth man.

"Four down," he announced. One reason for the report was to let Ceyx know he only needed to take down the final rebel. The other reason was to let Ceyx know where he was standing. It prevented the light infantryman from throwing a knife into his face.

"Done," Ceyx stated as the sixth man crumpled to the ground.

"Do you want to question any of them?" Alerio asked as he swung the blades over his shoulders and neatly sheathed both gladii.

Ceyx's back was turned to the Legionary as he searched a saddlebag. His hand touched a damp bundle of parchment.

"Normally, I'd like some intelligence," Ceyx informed Alerio. "But seeing as we know their mission. And already have one prisoner more than I prefer, the answer is no."

Both Legionaries pulled their knives and slit the throats of the six rebels. When they finished the grisly task, Ceyx held out his hand.

"Give me your knife and rebuild the fire," he ordered.

While Alerio collected stray pieces of wood and kicked the burning sticks and embers into a pile, Ceyx rested the knife blades over a hot spot. When the steel began to glow, he wiped them on the blouse of a dead revolutionary.

"What's up?" Alerio inquired. He was watching with his hand out expecting the return of his knife.

Ceyx turned his back again and chopped something. When he turned around, he held out Alerio's knife. On the blade was a chunk of meat.

Alerio sniffed and declared, "Fresh beef."

"Breakfast courtesy of Speckled Pheasant and these lads," Ceyx exclaimed. Then he began to look around saying. "Vino? Not the watered stuff we have. Real vino, full strength and right out of the barrel. Here put my beef in the fire with yours. If they have beef, there's bound to be vino."

Chapter 65 - Dangerous Travels

As dawn drove back the night, Ceyx went to count the ponies brought by the failed rescue team. Alerio busied himself with collecting weaponry. Most of the knives were cheaply made and the two swords weren't of much better quality. Still, he found four bows and four quivers stuffed with arrows. Almost as an afterthought, he selected a man with big feet and took his boots.

"Seven ponies," Ceyx reported as he led the animals to the camp. "I wonder which of these poor beasts was intended for Speckled Pheasant's fat cūlus."

"Four of the renegades were bowmen," Alerio announced holding up a bow and a quiver. "If we hadn't seen them, we'd have woken up to a breakfast of arrowheads."

"Not very appetizing," replied Eolus. "From here on, we ride. And we lighten the cart by using the extra ponies as pack animals. Altogether, we'll make better time."

The next day on the trail, Alerio rode one pony with three others on lines. Ceyx followed on another with a line to the mule.

"Get them away from me," shouted Speckled Pheasant.

The final two ponies were sociable. From where they were tied, they could easily place their muzzles into the cart and sniff the rebel Captain.

"He doesn't seem to like the company," observed Alerio with a nod towards the obese insurgent. "I guess he wasn't lonely after all."

***

They traveled for four more uneventful days. With the weight distributed among the ponies, they made better time. The mountain tops grew and the vegetation on the lower slopes became identifiable as trees.

On the morning of the sixth day, a cloud of dust rose in the distance. A long time later, the cloud formed a vee-shape pointing directly at the small caravan.

"What's that," Alerio shouted back. He was on the lead pony and guiding the mule. "A caravan?"

Ceyx stared off at the boiling dust for a long time. So long, in fact, Alerio got a creak in his neck and faced forward.

"Trouble," Ceyx finally replied. "Big trouble."

"More rebels?" asked Alerio.

"No. Worse. A war party of Frentani. Probably, eastern plain's tribesmen," Ceyx explained. "Pull the cart off the road and unharness the mule. Then circle the ponies around us and the cart."

"Form a defensive wall with living ponies?" asked Alerio. "Not much good if the wall can shy away with a single swat."

"Hopefully, they won't shoot the ponies," Ceyx explained. "Maybe it'll give us time to talk with them before they murder us."

"That easily?" inquired Alerio. He looked into the cart and Speckled Pheasant's eyes were wide open and the fat man was sweating.

"Not if we had two squads of heavy infantry with their big shields," Ceyx stated. "You wouldn't happen to have two squads in your kit?"

"No, of course not."

"In that case, yes, they can kill us that easily," pronounced Ceyx as he began tying ponies together nose to tail.

They sat on the cart surrounded by confused ponies and one mule that didn't seem to care about anything. The dust in the distance billowed to form a low swirl of boiling, brown clouds. Soon a line of men and ponies appeared on the leading edge of the dust.

"The Frentani tribesmen are from the high plains far north of here," Ceyx explained. "They migrate in hoards and send out foraging parties. Actually, more like war bands. Everyone who's confronted them is dead. The caravans simply pay them to go away."

The riders went from a gallop to an ordered stop. None of the tribesmen used a rein. Pressure from their knees guided the ponies so their hands were free to hold short, sturdy bows. One trotted forward, halted his mount, and crossed a leg across the pony's neck. As he relaxed, the tribesman observed the caravan.

A ring of fine ponies and an ugly mule circled a two-wheeled cart. On the cart were two men in leather armor and a fat man in a woman's vest. The war leader laughed at the man.

He raised an arm, pointed, turned his head and said something to the riders behind him. They laughed as well. Not seeing any of the three holding a bow, he nudged his pony closer to the strange formation.

Despite his shortcomings with the weapon, Alerio reached down for a bow.

"Don't," Ceyx ordered placing a hand on the young Legionary's arm. "Let's see if he'll bargain."

The Frentani war leader edged closer. From his pony's back, he leered at the caravan as if it were no more dangerous than a herd of sheep.

"Is that your man-woman?" he asked indicating Speckled Pheasant. "She's nice and fat, but she is ugly. I bet she likes the big boy best."

Alerio's spine straightened and he tensed up. The war leader had no respect or caution in his tone. His insulting confidence stung the young Legionary.

It took an elbow in the ribs from Ceyx to stop Alerio from drawing his gladii.

"But your ponies are nice," the Frentani war leader added. "I'll take them after you're dead."

The threat was too much for Alerio. He jumped up on the cart and blurted out, "You want me dead. Fine, fight me."

Ceyx cringed and the war leader laughed.

"I'll use a bow from the back of a flying pony," he bragged. "Where are your weapons?"

Alerio reached over his shoulders and drew both gladii.

"These," he said as he stepped down from the cart. After ducking under a pony's neck, he strutted to within four paces of the tribesman. "These are my weapons. You want me dead. I challenge you. My gladii against your bow and your pony."

The ten Frentani plainsmen trotted up as Alerio moved. They all had arrows notched and aimed at the Legionary.

Ceyx held his breath as the war chief looked around at his warriors. Some shook their heads no. Others shrugged noncommittally. Most indicated their excitement by rapidly jabbing their bows at the Legionary.

"I am Wolf Shout, a war chief of the Frentani family," the war leader stated. "It is our custom to know the names of the men we kill in single combat."

"Alerio Sisera, Decanus of the Republic Legion," Alerio replied. "We have no…"

A wineskin slammed into his chest.

"We also have a custom," Ceyx announced. Then out of the side of his mouth whispered. "Take a drink and salute the Frentani war chief."

"But I'm not thirsty," Alerio complained as he placed a gladius under an arm and took the wineskin.

"Just do it," insisted Ceyx. He turned and offered up another wineskin to Wolf Shout. "Our custom is to drink with our enemies, before killing them in single combat."

The war leader started chuckling before throwing his head back to allow a belly laugh to break over the assembled warriors.

"Drinking and killing," Wolf Shout explained. "Two of my favorite things."

Alerio pulled the stopper, lifted the wineskin above his head, and sent a stream into his mouth. Disappointingly, it was the weak watered vino they carried on the trail. At least, he thought, Ceyx could have given him the strong red they'd liberated from the dead rebels.

He held out the wineskin in salute. Wolf Shout followed his example. As the vino streamed into the war chief's mouth, Alerio could tell it was the strong red wine.

"Wolf Shout. To you, who is about to die," Alerio announced taking a second drink. "I salute you."

"Alerio Sisera. To you, who is about to die," the Frentani mimicked with a laugh and a drink. "I salute you."

"To the Consuls, vaulted Leaders of the Republic," Alerio said before pouring in a mouth filling stream. "I salute you."

"To the old fathers, esteemed by the Frentani family, and feared by our enemies," Wolf Shout said. He also drank with vigor and finished. "I salute you."

"To my comrades, living or dead," Alerio proclaimed. Now he was struggling to find more ways to keep the salutes and the drinking going. "I salute you."

"You honor your dead?" challenged Wolf Shout.

"I do," replied Alerio. "To those who have laid down their shields and no longer fill our earthly ranks. I salute you."

He took a hardy drink. The smile on the Frentani chief's face vanished and was replaced by a serious scowl. Alerio figured he had made a mistake. But what the Hades? If he truly was about to die, it couldn't hurt to honor those he was about to join.

Chapter 66 - Duel in the High Desert

"We also honor our dead," Wolf Shout stated as he pulled his leg from the pony's neck. He straightened, held the wineskin out, and shouted. "To our forefathers."

As he took a drink, the ten Frentani tribesmen behind him repeated the line.

"To the ground that guards their ashes," he said taking another drink.

Again, as if a choir, the tribesmen repeated the phrase.

"To the sun and stars that guide our way," he announced.

He drank while his warriors echoed his words.

Ceyx snapped his heels together and slammed a loud, cross fist salute into his chest. The salutation didn't go unnoticed by Wolf Shout. Alerio was a heartbeat behind. He raised his gladius to his chest to add his own salute to the ritual.

"To the wind that carries the whispers of our ancestors," Wolf Shout declared.

He drank. His men repeated.

"To the rain that waters our ponies," he roared.

His men replied in full voice while he drank.

"To the trail forward, which leads eventually to the ground," he said lowering his voice.

The Frentani tribesmen also lowered the volume as they uttered the words.

"To the ground, where our ashes will join with our forefathers," the Frentani chief almost whispered the final words.

The tribesmen mumbled those words as Wolf Shout took a long pour from the wineskin.

"We also honor our dead," slurred the war leader to Alerio. "Now we fight."

The pony responded immediately to the knee pressure and pivoted. Wolf Shout wobbled on the back of the animal as they trotted away. At fifty feet, the pony spun about and the Frentani over rotated before righting himself.

"How drunk do you think he is?" asked Alerio.

"I have no idea my friend," Ceyx replied. "Hopefully, enough. I think I'll watch from the cart."

"You do that," Alerio remarked as he dropped the wineskin and adjusted his grasps on the gladii.

Ceyx made it to the cart before Wolf Shout notched an arrow in his bow. Two additional arrows were clutched in his teeth. As he kicked the pony into motion, all signs of inebriation vanished.

The instructors in Legion recruit training had four words of advice when facing an archer; duck behind your shield. Unfortunately, he didn't have a shield. Beyond the advice, none of the lectures covered defense against a mounted archer.

Alerio didn't watch the pounding hooves or the bow and Wolf Shout's body. He focused on the tribesman's eyes. While an opponent's eyes, in a swordfight, weren't always reliable for judging a blade's path, an archer would need to aim. Or, did he?

Apparently, the wandering Frentani warriors from the high plains didn't aim like Legion archers. The arrow launched, from hip level, at twenty feet. While Wolf Shout failed to sight along the actual arrow, his eyes did lock on to the area he targeted.

Alerio raised both gladii in front of his face and held them together. One blade rocked back as it deflected the arrow. Rapidly, he lowered the blades to cover his midsection. It was a guess. If his head had been the first target, and it was protected, the next logical target should be his belly.

A blade rang as the second arrow impacted and ricocheted off the steel. Alerio spun to keep his gladii between him and the passing pony.

He dropped to a knee reducing his silhouette and flipped the blades up at an angle. Wolf Shout twisted around and released the third arrow. The arrow struck the blades and bounced high into the air.

Wolf Shout nudged the well-trained pony and it turned in a tight half circle. As the animal came about, Alerio stood. At the position of attention, he saluted with one of his gladii. With the other, he motioned for the tribesmen to come at him again.

There was no delay. While the pony was digging in his rear hooves, Wolf Shout notched one and placed two more arrows between his teeth. As if shot from a ballista, the mounted archer raced forward.

Alerio turned sideways to the charging pony. One of his blades was facing up while the other faced down. It looked ridiculous as if the Legionary was attempting to hide behind the blades. At their widest, the gladii were just under three inches in width.

The first arrow came at his knees. With a clue from Wolf Shout's eyes, Alerio rotated the top blade downward and used both to shield his knees. Just in time it seemed. The arrow immediately deflected off a blade.

Wolf Shout notched the second as the arrow to the knees struck without doing any harm. He pulled and released the second arrow. After a lifetime of shooting from the back of a moving pony, aiming was as simple as looking where he wanted the arrow to impact.

He looked at the Legionary and released the arrow. The arrow left the bow and sped across the distance. But, the target was no longer there.

By standing sideways to the charging pony, Alerio's body aligned with the track of the rider. When Wolf Shout focused his eyes, Alerio figured the archer would release the second arrow. Instead of standing and trying to block the arrow, Alerio jumped and rolled towards the path of the charging pony.

His feet found the ground and once he stood, he was one-step from being trampled.

By extending a gladius, he managed to slip the blade between Wolf Shout's leg and the animal's flank. As the pony raced by, the leg reached the hilt. A hard shove on the gladius unseated the rider. It also spun Alerio back and to the ground.

The deadly bow flew through the air and landed between the men. Both scrambled to their feet.

"Now we're on my terms," Alerio sneered. "Go for the bow and you'll lose an arm. Pull your knife and we'll fight blade to blade. Your choice."

Wolf Shout pulled his knife, spread his arms, and positioned his legs.

"Blade it is," Alerio declared as he tossed one of the gladii to the side. "Oh, I'm sorry. Would you like that sword? It's longer. Tell you what. You get the gladius and I'll fight you left-handed."

He switched hands and stood waiting for the confused Frentani tribesman to decide. As the men stared at each other, the pony pranced up beside Wolf Shout. It was the proper place for a war pony, next to its warrior and ready to be mounted.

Wolf Shout, without taking his eyes off Alerio, gently ran a hand down the animal's flank. As if confused, he chanced a glance at the pony. Other than a shaved area where the sharp blade had slid along its side, the pony's skin was undamaged. He'd expected to feel blood pumping from a deep wound.

"The pony is unharmed," stated Wolf Shout. He was puzzled and curious so he asked. "Why?"

"It's you I have to kill," Alerio explained. "Not a well-trained pony."

"But you could have sliced my leg and ended the fight," the Frentani war chief suggested. "Your blade would have butchered the animal in the process, but I'd be out of the fight."

"Where's the fun in that?" the Legionary questioned with a smile. "See, you have ten mounted warriors watching. I kill you; I die. You kill me, I die. So why add a helpless pony to the killing."

"You are an odd man, Alerio Sisera," Wolf Shout observed.

"I'm a thirsty man," the Legionary replied. "Where is your wineskin?"

"We drink. Then we fight," announced Wolf Shout.

"If we must," Alerio answered slowly while looking around. "Or you could take the seven ponies, the knives, and the bows as barter."

"Barter for what?" demanded Wolf Shout.

"Our lives," Alerio said. "In trade for our lives."

Chapter 67 - Caravan Town

"Do you think you could have unseated him if he was sober?" Ceyx asked.

They were standing next to the cart, the mule, and Speckled Pheasant. Wolf Shout and his Frentani warriors were specks vanishing in a trail of dust. Along with the tribesmen, went the seven ponies, the rebel's weapons, and the last wineskin of the excellent vino.

"I don't know," admitted Alerio. "My ego says yes. But common sense tells me otherwise. Can we make camp here for the night? I'm a little tired."

"Of course, we'll camp here," Ceyx replied. "And for you, my grand swordsman, I'll prepare something special for dinner."

"Sounds good," Alerio admitted. "What'll you make?"

"Barley meal with goat jerky," Ceyx said as he walked away. "My specialty."

At the mention of the menu, Speckled Pheasant gagged as a bit of puke rose in his throat.

***

Days later, a town appeared on the hills overlooking the high desert.

"Civilization," announced Alerio indicating the single-story clay buildings.

"Civilization might be giving the caravan town a little more credit than it deserves," Ceyx corrected. "It's there to supply merchants crossing to the harbor. Or for those crossing the mountains or continuing north on the high desert route."

"Still, it should have a variety of food," Alerio said. Then realizing the statement might be insulting added, "Oh, no offense to your cooking."

"None taken."

They camped that night with the lights of the caravan town in view. It was only half a day's march away. But they agreed it was better to arrive in daylight. Finding supplies in the dead of night in an unruly, frontier town wasn't a good idea.

"Captain. When we get into town, don't try to enlist help," Ceyx warned Speckled Pheasant. "If you do escape, Lance Corporal Sisera will hunt you down and your hired help. Then, he will kill all of them, and you."

"Why can't I kill him first?" asked Alerio. "Or better yet, why not kill him now?"

"Hold on," begged Speckled Pheasant, "I'm not going anywhere. The Dulce Pugno will hear my side. And, they will murder both of you. Me? I'll be in a caravan heading back to the harbor while the vultures are still rendering the flesh from your bones."

"Are you sure I can't kill him now?" asked Alerio.

"We hauled this fat cūlus and put up with his merda, all the way across the desert," Ceyx explained. "At this junction, we might as well finish it, and take him to the Golden Valley."

***

They broke camp while it was early morning and still dark. As the sun rose, the rough clay buildings stood out in stark contrast to the green trees of the foothills. The pens and stockyards, where the merchant's draft animals were held, came into view. They led the mule and the two-wheeled cart between the fencing.

"Livestock pens available," a man shouted. "Feed, water, and guards throughout the day and night. You'll not find a safer place for your mule."

"We're just passing through," Alerio yelled back. He and Ceyx were dressed in woolen trousers and shirts. No one would recognize them as part of the Republic's Legion unless they identified the gladii hanging from their hips.

"Young, sir. Everyone here is just passing through," the man replied by holding out both arms indicating the caravan town. "Your stay will be better if you don't have to keep an eye on your ass."

The man and Speckled Pheasant laughed. Ceyx didn't.

"He's not kidding," Ceyx advised. "The only law here is the one you can enforce, personally."

"We're pretty good at that," Alerio suggested.

"That we are," Ceyx agreed but warned. "One of us has to keep the cart in sight at all times."

The small caravan passed through the pens and between open air buildings. Under the roofs and around cooking fires, merchant guards and drovers lay about relaxing.

Alerio and Ceyx failed to notice when two guards suddenly became alert as they passed by. The small caravan turned a corner and proceeded onto a well packed dirt thoroughfare. Once the subjects of their curiosity were out of sight, the two guards leaped to their feet and rushed out the far side of the building.

The thoroughfare was lined on one side by stalls offering supplies for caravans. On the other side of the street, more permanent establishments were housed in unfinished clay brick buildings. Some offered divided spaces for sleeping. Some beverages, food, and tables for dining. Some served as offices for trading houses. A few buildings were occupied by lawyers and doctors. Merchant business and injuries to the men working the caravans were ongoing concerns.

Further down the wide street, the trail leading into or down from the mountains bisected the town. Beyond the trail stood a cluster of warehouses. These were for the temporary storage of goods awaiting transfer between caravans.

An aroma of roasting venison filled the street. It was carried on smoke lazily arising from a fire pit. The smell was a superb advertisement for the restaurant. Alerio and Ceyx were entranced. Resupplies forgotten, they marched by shouting vendors and didn't stop until they halted in front of the restaurant.

A man stood turning the meat on a spit. Another man inside the building shouted out an order. The outside man stopped turning, pulled a sharp knife, and sliced off a healthy portion of moist venison. After slapping it on a clay platter, he passed the platter to the inside man. Then, he returned to rotating the venison.

Alerio and Ceyx stood mesmerized by the process.

"They do sell the meat," an exasperated Speckled Pheasant sneered. He crawled out of the cart and waddled towards an opening in the low façade of the restaurant. Knee high boards acted as a barrier between the dust and mud from the street and the slightly raised flooring of the restaurant. "Well. Park the mule lads, and join me," invited the rebel Captain.

The restaurant occupied a corner at the junction of the vendor's street and the mountain caravan trail. They should have backtracked up the street for supplies. At the moment, though, the smell and promise of a delicious venison meal seemed like the better idea.

The mule was led in a U-turn and tied to a post just passed the fire pit. After strapping on a feed bag, they made directly for the eating establishment.

Speckled Pheasant had already chosen a seat. After studying the location, Ceyx motioned him to a table with a better view of the cart.

"Meat, my good man," Speckled Pheasant ordered when the proprietor approached. "Venison for three."

"We have bread and mead, as well," the proprietor explained.

"Even better. Meat, bread, and mead," the dissent Captain said. "We'll take all three."

The man limped over to a wall of barrels and selected three clay mugs. While the honey wine splashed into the mugs, he spoke to a teenage lad. The lad was occupied coiling silk thread around the looped end on a line of waxed hemp.

"Bread will be out shortly," the man explained as he set down the mugs. "You want rib, rump, or shoulder?"

"Shoulder for everyone," Speckled Pheasant declared without asking either Alerio or Ceyx.

The man turned and shouted the order to the outside man. Then, he limped over and said a few words to the lad.

The teen carefully laid his project on a barrel before running out and disappearing behind the building.

As the proprietor laid the three platters on the table, Ceyx asked, "Are you the hunter?"

"Not me. I've got a bum leg," the man stated. "It's my son. A few years ago, a bow maker stayed with us. He took a shine to the lad and showed him how to make a bow and how to shoot. The hunting he learned by wandering the mountains. That's a new bow string he's tying."

The teen leaped the low wall while balancing an arm load of bread loafs. One he dropped on the table beside the platters of meat. The others he placed on a barrel before gingerly picking up the silk thread and hemp line.

"I used to barter for meats from hunters," the establishment's owner said with pride. "Now, the lad brings me all the stock I can cook and sell."

"He must know the mountains really well," Ceyx suggested. "to bring in that much game."

"That he does," admitted the owner. "And his bows are starting to fetch a hefty price."

While Ceyx spoke with the proprietor, Speckled Pheasant gobbled down his venison, half a loaf of bread, and drained his mug of mead.

"I'll have the same again," Speckled Pheasant ordered with a loud wet burp. "But first, I must relieve myself. Where is the proper place?"

"There's a waste trench out back, behind the ovens," explained the owner.

Alerio was only half way through his venison and Ceyx had taken just a few bites.

"Want me to go with him?" asked Alerio.

"No. He can't organize a rebellion in the time it takes to cacāre," Ceyx said. Then he told the renegade. "Be quick. Don't make me come looking for you, Captain."

"It'll take, as long as it takes," Speckled Pheasant said using the table top to push up. He waddled towards the entrance.

"For some reason, the food tastes better without all the slurping," Alerio said between bites and sips.

"I believe you are correct," Ceyx replied as he placed a piece of venison in his mouth. "It does taste better."

Chapter 68 - Divide, Conquer, or Die

The half loaf of bread disappeared swiftly.

"I'll get another," Alerio volunteered.

As he walked to the barrel to retrieve another loaf, three men entered. They took seats at a table behind Ceyx. Alerio glanced at the men and thought it strange when they ordered mead and declined the offer of venison. The teen's coiling drew his attention and he stepped over to watch.

"Tying bow strings properly takes patience and talent," Alerio observed.

"Mostly just time," the boy replied without looking up.

His fingers wrapped a loop of silk thread and pulled it tight. Finishing the loop at one end of the waxed hemp line, he measured out a length of the line between his fingers. At a specific place, he formed another loop and began to secure it with silk thread.

While Alerio was admiring the teen's skill at making a bow string, Ceyx cursed and stood up.

"Someone's a little too interested in our cart," Ceyx explained. "You stay and wait for the Captain. I'll go run him off."

The Legionary strolled through the entrance obviously in no hurry. Alerio took it as a good sign and returned his attention to the small tight coils the teen was making.

Ceyx's voice carried into the restaurant, "You! Get away from the cart. Now. Are you deaf?"

The urgency in his voice drew Alerio's focus. He strolled back towards the table to get a better view.

Ceyx shouted at a raggedly dressed and dirty man. The Legionary, probably repulsed by the filthy beggar, attempted to warn him off verbally from a distance.

Alerio understood the need for space to avoid the stink. Still, he was tickled by the frustrated expression on Ceyx's face.

Two men approached from further up the vendor street. Both men were also amused as demonstrated by the wide grins on their faces. They slowed to observe the show before stepping up their pace. As they drew abreast of Ceyx, one pulled a club from behind his back.

The club connected with Ceyx's arm and the Legionary was launched away from the cart and to the side of the street. He lay still and defenseless. The attacker swung the blunt weapon back and forth as he casually strolled towards his victim.

Alerio's mother preached as he was growing up, 'There was always time for good manners.' The lesson took. Before Alerio rushed to help his companion, he bent to lay the loaf of bread on the table. That crouch saved him from the full impact of a second club.

The club did strike the back of his head but it was a glancing blow. Alerio, disorientated from the crack, stumbled forward. His shins collided with the knee-high wall of the restaurant and he flipped over and landed in the street.

Laying on his back, Alerio shook his head attempting to fix his vision. A double image of the three men standing in the restaurant and looking down at him emerged. One held up a club.

"From the Captain," the man stated.

Alerio was in no shape to fight. His ears rang, he couldn't think, and the world was spinning around him. Anger flashed in his chest and he gritted his teeth. With effort, he rolled over, got his fists on the ground, and pushed up while driving forward with his legs.

He sprinted with slow unstable steps right into the side of the man standing over Ceyx. The force of Alerio's weight drove the man away from the Veles and into the second man. While the men tumbled to the ground, Alerio squatted, tilted on the brink of falling over before placing a hand on the road for balance. He snaked the other arm under Ceyx and stood them both up.

Three voices called out in anger from the restaurant. Alerio, in his dizziness, couldn't tell how far away the voices or the thugs were and didn't care to stick around and find out. The two Legionaries staggered down the vender street. They crossed the mountain caravan trail moving unsteadily towards the cluster of warehouses.

"What happened?" Ceyx asked. Alerio stumbled in reply but didn't answer. "I think my right arm is broken. If not, it hurts enough to be."

Alerio staggered again and Ceyx ordered, "Grab my belt for stability."

The five attackers were in no rush. Although their prey had crossed the mountain route, the two victims were weaving back and forth. Even better, they were heading for the storage buildings.

One of the attackers enjoyed their plight and direction more than the other four. It would be quieter with fewer witnesses between the warehouses. Sure, the Captain wanted revenge on the men who had taken him prisoner, but among the buildings was an opportunity. He would kill the Legionnaires and apologize when the Captain returned from the Golden Valley.

The other four didn't care one way or another. Two were the caravan guards who had recognized Speckled Pheasant in the cart. They had gone to a known revolutionary organizer expecting a small reward. Instead, they were offered a substantial fee to help in killing or capturing the men holding the renegade leader. Two unscrupulous drovers were also hired. The plan was to disable the men and hold them for the Captain.

The disgusting pig of a rebel had issued the orders while squatting over the waste trench. Their dislike for the fat dissent was offset by the promised coins.

Alerio chanced to communicate verbally as his head cleared a little, "You got clubbed in the street. Me, in the restaurant."

"Speckled Pheasant is resourceful," Ceyx admitted. He was cradling the injured arm and with each step pain radiated up and down the limb. "and lucky."

"No. We're lucky," Alerio observed. "If it weren't for my mother we'd be at the tender mercy of the Captain by now."

"I don't understand. But, if Mrs. Sisera had a hand in you pulling me off the street, I thank her," Ceyx said. "You know at this pace a two and a half-legged goat could catch us."

"I can run but I'm still dizzy," admitted Alerio. "I'll probably run into one of those fuzzy buildings up ahead."

"The pain is taking a lot out of me. I'm only good for a jog," Ceyx advised him. "Lean on me and I'll guide us. You supply the leg power."

The five attackers strolled casually behind their wounded prey. Why rush when you could easily stay within striking distance and the victims were headed in the correct direction anyway?

The Legion trains beyond long distance running. In combat, units were required to rush from one position or formation to another. To assure a smooth and efficient maneuver, each Legionary spent time running sprints. Full rations, half rations, or quarter rations, it all depended on foot speed over a relatively short distance.

Caravan guards and drovers didn't run a lot and they never ran wind sprint drills. When their prey suddenly straightened up and raced off, they picked up their pace but didn't run.

The Legionaries passed the corner of the first storage building. At the end of the warehouse, Alerio glanced at the space between the walls. He didn't break stride.

Ceyx didn't know or care about the choice. His eyes closed involuntarily against the jarring pain. His legs faltered. After a sharp turn, he stumbled. If it weren't for the young Legionary's strong hold on his sword belt, he would have face planted on the street.

Chapter 69 - Only Defenders Like Funnels

The dizziness and double vision faded as Alerio ran. Hopefully, the sprint had put distance between them and their pursuers. He dared not turn to check. Spying what he was looking for he made a sharp turn. Ceyx slumped and tripped.

"Only ten more paces, Decanus," Alerio shouted. "One, two, three, four..."

Ceyx, being slightly invigorated by the countdown, forced an eye open, regained control of his legs, and added his own voice, "five, six, seven, eight, nine, ten."

But they continued running. "I thought you said ten?" Ceyx asked breathlessly.

"I lied," admitted Alerio as they continued to cross between storage buildings. "Do you know any songs?"

"Songs?" questioned Ceyx.

For a moment, he became numb to the pain as he attempted to remember a tune. Then they passed into shadows. On either side, rough clay brick walls closed in blocking the sunlight. The deeper in they went, the narrower the space between the buildings. At the end of the alley, there was only room for a single man to turn sideways in order to squeeze through the opening.

Ceyx found himself leaning against the side of a building. His curved knife was placed in his right hand and the weight of his gladius lifted as the sword was taken from his scabbard.

"Lance Corporal Eolus. Watch my back," Alerio directed. Then asked again. "Do you know any songs?"

"Songs? What do you care about a song?" insisted Ceyx. "We're about to be murdered by a handful of renegades and you want to find your happy place?"

"No. Not happy," Alerio explained. "We have hard, hot work to do. Someone once told me, when the task is difficult and maybe beyond your abilities, find a rhythm and keep swinging until the end. So, give me a song."

"In that case," said Ceyx. He cleared his throat and in a high pleasant voice, he began to sing.

Oh, the wolves came down from the hills, they did

And the sheep dog watched in the night, he did

While the shepherd boy slept on rocks, he did

And the sheep stirred in fright.

Oh, the wolves came down from the hills, they did

And the sheep dog charged into the fight, he did

While the boy grabbed sling and rocks, he did

And the sheep stirred in fright.

Oh, the wolves came down from the hills, they did

And the dog and wolves exchanged bites, they did

While the boy hurled words and rocks, he did

And the sheep stirred in fright.

Oh, the wolves scurried back to the hills, they did

And the sheep dog hounded their flight, he did

While the boy hurled the final rocks, he did

And the sheep stirred in fright.

Oh, the wolves vanished in the hills, they did

And the sheep dog watched in the night, he did

While the shepherd boy slept on rocks, he did

And the sheep stirred in fright.

"Your people seem to prefer story verse," Alerio commented as five men rushed to fill the entrance of the alleyway. The Legionary swirled both gladii in figure eights. "It'll have to do," he said as he stepped forward to meet the first two assailants. "Please, Decanus Eolus, grace me with your song again."

"Oh, the wolves came down from the hills, they did. And the sheep dog watched in the night, he did," Ceyx sang. As the words flowed, he heard a distinct rough and out of tune echo of the song from the young Legionary.

Partially to drown out the harsh vocal rendition of a beloved family folk song, and partially so Alerio could hear over the yelling and clash of swords and knifes, Ceyx sang louder.

Alerio chose his spot in the alley. Just wide enough for two men to attack comfortably. The comfortable part was important so the men felt confident in a two on one attack. Apparently, they did as both men rushed forward.

Alerio engaged the first man by slicing across the knee with his right gladius. The man fell and Alerio lifted the blade awkwardly as if he couldn't believe the lucky strike. Of course, the man on his left swallowed the act and charged. His long knife held high for a stab to the chest.

"Oh, the wolves came down from the hills, they did. And the dog and wolves exchanged bites, they did," Alerio rasped out as he opened the man's gut. Then he jumped forward and caught another thug unready. *"While the boy hurled words and rocks, he did. And the sheep stirred in fright."*

Now in a rhythm, Alerio stabbed the fourth man in the solar plexus. His instructors always warned against a high center chest stab. Your blade might get caught between the flexible cartilage and the hard bone of the ribs. It was like getting your boot caught in mud. You could pull it out in time, but in combat, you don't have time. He left the blade in the man's chest and looked for the final insurgent.

The man was spinning on his heels and preparing to bolt from the alleyway.

"*Oh, the wolves scurried back to the hills, they did. And the sheep dog hounded their flight, he did,*" Alerio crooned as he threw his gladius. It didn't stick, however, the heavy steel sword landed with authority. The man fell. Before he could rise, Alerio had a foot on his back. "*While the boy hurled the final rocks, he did. And the sheep stirred in fright.*"

"You sing like merda, Legionary," the man mouthed.

"What? I am blessed by the Goddess Canens with a manly singing voice," Alerio stated. "But I'm finished singing. Now it's your turn. Who put you up to this?"

There was a scuffling sound behind him. He turned just as Ceyx stabbed the man with the knee wound in the heart.

"He didn't know anything," the light infantry NCO explained. "Then he began pulling my arm. It hurt like Hades so I stopped him."

"Fair enough," Alerio said before looking down at the renegade under his foot. "Well?"

"The Captain wants you dead," the man announced. "By now, he's already left for the Golden Valley. When he returns, he'll cut your heart out."

Alerio reached down and snagged his gladius from the ground.

"You know I'm getting mighty sick of the Captain and his threats," Alerio admitted as he rested the tip of the blade on the back of the man's neck. "I have one more question. How many men does the Captain have with him?"

"Six archers and four swordsmen," the man said gleefully. "Even if you catch him, you are a dead man."

Alerio slammed his fist into the bottom of the gladius and the blade penetrated three inches. Just enough to sever the man's spinal cord.

"What did he say?" asked Ceyx. The Legionary was having a hard time breathing and he held his injured arm delicately.

"Just that you and I are dead men," replied Alerio as he wiped the blade on the dead thug's back. "Let's go find you a doctor."

"What about Speckled Pheasant?" Ceyx asked before a coughing fit forced him to gasp for breath.

"He's long gone and traveling with a mixed squad," Alerio reported. "Right now, I'm more worried about you."

Chapter 70 - Rest, You'll be Fine in a Month

"Two cracked ribs and a broken humerus," the Doctor reported. "Happens every time someone stands behind a mule."

The Physician had spent fifteen minutes painfully poking and prodding Ceyx. The Legionary suffered the exanimation gamely, yet a few tears had dribbled down his cheeks.

"I'll wrap the ribs and put a splint on the arm," the Doctor explained as he wound a length of fabric around Ceyx's chest. "And put the arm in a sling. You should be fine in a month. No heavy lifting. Rest and let your body heal is my advice."

"What about something for the pain?" inquired Alerio.

"I don't peddle them any longer," admitted the Doctor. "See the old man at the herb tent. He under cuts my prices anyway."

They left the physician's small cubical in the professional building. On the way out, a man stepped in front of them.

"You can sue them," he stated.

"What do you mean?" Alerio asked.

"You can sue the merchant for lost wages," the man announced. "I'm a lawyer."

"I don't think the man who did this is in any condition to pay up," said Ceyx as he pushed by the attorney.

"Where to now?" Alerio asked.

"To see the herb man," Ceyx stated. "Then we're going back and get some venison. We never did get to finish our meal."

***

A short while later, they were devouring platters of meat. Alerio was hunched while Ceyx sat stiffly with his back tight. He lifted a piece of venison straight up until it was level with his lips. Then he pulled it to his mouth and began chomping.

"I need to get to the Golden Valley before Speckled Pheasant," Alerio whined. "But I haven't the foggiest notion how to get there. Or how to get past the rebel and his men."

"You're not going alone," Ceyx informed him. "Even if it kills me, I'm going with you."

"Can't you just give me directions?" suggested Alerio.

"Well that's a thing," admitted Ceyx. "It's off a main mountain route and kind of north of there. You see, I've never actually been to the Golden Valley. As a matter of fact, very few people know the way."

The Legionaries busied themselves with meat, bread, honey wine, and worries. All in equal proportions. It was late in the afternoon and the sun was about to touch the mountain top.

"I know the way to the Golden Valley," the owner's teenage son announced.

He had been at the barrels bending a bow to fit the new string. Because the establishment was mostly empty, he heard the entire conversation. After some thought, he marched to the table.

"I know a way to the valley," he repeated. "A short cut that will get you there ahead of any wheeled cart."

"And how would you know a shortcut to a place no one knows?" challenged Ceyx.

"Last year, I was in the high mountains hunting," explained the teen. "I was two weeks out and deep in a river valley. Suddenly, I heard a voice crying for help. It came from the river, and when I looked, I spied a lad being swept towards the rapids. Don't know why but, I dropped my gear and jumped in."

The teen shivered as if recalling the memory of the icy water.

"I got a hand on his shoulder and towed him to the bank. He was in bad shape but I rubbed his hands, pounded on his back, and lit a big fire," the teen reported. "He woke and I shared my rations with him. Sometime in the night, five more lads arrived. Most of them around nine years old."

"What were six nine-year-old kids doing out in the middle of nowhere?" asked Ceyx. "Was there an adult nearby?"

"There was but the adult dove into the water to save the lad," the teen stated. "They never saw him again. Here is the odd thing. The kids knew the way home but, they were too short to make the climb. Seems the adult would lift them over steep areas and let them walk when it was safe."

"So, where did the children live?" Alerio asked.

"The Golden Valley," the owner's son replied. "It took me three weeks of lifting the wee ones, one by one, over riffs, across streams, and up short cliffs. But I got all of them home safely."

"Did you get a reward?" Ceyx inquired.

"I make a good bow and great bow strings," the teen bragged. "Every time I finish one, someone from the Golden Valley shows up and buys it. They pay far more than I could get from any merchant."

"And you can show us the way to the Golden Valley?" Alerio asked.

"For a fee, of course," the teen assured him.

"What's your name lad?" Ceyx asked. "If you're going to be our guide, I'd like to have a name to call you."

"Brianus, or in some of the eastern languages, High Hill," the teen announced. "Hunter, bow maker, and guide, at your service."

"We leave at dawn," stated Alerio.

"Can he carry his weight?" Brianus inquired by indicating the bandaged Ceyx. "It's a hard climb over two mountains before the final climb to the valley."

"I'll carry his gear if need be," Alerio assured him. "We leave at dawn."

"You can pick up fur coats, mittens, hats, and packs at the tanner," Brianus explained. "Use my name and he'll give you a discount. I trade him my furs - he owes me. In the morning, we'll get food stock from my father."

The Legionaries finished their meal and feeling better about the odds of completing their mission, left the restaurant.

"The lad's quite the businessman," Alerio observed as they walked up the vendor street and away from the restaurant.

"We're lucky to find a guide, on the other hand, we're running short of coin," explained Ceyx. "We've enough for the teen guide, the food, and maybe the packs and mittens. The coats and hats, well, I wonder if the tanner gives credit?"

Chapter 71 - Coin of the Realm and Other Currencies

The tanner took pity on the Legionaries by offering to hold the moldy fur coats and hats until morning. It wasn't much of a deal as he was just closing up shop for the night.

Alerio and Ceyx left the tanner's dejected.

"We could always cheat Brianus," suggested Ceyx. "Send him the payment when we get back to the Raider Post."

"Sure, and have a friend of the Golden Valley mad at us," Alerio said. "Just what I need, two vendettas against me by a single assassin's organization."

"The Dulce Pugno can only kill you once," Ceyx explained.

"If I were on a Legion Post, how would I raise coins?" Alerio asked. Then, he answered his own question. "At the heavy infantry. They're always up for a bet."

"You mean men who make their living by the sword?" Ceyx said. "As in caravan guards?"

"Exactly," Alerio replied.

They continued to a cross street and turned west towards the stockyards. At the open-air building, they stepped into the torch light.

"Anybody care to place a bet against the best swordsman in the west?" Ceyx announced.

The response was under whelming. No one stepped up.

Finally, a man stood. He was massive with legs the size of Ceyx's waist.

"No one here sword fights," he rumbled. "You get cut; you can't work. You don't work, you don't get paid. So, no one swords fights."

"What do you bet on?" asked the Legionary.

"These," the man said holding up a club and laughing. "We have club fights. A man can work with a broken collar bone. Or a broken arm."

The club was carved from the wood of a hardwood tree. One end tapered to fit a hand or two, while the other end formed a knot of wood resembling a large fist; a crippling weapon as Ceyx's arm and ribs could attest.

"Alright, who's first?" Alerio offered while Ceyx was still thinking of the ramifications of being hit with the club.

"My oxen are the fastest on the caravan trail," the giant bragged. "Want to know why? Because I don't spare the club. I'm your first, swordsman. And your last."

A club came flying across the room. Alerio deftly snagged it from the air. He inspected the weapon. It was about an arm's length long and far lighter than a practice gladius.

"Are you going to fight him?" Ceyx asked. "He's a large man."

"The club isn't much different than a wooden gladius," Alerio responded. "Except, it's not sharp, it's longer, it's top heavy, and the other guy is a giant. All that considered, yes, I'm going to fight him."

Bets began to pile up. Alerio's held a few coins, most of them placed by Ceyx. The giant's pile in comparison loomed over his opponent's pile. There was a parallel there but no one in the building cared. This crowd enjoyed raw strength and skill regardless of the difference in height and weight.

The giant came in with a shoulder level sweep, designed to knock his opponent down and, more than likely, out. Most people would have ducked under the powerful arc to avoid the club's head. Alerio noticed the giant had all of his weight on his back leg leaving the forward leg free to strike out.

He wants to kick me, thought the Legionary as he jumped above the sweeping club. On the way down, Alerio shot out a foot and kicked the giant's front leg. The big man rotated on the over weighted rear leg and Alerio ran up to his blind side and clubbed him in the head. The giant toppled to the ground.

The oversized drover laid moaning and unable to stand. Even with the yells and words of encouragement from the spectators, he was incapable of continuing the fight.

"That went well," Alerio said as he walked to where Ceyx was counting their winnings.

"Better still," Ceyx observed as he placed the coins in a pouch. "One fight and because of the odds, we are done here."

"Hold on a second," advised Alerio.

He walked over to the giant who was struggling to stand. Alerio picked up the large man's club and spun both clubs around with twists of his wrists. After wind milling them so fast, they became a blur, he stopped and rested the clubs on his shoulders.

"Anyone else want a shot?" he asked.

A round of applause was his answer. He handed one club to the big man, set the other down, and marched with Ceyx out of the building. His display of weapons handling was impressive agreed most of the men in the building. One man who had ignored the fight suddenly took notice of Alerio and his performance.

He was a thick boned man with massive shoulder muscles. His posture was distorted because he stooped. Most knew him as a sullen person with a mean temper and few friends. He didn't pay attention to the fight, but when Alerio put on the show, he recognized the young man straight away.

The last time he had laid eyes on the farm lad, they were in a jail cell. Legionaries removed the drunken lad before the brute knew there was a bounty on the boy's head. The Cruor gang wanted the farm boy dead or alive. And, they would pay handsomely for either. His usual demeanor vanished and he smiled at the idea of the fates dropping a fortune into his lap.

Alerio and Ceyx strolled happily to the building with individual bedding areas. They paid for two, walked to the sleeping cubes, and separated. Exhausted, the Legionaries laid down without exchanging a word. It had been a long day and both needed rest. It would, after all, be an even longer day tomorrow.

The brute waited until the middle of the night. He knelt by the hostel manager's bedroll and woke him with the point of a knife.

"Two men rented beds. One wrapped in bandages," he whispered. "The other one is a big lad. Where is the younger one sleeping?"

"They wanted to be along the back wall," the frightened manager whispered. "The big guy is in the cell second from the right."

"Stay still and stay quiet," the brute ordered. "It'll all be over in a minute."

The cells were separated by chest high walls of wood. It gave the place a fresh smell and afforded some privacy and security for the guests. Between the cells, aisles led front to back, and rows ran between lines of sleeping areas.

The brute inched along the aisle and down the row to the right. At the second cell from the end, he stopped at the entrance to the cell. Alerio lay on his side cradling the side of his head. The knot on the back of his head was painful so there was no way to lay on his back. The brute raised his knife and paused. He wanted to study his cash prize for an instant.

The first dog sailed over the chest high wall and attached his teeth to the arm holding the knife. The second dog turned the corner and latched onto the brute's lower leg. Between the weight of the dogs, their leverage, and the pressure of the canine teeth breaking skin, they easily took him to the floor.

Alerio came up with the gladius in his hand. Before he could make sense of the growling and screaming, the manager came running up with a torch.

"Please, please everything is under control," the proprietor assured him. "Just a little disturbance."

To the dogs, he whistled three times. The dogs began pulling the injured brute down the row. At the aisle, the manager whistled twice and the dogs dragged him down the aisle and out onto the street.

Alerio followed and ended up standing beside the manager.

"He asked for your cell," the proprietor offered as he dispassionately watched the dogs chew on the brute.

"I wish I had an opportunity to speak with him," said Alerio.

The manager whistled once and the dogs let go and stepped back three feet.

"Take as long as you like," the manager informed him.

Alerio took a knee and shuddered at the sight of the half-chewed arms and legs.

"Why come after me?" he asked.

"The Cruor reward," the brute said. Then begged. "Please no more dogs."

Alerio stood. "He's all yours," Alerio announced as he walked to the manager's side.

The manager whistled four sharp notes. There was no growling this time. A single scream issued from the brute's throat before a dog ripped it out.

"Merchants stay here and they are targets for robbers," explained the manager. "Others stay here and they have enemies. All my guests are protected by my lads."

He whistled one long note and the dogs came trotting over to the manager. He bent down and ignoring the blood on their muzzles gave each a friendly rub on their head.

Alerio went back to bed but sleep wouldn't come. He lay there thinking about the Cruor gang and the Dulce Pugno. Both wanted him dead. He hoped to resolve the dispute with one in the next few weeks. And, hopefully, not disappoint the bounty hunters from the other, by dying.

Act 7

Chapter 72 - Mountain Trails and Quail

Brianus led Alerio and Ceyx across the mountain route, and behind the warehouses before climbing a foothill. Brianus and Alerio had no trouble with the steep but short slope. Ceyx on the other hand struggled.

They traveled along the crest of the hill for part of the morning. At one point, Brianus stopped, pulled a big knife, and proceeded to chop down a young sapling. He flattened one end and left two prongs on the other. After inspecting it, he handed the walking stick to Ceyx.

"Up hill, use it as a staff," he directed. "Downhill, use it as a crutch."

Without another word, the teen stepped off the crest and slid down the hill. At the bottom, he crossed a narrow basin and started up a much steeper rise on the other side.

By midafternoon, they left the foothills behind and were traversing the first mountain. Tough as iron Ceyx put one foot in front of the other and stayed with his two companions. When he finally stumbled, Alerio dropped back and took his pack.

"I can manage," protested the light infantryman.

"I know. It's just the thin air requires me to carry a heavier load," Alerio said with sincerity as he slung the pack's strap over his shoulder.

He stepped away and marched after Brianus. It took a few heartbeats for the exhausted Ceyx to process the concept.

"Wait. That doesn't make sense," pleaded Ceyx as he followed. "Thin air makes it harder to breathe."

"That's not how I heard it," Alerio replied looking back. He was happy to see Ceyx climbing faster without the weight of the pack.

They settled in a camp site and after dinner, Ceyx was the first to fall asleep.

***

In the week that followed, they climbed up a mountain and down the far side. Brianus knew the trails and when possible, selected gentle sloping paths. He even supplemented their rations with fresh meat.

As they started up the second mountain, Brianus held up a hand. The guide turned and placed a finger over his lips for silence. Alerio and Ceyx as trained Legionaries, took a knee to lower their profiles.

"The mountain quail are stirring," Brianus whispered after softly creeping back to them.

"What does that mean?" Ceyx asked.

"Quail are lazy cowards. When small animals move, the birds sit and watch," Brianus replied. "When something big moves through the mountains, the quail fly away. Up ahead, the quail are flying."

"So, what is it?" Alerio asked.

"If I knew that," Brianus bragged. "I'd be the greatest hunter, in all the mountains, in all the world."

He slung his backpack off and untied one of the three bows tied to it. After removing the leather cover, he bent the bow and strung the bow string.

"Wait here," he whispered before slipping away into the foliage on the side of the hill.

Alerio and Ceyx stayed diligent. They divided the area and one scanned in one direction while the other watched the other way. An hour later there was a crash in the trees, breaking branches and snapping twigs. The sound grew closer. Finally, Brianus appeared dragging a large boar.

"This is a problem," announced Brianus.

"Why?" asked Alerio.

"Because we need to stay here for a day while we smoke and eat as much pork as we can stuff into our mouths," the young hunter said with a smile.

"That is a disaster," Ceyx agreed. "a real shame."

The rest and the extra protein did wonders for Ceyx. While he still struggled over the next mountain range, he wasn't a drag on Brianus and Alerio.

***

A week later, Brianus pointed up at a steep ridge. They were in a saddle between higher peaks. The profile of the mountain dipped above them creating a passageway to the higher elevation.

"The Golden Valley is up there and to the right," he announced.

"Aren't you coming with us?" asked Alerio.

"I've never been there," admitted Brianus. "The children told me. When we arrived at this spot, three adults were waiting. They questioned me. Gave me supplies including two small jars of honey and sent me away. I stayed and watched the children scamper up the slope. If they can make it, you can as well. Goodbye, my friends."

The hunter spun and jogged into the tree line. In a few heartbeats, his form was swallowed by the dark green of the forest.

Ceyx and Alerio turned and eyed the slope. It looked just like the hundreds of others they'd climbed over the last few weeks. Hopefully, this one would lead to the Golden Valley and a satisfactory settlement with the Dulce Pugno.

Chapter 73 - Natural Defensive Position

Ceyx and Alerio found flat ground at the top with a thin forest of hardy mountain pines. As directed, they turned right and with pine needles crunching under foot headed towards the valley.

The ridge to their right climbed to the heavens and its broadening base forced them to angle towards the center of the flat land. Soon they walked in a mountain meadow with steep slopes rising on both sides. After a quarter of a mile of angling further to the left, they stepped from the pines and stopped next to a fast-moving stream.

On the other side of the creek, an over grown wagon trail meandered through the center of the dale. They hopped from rock to rock to cross the stream.

"Signs of human passage," Ceyx announced as he examined the wagon wheel marks. "Not much traffic but enough ruts to show years of usage."

"Any recently?" Alerio inquired.

"If you mean a two wheeled cart hauling a fat, ugly rebel?" Ceyx stated. "No, I believe young Brianus was as good as his word. We're ahead of Speckled Pheasant."

"Then let's find out what's ahead of us," suggested Alerio.

Ceyx used the staff to straighten up. Alerio helped him adjust his pack and they stepped off heading deeper into the valley.

"This is incredible," explained Ceyx. "In the legend, the escaping families fought snow and freezing weather to pass through this beautiful place. It doesn't seem so terrifying now."

"Look up at the high peaks towering over the ridges," Alerio suggested. "Even in summer, they're snowcapped. In winter, I expect the wind would blow feet of snow up this valley. It wouldn't be a pleasant place after a blizzard."

"Still, it's beautiful," insisted Ceyx. "I wonder how far it is to the Golden Valley."

"More importantly," Alerio pondered. "How far to the valley's defenses?"

They were just one hundred paces into the march when they discovered the answer to Alerio's question.

It started with being tracked. A bush ruffling, a twig snapping, and the flash of a small body racing between clumps of trees. Soon, the signs of being stalked vanished. Yet, the feeling of being watched was there and the rising hairs on the backs of the Legionaries' necks continued to warn them.

The uneasy silence followed them as they marched. Alerio held up a hand.

"We are being watched," he announced.

"You are a bright lad," teased Ceyx. "What was your first clue? The little lads running between trees or the lack of birds singing?"

"Let's invite them in for a meal and a conversation," suggested Alerio.

"Or to get our throats cut by assassins," Ceyx commented as he stepped off the trail and chose a spot next to the stream. "Here is as good a place to die as any."

While the Legionary had been joking, the camp site was carefully selected. Far across the valley, on the other side of the wagon trail, laid the tree line. Only low growth occupied the ground between the camp and those trees. An enemy would be visible while crossing the field.

On the backside of the camp site, anyone attacking from across the stream would need to wade through icy mountain water to reach the camp. The trees on the other side of the mountain stream grew farther back, probably from years of spring flooding that washed away any young trees trying to take root in the flood plain.

The final reason for the camp site was a large boulder resting on the edge of the stream. About shoulder high, it afforded a small defensive position against arrows. It also provided a wind break for the three campfires.

At each campfire, Ceyx skewed hunks of boar with sticks. Alerio tented green tree limbs to hold the meat over the flame. Soon, their area of the valley began to fill with the aroma of roasting pork.

"Why do you think our stalkers will be hungry?" Ceyx asked as he leaned on the staff and the boulder to ease his way to the ground.

"Because I'm hungry," replied Alerio. "And I couldn't smell smoke in the air. If the watchers patrol far out from the Golden Valley, they, like us, are eating jerky. Let's see if they'll come out for a hot meal."

Two of the campfires blazed and smoked on either side of the boulder. Ceyx and Alerio were sitting at the center fire. They could see around the sides of the boulder and use it for cover if attacked.

A man dressed in green and brown leathers came from the tree line across the wagon trail. His gait was smooth, a big hunting bow rested in his hand with a quiver of arrows strapped tightly to his hip and thigh. This was the tell. A hunter didn't care if his quiver moved as he would be stationary when going for a shot. A warrior required all of his equipment to be tightly strapped to his body to prevent snagging while he changed positions in battle.

"I assume this is an invitation?" the man stated as he circled around to one of the campfires.

He approached from the far side keeping the fire between him and the Legionaries. At the fire, he squatted and peeled off a piece of pork. The hot meat hovered in the air and he waited expectantly.

Alerio, seeing the delay, reach to his roasting pork and peeled a section. He shoved it into his mouth and began chewing.

"Yes, the meat is an invitation," Ceyx replied as he also took a piece.

"You're going the wrong way," the man said as he nibbled. "While I appreciate the hot meal. There's nothing up ahead for you."

"We're going to the Golden Valley," announced Alerio. "I have business with the Dulce Pugno."

The hunter ceased chewing and stated, "They don't take recruits."

"I didn't think they did," agreed Alerio. "Then again, they want their Nocte Apibus back."

"And what would you know about the Night Bees?" inquired the man.

"I have them," Alerio admitted. "Well, not on me. They're coming by caravan."

"Yes, the cart with the fat man, four swordsmen, and six archers," the man reported. "They're about a day's travel from here. So, we shouldn't kill them?"

"You can kill all of them except for the fat man," Alerio offered. "I need him and the cart when I speak with the Sweet Fist."

"What makes you think they would want to speak with you?" the man asked. Then he held out a palm to stop Alerio from answering.

He waved an arm and twelve men and lads emerged from the trees. Some hopped rocks to cross the stream while the rest moved from the wagon trail side.

"I'd like my fellow Watchers and their apprentices to hear this," the man said.

As the Watchers gathered around the fires and cut slices from the pork, the Legionaries got their first look at the unit's make up. For every adult male, there was a teen and a young child of about ten years old.

"Please. Tell us why the Dulce Pugno want to speak with you," the man ordered. "If your story is good, maybe we'll let you return from where you came. If not, there are many graves in this valley."

Ceyx looked around at the mountain splendor before saying to Alerio, "Yup, it's a good place to die."

"No one is dying today," Alerio assured him. "At least not us."

"You speak bravely for a man on restricted land in a dale that's hard to find," the Watcher stated. "Tell us why you are here."

"There are four Nocte Apibus missing," Alerio informed them as he stood. He unsheathed his gladius and tossed it to the other side of the fire. Next, he pulled his knife and it joined the sword. "I know there are four assassins dead and four missing Night Bees. I know this because I killed them."

Arrows were notched and bows aimed at Alerio.

"They were our friends and family," the Watcher explained. "Why should you live?"

"You keep threatening death," challenged Alerio. "There are three reasons to stay your hand. One, the Dulce Pugno wants retribution. I guess from your hesitation and questions; you are not with the organization. I am here to plead my case. Number two, the legend is that the man possessing a Nocte Apis must return it to the Golden Valley himself. I have four Night Bees. Number three, the man must face a trial to see if he lives or dies. Unless you consider my skill at roasting meat a test, I have yet to be properly tested."

He sat down and plucked a hunk of pork from the skew.

"Shoot or eat," Alerio ordered while holding out the food for people at both campfires to see. "I choose eating."

The Watcher raised a hand and indicated for the bowmen to lower their weapons.

"You require the fat man to live?" the man asked Alerio.

"Yes. The fat man and the cart must accompany me to see the Dulce Pugno," the Legionary replied.

"While we eat tell us how you killed four apprentices of the Sweet Fist," the Watcher suggested.

Everyone stopped eating and leaned forward. Apparently, they were in awe of the Dulce Pugno and wanted to hear how he had managed to kill four of the assassins.

"You say they were apprentices," Alerio responded. "That explains why they came at me like a pack of vicious dogs. No tact, just a blind attack. It helps that I am a better swordsman than most. Still, whoever trained them is a poor instructor. Over confidence and rash tactics is why they died."

"You just saved me from a long lecture," the Watcher leader exclaimed. "The fat man and the cart will be brought to you. Do not move from this camp. Do not, unless you seek death."

The Watcher and his unit stood and dispersed. Soon, they had all faded into the surrounding forest.

"That went better than I expected," Ceyx said laying back against the boulder. "You know Alerio, one of these days your mouth will get you into real trouble. I thought it was today. And, we were going to die."

"Not today," stated Alerio as he also leaned back against the hard granite stone. "Not today."

Chapter 74 - Entrance to the Golden Valley

Two days later, they saw a pleasing sight. Or, a sad sight if you were Speckled Pheasant. The rebel Captain walked beside the mule as five little lads herded them along the trail. Each little Watcher had an arrow laying across their bow and seemed prepared to use it.

The revolutionary looked road weary and foot sore. As he stumbled up to the Legionaries, he exploded.

"I am going to kill you both slowly," he bellowed. "I'll skin the flesh…"

Shouting him down, Ceyx announced, "We're moving. Try to keep up."

Alerio and Ceyx marched off. When Speckled Pheasant hesitated, one of the little Watchers poked him with an arrow. The rebel jerked hard on the lead and he and the mule followed.

A few miles later, they arrived at a dam. Behind it, a lake occupied half the gorge. While the main trail tracked around the earthen dam and deeper into the narrowing dale, the little Watchers guided them off the path.

The new course took them over a wooden bridge spanning the stream Alerio and Ceyx had camped beside. At the far end of the bridge, they entered a village of craftsmen. A wheelwright's hut and work area strewn with partially constructed wheels was the first. Next, a blacksmith's forge glowed and the ringing of a hammer on an anvil echoed over the water. After these trade areas, they passed a cooper shaving slats for barrels and a carpenter's stand where boards were being fitted together. Between the carpenter's yard and a work area with a potter's wheel and kiln, the little Watchers pointed to an empty hut.

"Finally. I can't go on," exclaimed Speckled Pheasant spotting a bench at the hut.

He dropped the mule's line and staggered to the bench and plopped down.

Alerio took the opportunity to inspect the cart. After checking a pouch for the Nocte Apibus, he lifted it out and dropped its strap over his shoulder. Then, he lifted out the dual gladius rig, slung it onto his back, and tied it down.

"Think we'll need our armor?" Ceyx asked as he reached into the cart.

"Him, not you," the Watcher in the green and brown leathers stated. The man had appeared out of the twilight like an apparition. "Him and him," he repeated while pointing to Alerio and Speckled Pheasant. Then he pointed at Ceyx. "Not you."

"Hold on," complained the Legionary. "If Alerio is going, so am I."

"He will be tested," the Watcher explained. "You will not. So, stay and wait, or die. Please make a choice. We'll gladly fulfill your request."

Up and down the row of huts, all the craftsmen and their assistants had exchanged their tools for bows. The bows had notched arrows resting on the strings and they were all aimed at Ceyx.

"I'm sure you'll be comfortable here," suggested Alerio. "I bet they'll feed you. Maybe they'll have barley mush and goat jerky."

"I'd rather die," Ceyx replied before realizing what he said. "No, I'll stay. Here's me staying."

The Legionary stepped purposely to the bench, used his walking staff to shove the Captain over, and sat down.

The sunlight faded as the sun dipped below the high mountain peaks. Darkness descended and cooking fires were lit. As the aroma of boiling stew drifted over the craftsmen's village, the Watcher walked to Alerio and Speckled Pheasant.

"You will follow the path to the Golden Valley," the Watcher advised while pointing to the bridge.

Chapter 75 - The Golden Valley

Alerio and Speckled Pheasant marched stiffly back over the bridge. Neither man spoke. The mistrust and dislike between them was almost a physical presence.

At the path where the Watchers had them veer off towards the bridge, they turned toward the Golden Valley. A few yards away, torches lined the trail. Along with the sunlight, the warmth of the day vanished. They shivered in the cold of the mountain night.

Alerio and Speckled Pheasant followed the torches until they reached a wooden wall. A doublewide gate opened and they stepped through.

The chill vanished. Almost as if the warmth of the sun had reappeared, the air temperature rose to a comfortable level. In front of them, torch lined paths meandered through the dark. Bright spots of light identified widely spaced huts. Some huts near the gate were opened sided, as if work areas, while other huts had doorways.

Three men stood waiting for them inside the gate.

"Captain. Welcome to the Golden Valley," one of the men said pleasantly. "Please come this way. We have refreshments and a place for you to rest after your long journey."

As the rebel began to follow the pleasant man, he turned and flashed an evil grin at Alerio.

"Legionary. Come with us," another of the men ordered.

He motioned and stepped off. Alerio followed. The last man fell in behind them.

They wandered along one of the lighted paths. Alerio marveled at the well laid black stones under foot and realized the warmth he felt radiated from the ground. The path snaked around but, generally favored one side. Just when he thought they would have to climb the mountain to go farther, the path made a sharp turn. They arrived at an entrance set in the side of the hill.

Inside, Alerio looked around and marveled at a large cavern. It was dome like with several small round tunnels leading off into darkness. Some openings were overhead, others head and shoulder high, and a few sat at floor level. His escorts indicated one at floor level. He and the men marched to the back of the dome.

The tunnel ran straight before it turned and the floor angled upward. A short while later, it intersected with other passageways. Here, the walls changed from smooth to showing signs of pick and ax work. Some distance into the warren, his guards stopped and indicated an opening.

"In there," his escort instructed.

If it was a cell, his jailers didn't know what they were doing. First off, the door was constructed of stretched leather. He could easily rip the material off the frame. But where would he go? Secondly, they hadn't taken his gladii or his knife.

A bed had been chiseled out of the stone, a bedroll lay on one end, and a burning torch lit the small room. He laid on the stone and closed his eyes.

A noise caused him to look as the flimsy door opened. Two men walked in with trays. Behind the men, faces peering in lined the entire door frame.

"Refreshments, honey wine, and water," one of the men stated as he and the other man set the trays on the bed. "You have time."

"Time for what?" Alerio asked. The men didn't answer. They walked out shutting the door behind them.

Alerio, being a young guy, was always hungry. He tossed back the cloth covers and dug into the food. The best part he decided was the honey in the clay pots. After eating, he stretched out and fell asleep.

Act 8

Chapter 76 - The Return of Four Nocte Apibus

"Legionary. Awaken please," a high-pitched voice announced.

Alerio shook himself awake and sat up. The voice belonged to a lad about ten years old. He was standing close to the foot of the stone bed.

"Good morning young man," Alerio said with a smile. "Is it time?"

"It is," the lad replied as he walked to the doorway. "If you'll follow me?"

Alerio picked up on a bit of nervousness in the lad's voice. But the little one didn't display any outward sign of his apprehension as he marched steadily out of the cell. After all the faces peering in when the food was delivered, Alerio was surprised to find the tunnel empty.

His small escort guided them up and down through new tunnels. Alerio was completely lost when the lad held aside another sheet of leather. For a heartbeat, the Legionary thought it led to another cell. It wasn't.

The circular room with the black sand floor could have been called an arena. Tiers of ledges circled the room. Over a hundred people sat quietly on those shelves watching the Legionary walk to the center of the sand. Some tiers were low enough to easily reach with a jump from the gritty floor. Others were so high, Alerio needed to crane his neck to see the upper level. It was a fighting pit, he decided.

"Lance Corporal Alerio Sisera," a voice called out. "Why have you invaded the Golden Valley?"

Alerio spun around seeking the source. Three people occupied a wide space on the second tier. One stood in front of her chair and the other two were sitting in high-backed seats. Speckled Pheasant was one of them. The rebel raised a clay mug and saluted Alerio. After taking a drink, he smirked in an irritating I-told-you-so manner.

The Legionary reached into the pouch and pulled out the four knives. With two in each hand, he held the Nocte Apibus above his head.

"I've come to return, four Night Bees," he announced.

A murmur ran through the crowd.

"And how did you come to have, four Nocte Apibus?" asked the woman.

"I killed four of the Dulce Pugno," stated Alerio. "and took their Nocte Apibus."

"Do you mean you were part of an Infantry squad?" the woman challenged. "A squad that caught our friends inside the Legion Post and killed them before taking the Night Bees?"

"No, ma'am. I killed them single handedly," Alerio boasted. "I alone killed your assassins."

More murmurs ran through the crowd. This time words rose above the buzzing. In essence, they all said the same thing, "Kill him. Kill him."

The woman sounded unsure about Alerio's statement, "For now, it'll stand as you state." Then she looked around Speckled Pheasant and spoke to the man in the other chair. "Brother. By what terms did we commit ourselves to the contract."

The man on the rebel's left stood and the woman sat. Speckled Pheasant glanced from side to side at the woman then at the man, obviously confused by the proceedings.

"The Captain contracted for our services," the man boomed so everyone on the ledges could hear him clearly. "He refused our first offer to use experienced craftsmen. Pleading low funds, the Captain negotiated with our representative. It was agreed upon to use four apprentices. Each apprentice would sting twice with the Nocte Apibus before leaving. These were the basic terms of the contract."

Speckled Pheasant's head nodded enthusiastically all through the speech. The man sat and the original speaker stood. The revolutionary ceased his head movements and settled for glaring at Alerio.

"There are no witnesses to consult, except for Decanus Sisera," The woman said before asking. "Lance Corporal. What are your recollections of the events the night you captured four Nocte Apibus?"

"I was walking a guard post. The guard on the next position failed to report," Alerio described. "I left my post to check on him. When I tripped over the guard's body, I shouted for reinforcements. That's when I saw the shadows coming over the wall."

"Point of clarity, Decanus," she asked. "They came over the wall? From outside or inside the Post?"

"From outside the Post," Alerio replied. "I saw their shapes because they were backlit by the lights from Crotone's harbor. As I shouted for the Sergeant of the Guard, the four men attacked. Two came straight at me. For assassins, they lacked discipline and so they died. The other two divided, attempting to hit me from the sides. I downed one but lost my helmet. The last of your lads sliced my scalp before I could bring my blade around."

"You were wounded?" the woman asked. "Where?"

Alerio pointed to his head and traced the half-moon scar with a finger.

"Doctor. If you would?" she called out.

From another entrance, a man walked briskly to the Legionary. He held the torch he carried over Alerio's head and probed the scar tissue. Three times he traced the line of stitches using different pressures on each pass.

"The scar is indeed the sting of a Nocte Apis," the man announced before exiting as rapidly as he arrived.

Again, restless mumbling rose from the tiers. The standing questioner leaned over and look past Speckled Pheasant's belly.

"Subtext?" she asked of the man on the other side of the rebel.

"Yes. Two points," the man on the renegade's left side said as he stood. The woman sat down.

"The Captain's men were to remove the guards from the wall," he reported. "Allowing our less experienced assets to infiltrate the Post. It appears this section of the agreement was not executed."

Speckled Pheasant shifted uncomfortably. Alerio enjoyed his uneasiness until the man continued with the second point.

"Failure to clear the wall was a grievous breach of the contract," the man stated. "Nevertheless, one guard should not have been a hindrance even given the youth of our dead. Therefore, it is my opinion the contact be voided and declared null with the Captain forfeiting his payment."

The man sat and his female counterpart on the other side of the rebel stood.

"Are you in agreement with the findings, Captain?" she challenged.

Speckled Pheasant sat thinking for several long moments. Maybe he could ask for a partial refund. After all, the man had said the one guard shouldn't have been a problem. While he thought, he eyeballed the shadowy figures on the shelves around the dome and remembered he was as much a prisoner as a guest in the Golden Valley.

"The terms of the contract shall be voided," he announced. "May I go now?"

"Not just yet, Captain," the woman replied. "There is the matter of retribution for the lost Nocte Apibus."

Alerio tightened his back, expecting any second, the sharp pain from a spear or an arrow. With the revolutionary seemly off the hook, the price of retribution most certainly would be his life.

"We test all who return a Nocte Apis," the woman announced. "However, in all the years of the Dulce Pugno, never have we lost, and needed to recover four Night Bees."

The evil grin was back on Speckled Pheasant's face. Alerio ignored the fat rebel and began exercises to loosen his shoulder muscles. If combat was the test, he might go down, but he'd go hard, taking as may assassins as possible with him.

Chapter 77 - The Retribution Trial

"All parties concerned have agreed to void the contract," the woman explained. "There remains only the matter of the guards left on the wall. Were our apprentices unready for a mission beyond our Valley? Or, did they meet an unusually skilled swordsman?"

A hush fell over the crowd and all eyes in the dome were on her.

She inhaled deeply. As her chest fell from letting out the breath, she pronounced, "If they were ill trained, the fault is ours. The failure to remove a guard would have made no difference. Conversely, if the failure to remove the guard placed them in the path of a deadly warrior, the fault rests with the Captain. Therefore, Lance Corporal Alerio Sisera will be tested. If he truly is an exemplary fighter, he will pass the trial. In that case, he and the Captain will be free to go."

"But, if he fails," the woman continued. "It proves the Dulce Pugno were not ready. This makes the removal of an ordinary soldier off the wall paramount to the successful completion of the contract. In that case, The Lance Corporal and the Captain will die."

Speckled Pheasant jumped up from the chair. "This isn't part of our agreement," he yelled. "Even if my men didn't remove enough guards, I shouldn't have my fate tied to the Legionary. He killed the Dulce Pugno. He took the Nocte Apibus. He should pay the price."

Alerio was struck dumb. His life or the dissent's, he understood. Having both their lives depending on his success was confusing and somehow comforting. He gazed up at the antics of the fat man and laughed.

"Sit down, Captain," the woman ordered. Then she turned to Alerio and instructed. "Lance Corporal Alerio Sisera. Your test began earlier. Ponder this as you proceed with each coming phase."

Alerio began mentally retracing everything he had experienced since arriving at the Golden Valley. Nothing came to mind and his ponderings ended when hemp lines dropped from the dome above. He reached over his shoulders for the gladii.

Five young lads came sliding down from the dark. They hit the sand too hard and each staggered from the impact. Alerio released his grip on the hilts. For a second, he almost went to help the awkward lads collect themselves.

One at a time, they pulled foot long wooden tubes from their belts. One end of each tube was cut on a gradual angle. Not sharpened enough to stab with any efficiency and from the way they handled the wooden instruments, not heavy enough to use as clubs.

The boys spread out in a semi-circle and advanced towards him. It was ridiculous. Alerio glanced behind and above to see if the little lads were a decoy for a deadlier attack. Nothing showed itself but, these were assassins, so in his cursory look, he might have missed something.

Three of the lads had their wooden tubes held up as if to stab downward. He couldn't help himself.

"What manner of wood is that?" he demanded.

"Bamboo," two of them replied.

"I've heard of this reed," he said. "Now, switch your grips. In a knife fight, you wouldn't have a chance to stab downward. You need to jab or slice your foe."

One of the boys held out his tube. Alerio took it and demonstrated the proper grip.

"Stab or slice," he said. "Also, feet, all of you stand with your feet a shoulder's width apart. One foot should be slightly behind the other."

As if he were their instructor, they all fell into the correct fighting form.

"Class is over," he said. Then just to see how they would react, he ordered them. "Drop your weapons, and leave the dome."

The little ones marched by him setting down their weapons until he had a stack at his feet. Alerio glanced up at the woman and man on either side of Speckled Pheasant. Their expressions gave no clue if the little ones' harmless assault was a part of the test or not.

A sound carried across the pit. It resembled the noise made by handfuls of sand running between fingers. Alerio spun around to see four figures emerge from the black sandy floor. He hadn't noticed any lumps or movement in the sand when he'd looked before.

With both hands up ready to unsheathe his gladii, Alerio waited to see what form the attack would take. Bamboo poles, about six feet in length, were held above the heads of four lads. The boys were about twelve years old. He dropped his arms into an empty-handed guard position. The four assaulters spread out and moved forward until they surrounded the Legionary.

From the high tier, Speckled Pheasant shouted, "Pull your swords, you idiot. Pull your swords and kill them. What is wrong with you? Kill them."

Alerio ignored the rebel. He could only see two of the attackers at a time but two was enough. A tiny nod from one and lip movements from the other tipped him off to their tactics.

The nod started a countdown and the lip movements were the count. Alerio would know the order of attack once one moved. An almost imperceptible shuffle of sand identified the first attacker. He was behind and to Alerio's right.

Alerio waited until the shuffle revealed a full step. He dropped to one knee, reached over his head and caught the bamboo pole. By pulling the pole and the youth forward, he managed to capture the boy's wrists. A jerk and the lad went flying over Alerio's head. He landed hard enough to knock the breath from his lungs but not hard enough to break bones.

The second attacker was in motion. He was to the Legionary's left front. Again, the pole was caught, the wrists captured and the boy sent flying through the air.

Alerio didn't wait for the third attacker. He jumped at the lad to his right front and snatched the pole. A simple leg trip and the Legionary had spun away before the youth hit the gritty surface. The bamboo pole of the fourth attacker was knocked aside, and Alerio punched him in the chest with an open hand. The youth sailed back a couple of feet before plowing into the sand.

After picking up all four poles, he stepped back so all the youths were in view.

"You divulged your tactics by waiting for your formation to set," Alerio explained. "If you had attacked before waiting for perfection, you might have succeeded. Four surrounding one opponent is unnecessary. Two to a side working together is more powerful than a crossed single attack."

To everyone in the dome's surprise, he tossed the poles back to the startled youths.

"Do it again. Attack me, two to a side," he ordered. "Do not delay."

The lads didn't. While Alerio received a few taps to his arms, the boys suffered the same fate as before. They all ended laying in the sand with their poles in the Legionary's hands.

"Better," he informed them. "Next time have one come in high and the other attack low."

The youths jumped up and crowded together in front of the Legionary. They just stood there as if waiting for something.

"Leave the dome," Alerio instructed wondering if they would obey.

The four lads scrambled for an exit tunnel leaving Alerio standing in the sand holding four bamboo poles. He stood baffled at the nature of the test, until a burning sensation tore down the back of his left arm.

He did three things that saved his life. One, he didn't waste time turning to see who or what had attacked him. Two, he swung the bamboo poles over his head. They connected with something as he did the third thing that saved his life. He kicked out a leg as he spun down to the sand. By rotating his body, the leg swept around and caught the attacker in the knees.

The attacker continued jabbing with his knife as he went horizontal. It was a good tactic except Alerio had curled his upper torso to bring his arms and shoulders around. While the knife jabbed where his head should have been, Lance Corporal Sisera's arm was inside the attacker's forearm.

Alerio's elbow followed the assassin to the sand and pounded into his chest, breaking a rib when he landed. After prying the knife from the attacker's hand, Alerio hovered it over the man's eye socket. He was a heartbeat and two inches from scrambling the man's brain when Speckled Pheasant yelled.

"Kill him. Kill him, yes, kill him," the Captain screamed incessantly.

Bile rose in the Legionary's throat at the sound of the voice and the sour taste reminded him of how much he detested the renegade Captain. Alerio flipped the knife into the air, caught it by the hilt, and pounded the butt end into the attacker's forehead. The man would have an epic headache tomorrow, but he would live.

Alerio didn't look up at the spectators while reaching around to check his wound. Instead, he began to slowly turn in circles while his fingers explored the injury. It was a long deep scratch. More than likely, the attacker had run at his back. His error was over extending the knife for the initial attack. Only the tip of the blade had touched the arm. It was enough to open a wound but the bleeding wasn't the streaming flow he expected.

Playtime was over. Alerio reached to his shoulders, gripped the hilts, and drew both gladii.

"Who is next!" he shouted while holding out the blades. He continued turning and scanning the pit.

Then, the crowd heard something funny. The Legionary was humming. They couldn't tell what song as the tune had no rhythm nor did it follow any musical pattern. Nonetheless, the humming was soon accompanied by sword drills. They observed fascinated as the blades flashed faster and faster and Alerio flowed smoothly from one position to another.

He wasn't showing off or putting on a show. These were assassins, and as he experienced in the last attack, the next one could come from any direction.

The assailant on the ground groaned and pushed up to his knees. Alerio strolled over and his blades blurred in circles on either side of the assassin's head. Still, on hands and knees, the assassin looked from side to side at the spinning steel blades.

Alerio leaned forward and whispered, "Run."

A roar of warning came from the spectators as the assailant rose to a sprinter's position between the confines of the blades. Then he rolled straight back and gathered his feet under his hips. Alerio watched as the dizzy man ran and staggered to an exit tunnel.

The Legionary resumed his vigil of turning and watching for the next attack.

"Decanus Alerio Sisera," the woman on the tier called out.

"Yes, I can hear you," Alerio replied as he spun and scanned.

"The test is done," she announced. "Please put away your swords and follow the lad."

The ten-year-old who had guided him to the fighting pit was standing at an exit. A huge grin plastered on his face, he beckoned to the Legionary. Alerio hesitated at the abrupt ending of the trial. Slowly he sheathed the gladii and marched across the sand towards the youth.

Chapter 78 - Honor Among Assassins

The boy guided him down different tunnels. Before they arrived, Alerio smelled food and heard the low hum of conversation. When they stepped into a dining hall, he was shocked when a woman waved him to a chair at the head of a table. He paused and glanced at those already seated.

Sitting at the table were the five little lads. All grinning and nudging each other at the sight of the Legionary. Next to them were the four teens trying to look stern and adult, except their wide eyes displayed their adulation and spoiled the act. The last occupant was an older man. A bandage circled his head and his ribs were wrapped tightly with more cloth.

"Our guest, Lance Corporal Alerio Sisera of the Legion," a familiar voice announced. It was the woman from the chair to Speckled Pheasant's right. "Please Decanus, sit," she ordered. "We don't get much company in the Golden Valley."

The woman waved an arm at a chair as she entered the room.

"Is the food poisoned?" Alerio asked. "Or do I get a Nocte Apis in the back after a last meal?"

"Goodness no," she explained. "You passed the test with honors."

"It wasn't much of a test," confessed Alerio. "I've had harder fights."

"Oh, we already knew you could fight," she advised him. "Anyone who can kill an associate of the Dulce Pugno is already a proven warrior. No, we test for character. A raging killer, an arrogant cūlus, or a braggart would have failed the test."

"But you placed the lads in the fighting pit with me?" Alerio warned. Then looking as the little ones slumped and shame washed over the teens, he added. "Although they displayed bravery and deadly skills, it was dangerous."

The woman beamed at the table of young people who brightened at the praise, before responding.

"Not as dangerous as you might think," she reported. "We had seven archers on the upper tier targeting you."

Alerio understood if he had hurt one of the youths, he would have become a pin cushion before he could hurt another.

He asked, "You said the test started before the pit. What did you mean?"

"The boy who fetched you from your room," the woman explained. "He was close enough for you to strike or to scold for sneaking in uninvited. Had you abused him; the test would have been very different."

"So that's it," Alerio said hopefully. "I can leave and return safely to my Century?"

"No, there is one more aspect that only applies to those passing the test," the woman admitted. "It doesn't affect those who fail, as they can't talk about what they've seen or done here. You can."

Alerio sat down stiffly when the woman paused.

"So, the final retribution is, you must leave our region," she announced. "In other words, you are exiled. We can't have anyone pointing you out as the man who killed four Dulce Pugno. The Golden Valley doesn't have an army to protect it. The survival of every man, woman, and child depends on fear of Dulce Pugno to deter our enemies."

"How long do I have to pack?" asked Alerio sarcastically.

"From the time you reach your Legion Post," the woman replied. "Thirty days. After that, if you're found on our shores, you will be murdered in your sleep along with anyone near you."

There was a noise at the entrance and trays of food appeared. Ham baked in a honey glaze, fresh biscuits, butter mixed with honey, and steamed vegetables were placed on the table.

Alerio inhaled and his mouth watered at the aroma.

"In case you attempt to stay by changing your name," the woman added. "Remember, everyone at this table knows your features. Now for something more pleasant."

Ten pairs of eyes peered at him. Gone were the looks of awe. They had been replaced by studious stares. Under the glares, the aroma no longer seemed so appealing.

One of the little boys pushed back his chair and marched to a side table. He picked up an object wrapped in a white cloth and carried it to Alerio.

"For you, master," the boy said as he handed over the package.

Despite the test, the exile, and the promise of death, his mother's reminder to always be polite echoed in his mind.

"Thank you, little Dulce Pugno," Alerio said graciously. He was rewarded by a wide smile which displayed missing teeth.

The child returned to his seat as the Legionary peeled back the fabric.

"As I explained," the woman said as the layers fell away. "You passed the test with honor. Your bravery and good heart were displayed when you spared and then taught each group of students. For that, you are deemed an Ally of the Golden Valley."

Alerio folded back the final corner. In the cloth laid a long-curved dagger with a wide yellow band in the center of a black hilt. He drew the weapon. A small engraving of a bee hovering over a flower was etched in the upper part of the blade.

"We have friends and associates around the Republic, and in the kingdoms across the sea," she declared while pointing to the dagger. "This is a symbol of our allies. While it doesn't allow you to send us to kill for you, the symbol will get you sanctuary, protection, medical attention, and any information we are privy to. Also, the Dulce Pugno will not accept a contract on an Ally of the Golden Valley."

"What about an exile who stays?" Alerio asked hopefully. Then another thought occurred to him and he added, "Is Speckled Pheasant banished?"

"You must leave our shores," the woman explained. "As for the Captain? He didn't kill a Dulce Pugno nor does he know anything about the Golden Valley."

"I haven't seen much of the Valley either," admitted Alerio.

"The Captain was brought in one entrance and placed in a luxury suite," the woman stated. "From there, he went directly to the arena. Also, he left before daylight so he has no knowledge of the Valley's layout. You will, and we trust you to never divulge the information, Ally of The Golden Valley."

As the woman left, Alerio looped the dagger on his belt and filled a plate. The first bite of food revived his hunger and he dug into the ham and vegetables.

"You fight two handed?" asked the man in the bandages. "How is that possible?"

Alerio began telling him about the need to switch hands when he was smaller. During the explanation, the teens and children began dueling in the air with a fork in one hand and a knife in the other. He wasn't sure but, he might have just added a new technique to the assassins' arsenal.

Chapter 79 - Daylight in the Valley

When the meal ended, all ten of his breakfast companions filed by and touched his shoulder before leaving the room. As the last stepped through the doorway, his ten-year-old guide stepped into the room.

"Please follow me," he said with a grin.

"Whose soup did you pee in?" Alerio inquired as he stood and stretched.

"Pardon? Soup?" the puzzled boy asked.

"Who did you anger to draw the duty of guarding me?" the Legionary asked as he walked towards the lad. "Shouldn't you be off training to be a Sweet Fist?"

"Oh, after my time in the outside world, I'm going to be a Watcher," the boy said with pride. "I like hunting and tracking. But mostly, I like fresh air."

For the first time, Alerio noticed how hot and stuffy it was in the tunnels. It's why, as they walked, he knew when they approached an exit. A breeze of fresh, cool air caressed his face.

They emerged high up on the side of the mountain. Spreading out to the far side of the valley were huts, work sheds, fields of crops surrounded by rings of flowers, and beehives. So many in fact, the beehives outnumbered the huts.

Though, something was missing. In a sprawling village such as the Golden Valley, one would expect lingering smoke from morning cook fires. There was no layer of smoke hanging across the huts and fields.

All along the black stone paths, people moved slowly. Some carried buckets, other hoes or rakes, and others toted baskets. The one thing they had in common was they were all traveling in a precise manner.

"We will descend on the path," his guide informed him. "At the bottom, there will be bees. If one comes close, do not shoo it away. If one lands on you, do not swat it. Bees are our livelihood and are sacred. Move slowly and follow me."

"Does no one here breakfast?" Alerio asked. "There are no cooking fires."

"Fires and fast movements are allowed only after sundown," the future Watcher replied. "In the Golden Valley, daylight is bee time and we do not disturb our benefactors as they go about the work of producing honey."

"A strange but understandable rule," Alerio observed.

They sneaked heal and toe along the paths, being extremely careful where they stepped. Three times during the odd stroll bees landed on Alerio. Each time, a handler would hold up a hand for them to stop. After long stretches of waiting for the handler to come to them, a feather fan was gently waved until the bee took flight.

It took a large part of the morning to cover what should have been a leisurely stroll.

"Thank you, young Watcher," Alerio said as he stepped through the gate.

"Go in peace Ally of the Golden Valley," the youth responded as he closed the gate door.

Now free of the movement constraints, Alerio jogged down the trail, over the bridge, and into the craftsmen's village.

"Ceyx. Ceyx," he called out. "Gear up. We've got to catch Speckled Pheasant."

Lance Corporal Eolus ducked through the door of the hut. He walked out a few steps before stopping, raising his good arm above his head, and stretching.

"Why?" he asked as he yawned. "The rebel is gone."

"We have to catch up with him," Alerio explained. "I'm going to kill him. Now hurry."

"There's no rush," Ceyx said which obviously agitated Alerio. "They put him in a two-pony cart before daybreak. We'd need to be mounted on ponies to catch him. But guess what? In all of these mountains, there's not a pony to be had. Or bought. Or stolen. Or…"

"I get the picture," Alerio said in defeat. "Let's gear up. I need Optio Horus' sage counsel."

Act 9

Chapter 80 - Down from the Mountains

"I see you have a new tool," observed Ceyx as the Legionaries marched beside the mule.

They had decided to take the trail through the mountains. With their gear and the slow-moving mule, it would have been impossible to backtrack along Brianus' narrow and twisting short cut.

"A gift from the Dulce Pugno for returning the Nocte Apibus," Alerio replied.

"When you left with Speckled Pheasant, I figured it was the last time I'd ever see you," Ceyx admitted. "Now, here we are and you have a new dagger. What was the test? What was it like in the Golden Valley?"

"I guess they liked my face," Alerio said avoiding the question. "The knife was a reward for returning the Night Bees."

"I've never heard of a reward from the Dulce Pugno," Ceyx said. "Unless you count them sparing your life as a reward."

"I do," was all Alerio said as they hiked to the top of a steep grade.

Two Watchers stood at the edge of the forest observing the Legionaries. One raised a hand and pounded it into his chest as a salute.

Alerio and Ceyx returned the salute before stepping over the crest of the hill.

"The Watchers and craftsmen are very cosmopolitan," noted Ceyx. "Surprisingly so for mountain dwellers."

"Probably just knowledge picked up during the travels of the honey caravans," Alerio replied.

He didn't inform Ceyx the residents of the Golden Valley had expatriates placed in major cities around the Republic. Or that the Dulce Pugno, could be reached by visiting any of the luxury trading houses.

Six weeks later, the caravan town came into view. From high up, they could see the roofs and tents of the supply merchants. Further out, beyond the stock pens, lay the edge of the flat plains and the eastward road leading to the Legion Raider Post. But they focused on one building, specifically, as they descended the mountain trail.

It was late in the afternoon and the fire pit was glowing and the meat on the spit was dripping. Together they created aromatic smoke that seemed to climb the mountain trail directly to the Legionaries' noses. Hunger put a bounce in their steps and they wanted to race downhill for the inn. But the stubborn mule, wouldn't be rushed. He slowed and placed each foot carefully on the steep trail. As a result, they arrived well after dark.

"Proprietor, meat and mead," Ceyx called out as he tied the mule's lead to a post.

The happy vision of a large slab of roasted venison caused Alerio to fumble with the feed bag as he rushed to strap it over the animal's head. Although the spit and roasting meat were gone, the aroma lingered. His spirits sank at the reply.

"Sorry gentlemen," the owner reported. "We're closed for the evening."

In the lantern light, Alerio observed Ceyx's head drop in disappointment. Another dinner of barley mush and jerky was almost too much. Alerio attempted a different ploy.

"Is young Brianus around?" the Legionary asked. "We're clients of his."

There was a pause as the owner looked towards the back of the restaurant. From the shadows, the hunter emerged and studied the Legionaries.

"Alerio and Ceyx," Brianus said in surprise. "When the Captain came through, I assumed you were dead. Claimed by the mountains, his guards, or the defenders of the Golden Valley."

"When did Speckled Pheasant arrive?" inquired Alerio. "But more importantly, is he still here?"

"Ignore my vengeful friend," interrupted Ceyx. "Do you have any venison left. Scraps will do. By Hades, do you have any remaining burnt skin? That'll do."

"We can do better than that," Brianus announced. "We were just sitting down for supper. Come, join us. Father, with your blessing?"

"Of course," the owner replied. "Please join us."

While Ceyx and Brianus talked with the hunter's father, Alerio sulked after learning Speckled Pheasant had passed through only four days ago. Even with two ponies, the fat revolutionary had only been four days ahead of them on the trail.

In the morning, they guided the mule and cart through the stock pens and started the journey eastward.

Chapter 81 - Legion NCOs Fix Stuff

Sergeant Horus was waiting in the command tent when Alerio and Ceyx entered. Dirty and dusty from the trail, the two Legionaries looked as if they would fall over from exhaustion.

"Well, you're obviously not dead," pronounced the Optio. "So, I assume the stuff with the Dulce Pugno is settled?"

"Not exactly," Alerio explained. "No one is in danger from an attack by the assassins. However, I have a problem."

Alerio paused and chewed on his lip while gathering his thoughts before continuing.

"Spit it out Decanus," Manfredus ordered. He was at his desk making entries in the Century's log.

"Give him a second to collect himself, Corporal," Centurion Stylianus urged. "He looks troubled. Come on son, just say it."

The Centurion was totally healed and all the bruises had faded.

"I am banished from the Eastern region," the words burst from Alerio's mouth and he hung his head. "I don't know what to do. If I'm here in thirty days, I'm dead as well as anybody sleeping near me."

Corporal Manfredus dropped the quill on his desk and stared open mouthed at the Lance Corporal. Centurion Stylianus wasn't as dramatic. He settled for stroking his chin thoughtfully. It was the Sergeant who spoke first.

"Sir, I believe we need to put in transfer papers for Decanus Sisera," Horus suggested. "Rush orders at that."

"I will sign the transfer. The Colonel's staff will pass it through," Stylianus said. "But we haven't had a request from another Legion for any personnel. We can't just ship him off to another unit unannounced."

"Perhaps, the Southern Legion," Corporal Manfredus suggested.

Ceyx and Horus groaned. Even Stylianus allowed a little discomfort to spill out in the form of an ouch.

"Pardon me, sir. But what's wrong with the Southern Legion?" asked Alerio.

"Nothing Lance Corporal," Centurion Stylianus answered. "It's a fine posting."

"Except for the heat," Manfredus added.

"And the wild, crazy mountain tribesmen," added Ceyx. "and the soldiers from Qart Hadasht across the strait."

"Or the rocks along the shore," Horus said. "Oh, and the Pirates."

"And the sea storms," Manfredus added piling onto the benefits of the Legion posting. "Can't forget the sea storms."

"In short, it's the cūlus of the Republic," Horus summed up. "and the Legion isn't much better."

"Now hold on Optio," scolded Stylianus. "As an officer of the Legion, I simply can't stand by while you besmirch the integrity of a Legion of the Republic."

"Sorry, sir. I wasn't aware you served in the Southern Legion," admitted Horus.

"I haven't," explained the Centurion. "And I must add if ordered there, I'd resign my commission. I have that option. You, Decanus Sisera, do not."

"I understand, Centurion," Alerio stated. "There is another favor I'd like to ask for."

"Speak up Legionary," Stylianus ordered.

Chapter 82 - The Harbor at Crotone

A week after the return of Lance Corporal Ceyx Eolus and Decanus Alerio Sisera and the meeting in the command tent, the harbor town rested in the early evening. As with all evenings, the town seemed to breathe a sigh of relief after the heat of the day. Good people were in their homes enjoying supper with their families. The few people out were either workmen grabbing a last beverage after a hard day's work or shopkeepers closing for the day.

Evening watchmen on the anchored ships strolled the upper decks. From the merchant's large transports to the small sloops, and the Republic's triremes tied to the pier, everyone watched for two things. People attempting to stowaway and fire. One was a bother and the other a life-threatening disaster. None of the watchmen were prepared for the stomp pause stomp that preceded the arrival of a squad of heavy infantrymen.

From the direction of the Legion Post, the Legionaries marched directly to the pier where the Navy warships were anchored. As they moved along the dock, Legionaries, in full armor with javelins and massive shields, fell out of line and assumed sentry positions.

One of the Navy watchmen shouted down, "Lance Corporal. What's happening?"

"You sail on the morning tide?" the infantry squad leader shouted back.

"Aye, first thing, just before sunrise," the sailor replied, "So why are you here?"

"We're here to keep the rats off your boat," the Decanus answered.

While the Lance Corporal and the sailor exchanged words, two cloaked figures came from an alleyway. In the lantern light of the harbor boulevard, they appeared to be two workmen heading for a pub for refreshments. When they turned and entered a drinking establishment, it was confirmed.

"You don't have to do this," Sergeant Horus grumbled as he tossed back the hood on his cloak. "We'll get to him later."

"As our Centurion explained, politically, the Legion can't start a brawl in the business district with the rebels just to extract revenge on one man," Alerio explained. He stopped talking as the bar maid approached.

She took orders for two ales from the men sitting in the darkest corner of the pub. Once she had waddled away to fetch the drinks, Alerio continued.

"I'm sailing on the morning tide," he said. "Even if the civilian authorities investigate, the only person to charge will be in a different region of the Republic."

"There's little likelihood of them issuing a warrant for a brawl in a pub," Horus admitted.

Their ales arrived and the men sat in silence sipping from the clay mugs.

On the pier, the Decanus of heavy infantry stopped at each of his men, said a few words before moving on to the next Legionary. At the end of the dock, he stopped. Four men in workmen's clothing strolled up to the Lance Corporal.

"Pleasant night," one of them said to the Squad Leader.

"Good evening, Corporal Thornernus," the Decanus greeted his NCO.

"When the package arrives," Thornernus ordered. "Get it aboard the ship. Dead, bleeding out, or alive and kicking, the package must be on that ship when it sails. Understand?"

"He'll be on the ship," the Squad Leader promised. "You can depend on us."

"I do Lance Corporal," Thornernus assured him. Glancing down the boulevard, the Corporal saw seven men strolling toward the door to the tavern. "Show time," he announced.

Alerio and Horus dropped their heads and studied their half empty mugs when the door opened and two men stepped in and scanned the pub's interior. With just a few patrons in the bar and none seemingly dangerous, one of the men stepped outside. A moment later, Speckled Pheasant bristled through the doorway followed by five men.

The rebel Captain sat and two of the men selected seats facing him. While the leaders of the insurgency conferred, the four guards eyed the room. The talk stopped when drinks arrived. Once the barmaid was clear, the three continued their conference.

Four masked men burst through the door. Two of the guards were immediately downed by bludgeons. The other two pulled swords and faced off against the four strangers. Both dropped as flats of gladii blades slammed into their heads from behind.

Speckled Pheasant and his Lieutenants shoved back their chairs and jumped to their feet. With all of their guards down, the Lieutenants attempted to shield their Captain.

Nevertheless, five trained Legionaries against the two renegades soon separated the rebel leaders. The

Lieutenants were pushed to the side and restrained. Speckled Pheasant stood alone in the center of the pub.

"Hello Captain," a voice spoke from the dark corner of the tavern.

"Alerio Sisera. I thought you died in the mountains," sneered the rebel leader. "Are these your Raider friends? I also have friends. Two kinds actually. One kind are magistrates and civic leaders. They'll bring the Republic's law down on you and your unit. If they have a chance. See, I have other friends. The kind who will stab you in an alleyway or gut you on the street. You and your friends are dead men."

"Funny you should mention the Raiders," Alerio replied. "I believe they are all standing a general inspection. This very night, they are dining with the Battle Commander who is visiting the Raider Post. Imagine the embarrassment of a civilian court questioning the word of a Legion Colonel."

"As for your thug friends," Alerio continued as he stepped out of the shadows. "It seems I'm being transferred. Unless your friends care to track me across the Republic, I won't be available."

Reaching over his shoulders, the weapon's instructor and drew both gladii.

"Strangers. Please remove the customers, the barmaid, the bartender, and the guards," Alerio instructed. "I have things to discuss with the Captain and his Lieutenants."

After everyone was herded or dragged out, the last masked strangers stopped and dropped the Lieutenants' swords on the floor at their feet.

"Oh, this is rich," crowed Speckled Pheasant as his officers bent and retrieved their weapons. "I'll not be bothering my friends. Because, boy, you are already dead."

After a speech with as much bravado as that, Alerio expected Speckled Pheasant to attack. But like all sadistic bullies, the Captain was a coward at heart. While he talked a good game, he wasn't about to attack the young Legionary. Instead, the leader of the insurgents reached out and shoved one of his Lieutenants in Alerio's direction.

The man stumbled forward. Off balance, he swung high, probably hoping to drive back his foe and give him a chance to get himself steady.

Alerio didn't give him the opportunity. He dropped to a knee and drove the tip of his left gladius up through the soft tissue under the man's chin. But the man didn't stop coming. Speckled Pheasant was behind his dying Lieutenant, holding the body up, using it as a shield while stabbing over the man's shoulder.

The Legionary pivoted on the down knee away from the charging Captain. He engaged the advancing second rebel Lieutenant. With blades clashing, Alerio rose and took a giant step to the side. Now the Lieutenant was between the Captain and the Legionary.

The Lieutenant was an excellent swordsman. His legs were set properly for advancing or retreating. His shoulders rotated to provide the smallest target. And, his sword held up to parry or attack as the fight progressed. Unfortunately, it wasn't a fair fight.

Alerio allowed a flurry of clashes with his left gladius against the Lieutenant's right-handed sword. Then, the Legion weapon's instructor parried the Greek officer's blade to the side while stabbing with his right blade. The rebel Lieutenant folded up around the deep belly gash and sank to the floor.

Speckled Pheasant could have joined in the fight sooner. But he was delayed by the weight of the dead Lieutenant's body. If nothing else, the Captain was persistent. His fixation on having a shield was time consuming and, by the time he turned the dead man to face Alerio, the second revolutionary Lieutenant was laying and dying in a pool of blood.

"One thousand Republic gold," Speckled Pheasant said.

Whether it was an offer or just to see if he could distract Alerio, didn't matter. The Legionary stabbed through the side of the dead Lieutenant and skewed the fleshy flank of the rebel Captain. In pain and surprise, Speckled Pheasant dropped the body. As it fell, the tip of the gladius tore from his side, widening the stab wound. Speckled Pheasant sank to his knees.

Alerio retrieved his gladius from the dead man and wiped the blade on the man's shirt. Then, he angled both gladii over his shoulders and slid them into the scabbards.

"Speckled Pheasant. Pay attention," he said standing over the bent and crying Captain. "You are about to die. Make peace with what every God will have you."

The Captain lunged with his knife. It slid along the underside of Alerio's left forearm. As blood poured from that arm, the Legionary used his right hand to pull the curved dagger with the yellow band on the hilt.

It flashed once horizontally. Speckled Pheasant began to gurgle as bubbles of blood formed at his neck. His eyes opened wide, staring at the Legionary.

"Goodbye Captain," Alerio said as he drove the dagger tip through Speckled Pheasant's eye and into his brain. "Giving you a chance to pray was a mistake. I was taught better. The next time, I'll remember to never give my opponent a chance to counterattack."

Alerio flipped up the hood of his cloak and strolled behind the bar. After snagging a clean bar rag and wrapping his forearm, he headed for the door.

Outside, Horus paced back and forth. The rebel guards were tied up and lying face down. The bar owner and everyone else had run off. Most of them didn't want to be involved. But, one man decided there might be a reward if the renegades knew their Captain was in trouble.

Alerio pushed through the door while holding the wound closed.

"Can you run?" Horus asked as he rushed to the young Legionary's side.

"Yes. Just a little leak," Alerio replied then he staggered.

Horus grabbed one arm while Corporal Thornernus took the other.

Before they stepped off, Thornernus looked over his shoulder and ordered, "Scatter."

The three masked Legionaries dashed off into the night. Alerio matched the pace of the two men holding him up as they jogged down the boulevard towards the dock. Behind them, like rats emerging for cheese, thugs began to stream from alleyways.

By the time they had the four rebel bodyguards untied and a direction, Alerio was already handed off to the heavy infantrymen. Horus and Thornernus drifted away into the shadows. In five heartbeats, a gang of renegades gathered on the boulevard at the end of the pier.

"We're going to search that ship," one stated. "Move aside!"

The Decanus glanced over his shoulder then back at the rebels.

"What ship?" he asked.

"That ship. The ship where you took the killer," shouted the thug.

"If there's no ship," the Squad Leader asked. "How could we have loaded a killer on it?"

"What are you deaf as well as blind?" demanded the rebel.

The Lance Corporal looked over his shoulder at the two heavy infantrymen standing behind him.

"Did they just insult the Consuls?" he asked. "And threaten the stability of the Republic?"

"That's what I heard," one replied.

"It's treason to call the Consuls blind as well as deaf," the other replied.

"Half squad. Form up," the Decanus ordered. "Forward march."

Suddenly, the dock shook as their left feet came down and when the right stomped, the dock thundered.

The thugs failed to grasp the significance. Five infantrymen slammed big shields into the rebel's faces knocking the men to the pavement. Then after a painful hammering, the Legionaries stomped and ground the agitators into the stones of the pier.

Alerio heard the stomp and cries of agony as the ship's medic guided him down to rower's deck.

"What was that?" the medic inquired.

"Oh, just the infantry keeping the ship clear of rats," the sailor on watch replied.

"That's excellent," the medic observed. Then to Alerio he said, "Come on young man, let's get that arm sewn up."

The End

A not from J. Clifton Slater

Thank you for reading the 1st book in the Clay Warrior Stories series. While Clay Legionary incorporates fantasy elements in the form of Alerio fighting with two gladii and the introduction of the Sweet Fists, at its heart the book is historical fiction.

The Legions of the mid Republic period were not the regimented standing armies of the Imperial Roman Legions. Disbanded after every Consul/General returned to the senate, a majority of the time the Legions were garrisons in strategic locations. However, the training of recruits made even the early Legions a formidable fighting force.

In future books, Alerio will encounter politics, treachery, and conflicts between the powerful city states of the era. Hopefully, you enjoyed the historical adventures as much as I enjoyed researching and writing them.

If you have comments please contact me.

J. Clifton

E-Mail: GalacticCouncilRealm@gmail.com

FB: facebook.com/Galactic Council Realm & Clay Warrior Stories

Military Adventure both future and ancient
Books by J. Clifton Slater

Historical Adventure – 'Clay Warrior Stories' series

#1 Clay Legionary   #2 Spilled Blood   #3 Bloody Water

#4 Reluctant Siege   #5 Brutal Diplomacy   #6 Fortune Reigns

#7 Fatal Obligation   #8 Infinite Courage

#9 Deceptive Valor   #10 Neptune's Fury

#11 Unjust Sacrifice   #12 Muted Implications

#13 Death Caller $#14 Rome's Tribune

Fantasy – 'Terror & Talons' series

#1 Hawks of the Sorcerer Queen

#2 Magic and the Rage of Intent

Military Science Fiction – 'Call Sign Warlock' series

#1 Op File Revenge   #2 Op File Treason

#3 Op File Sanction

Military Science Fiction – 'Galactic Council Realm' series

#1 On Station   #2 On Duty

#3 On Guard   #4 On Point

Printed in Great Britain
by Amazon